MW00880505

i

T. L. Scott

Levels

T. L. Scott

16 August 2018

This book is a work of fiction. Names, characters, places, and incidents either are products of the author's imagination or are used fictitiously. Any resemblance to actual events or locales or persons, living or dead, is entirely coincidental.

Levels

This story is dedicated to those who ask the brave question: What if?

Keep using your imagination and seeking answers.

I could not have done this without some major support. Thank you to all of you brave souls who agreed to read the advance copy. Your feedback shored up the story where it needed it the most. To my editor, Kelly Lamb, your sharp eye and dedication to this story are greatly appreciated, the very talented Elizabeth Gauthier for designing this fantastic book cover thank you.

To the precocious imp that always inspires me and keeps me true to the story I am forever grateful for you.

And to you, dear reader, thank you for taking the time to go on this journey with me. I hope it is as enjoyable for you to read as it was for me to write.

Scott

Levels

Chapter 1

Jake leaned his head against the cool glass of the window. The air conditioning in the car was on, but it wasn't doing much. It had been in the upper nineties for the past week, and the app on his phone didn't show any change coming. Jake didn't mind the heat too much. He usually just took things in stride.

He sat forward, trying to catch some of the air blowing from the vents. It wasn't much cooler even though it was set on max chill. He arched his back, his focus fully on a bead of sweat as it rolled down his spine. He mentally tracked it all the way down to where it met his underwear and disappeared.

He sat back and rested his head against the window again, at least it felt cool. He thought about rolling it down and sticking his arm out. He imagined feeling the resistance of the wind on his hand. Mentally he cupped his hand in the current to direct some air into the car. He knew better than to ask his dad if he could roll it down. He had a thing about the noise with the windows down.

Jake looked to the east as they drove across the Manchester Bridge, crossing the James River. It hadn't rained for a few weeks, and the water level was low. You could almost walk across the river, hopping from boulder to boulder out to Mayo Island.

Jake liked the sound the tires made on this part of the bridge. They sounded like they were zinging along. The sections of the bridge added a counter-point to the zinging sound. They made a rhythm as they crossed each joint: thum . . .zing… thum . . .zing… thum . . .

As much as he liked the sound as they drove, he didn't like bridges. He looked at his reflection in the window and saw a scared little boy.

It didn't happen every time, he reminded himself. He never knew when or where it would, but there was almost always something when they crossed a bridge. He forced himself to breathe deeply.

A metallic taste flooded his mouth making it fill with spit. He quickly swallowed it down. His throat clamped tight. He kept swallowing, trying to keep it under control, forcing it down his throat without puking.

He took in a ragged breath and focused intently on something, anything, else. They had passed the mid-point of the bridge. He focused on the soothing sound of the tires and the cool feeling of the window.

Levels

He stared at the metal bridge downstream by Mayo Island. It had one train track and looked old. He had no idea just how old. He didn't even know if it was still in use. It looked cool though. The structure looked solid even if it was rusty.

"You okay back there, kiddo? Just a little bit further and we'll be over it."

Jake looked up at his dad's gaze in the rearview mirror and nodded his head. He felt it releasing its grip on him. It wasn't over, but it was passing.

It was weird. He wasn't afraid of heights. He wasn't worried about the bridge collapsing. Strangely, when the feelings hit him, he felt afraid of being alone, of being abandoned. His mind flashed to the time when he was little, and they'd been at the aquarium. He'd become separated from his dad for a few minutes. He remembered how scared he'd been, but that wasn't on a bridge. It didn't make any sense. He felt the fear rushing back as a blurry memory bubbled up. He quickly pushed it down. *That wasn't real. It didn't happen. It was nothing but your imagination. You remembered it wrong. It was probably from a nightmare, and you made it part of that time at the aquarium.*

He shook it off and sat forward again.

"Better, Jake?" asked his dad.

"Yeah," he said, relaxing his hands. The white marks on his legs began to fade where he'd been gripping them so tightly.

The buildings of downtown Richmond filled the windshield. He had always liked the look of the Federal Reserve Building. Its lines were simple and powerful. They made it look like it was soaring into the sky. The two buildings on the other side of the street, the BB&T buildings, were cool but in a different way. They were solid looking.

He felt excitement take the place of the nausea in his stomach. They were going to Wentley's department store because he needed new cleats for soccer. He knew which ones he wanted: the new model. They were so cool. They were also expensive, but he had a plan to convince his parents to let him buy them. He kept rehearsing it in his head.

He wasn't surprised his mom was still on the phone. They weren't even five minutes into the drive before it rang. It was Saturday. Couldn't she have the day off?

She looked back at him. "I'm sorry," she said putting her hand over the phone. She gave him a wink. "I'm almost done, I promise."

They'd turned into the parking garage and were cruising for an open space.

Levels

"Dad, over there, on the right," said Jake, pointing to a spot close to the entrance.

"Good eye, kiddo. This must be our lucky day."

It wasn't an ideal spot. His dad made it work though. They were between an SUV that was parked over the line and a Mini Cooper. Their car was small, but it was a good thing that the Mini Cooper was smaller yet. Jake still had to squeeze to get out of his door.

They were on the second level of the parking garage. The entrance to the store was on this level and the first one. They almost never parked on the ground floor. It was always packed with shoppers from the grocery store.

Halfway to the automatic sliding doors, his mom finally ended her call. From the sound of it, the signal had degraded to the point she couldn't hear the caller anymore. *It wasn't like she had ended it by choice*, Jake thought with uncharacteristic bitterness.

"Guys, I'm sorry, but I need to finish this call. Something serious has come up," she said, already distracted.

She walked away from them, her attention fully on the phone. "I need to find a signal."

She stopped waving her phone around in search of that all elusive signal long enough to look at her family. When she saw the look on both of their faces, she took a breath and lowered the phone to her side.

"I'm sorry, but this really is important." She walked back to them and wrapped her arms through both of her guys' arms. "What do you say we grab a coffee?" She saw the looks on their faces. "I promise! I really will make it quick, okay?"

"Coffee? Yuck! I think I'll get a Red Bull instead," said Jake.

"Nice try, but no," said his dad with an eyebrow raised. "You can have a Coke instead. You know how bad those drinks are for you, Jake."

"Hey, a guy's gotta try, right?"

"Honey, you know what I want," his mom said as she brought the cell phone up to her ear. She mouthed, "I'm so sorry," waving her hand and then pointing at the phone.

Jake was already done with his Coke and it didn't look like his mom was any closer to finishing her call.

His dad took the last couple of drinks from his coffee then looked over at his wife. The only change to her soy latte was that the foam had settled. There wasn't even the tell-tale sign of her

Levels

lipstick on the rim. It was evident that she hadn't even paused her conversation long enough to have a drink. It had sat there and gone cold.

Jake could tell by the frustrated look on his dad's face that he was tired of it. Like most kids his age, he knew when there was trouble at home. As much as the adults tried to keep up the appearances that everything was great, kids knew. He didn't think it was a serious problem yet, but it was getting worse.

His mom didn't notice. She was lost in her call. That was the thing with her; she was very focused. Unfortunately, the focus had been more and more on work and less and less on them.

Jake was tired of waiting. He was patient, but he was a kid.

"Dad, come on, let's just go. I bet we'll be back before she's finished."

Sadly, his dad agreed with him. He waved his hand to get her attention.

She automatically raised her index finger. "Just one more minute, honey," she mouthed before going back to her call. She hadn't even looked at him.

He'd had enough. "Let's go, son," he said standing up from the table.

She looked up at him. "I'm so sorry. Two minutes," she mouthed to him.

"We're going in," he said to her, his voice barely a whisper. He then held his pinky and thumb up in a classic call me sign.

She gave a thumbs-up and went back to her call, oblivious to his sarcasm.

"Well, kiddo, I guess it's just us for now."

They walked for a couple of minutes, merging into the flow of the other shoppers. They passed a couple of stores without saying anything to each other.

Jake felt his dad's strong hand on his shoulder.

"So, tell me again why you need those cleats?"

"Okay, first of all, the cleat pattern has been designed just for us strikers. The angle is designed for better traction for quick starts. They also made them lighter . . ." Jake went on, animatedly telling him all the reasons why he had to have them.

"So, how much do they cost?"

Jake moved to the side of the walkway, near the rail that overlooked the ground level and out of the flow of traffic. The back to school craziness had passed, and the crowds had returned to normal. At this time of the morning, foot traffic was still light.

Levels

"Dad, these are not just any shoes, alright?" Jake liked to talk with his hands when he was excited. He was using them to accentuate his points. He was so animated his dad had to fight to keep the smile off his face.

"They're really high-tech. They are designed to take the game to a whole new level. A lot of the pros are already using them." A very serious look came over him. It was time to close the deal.

"You know I need new cleats. The old ones don't fit anymore, so we have to buy a pair anyway," he reasoned, with his hands spread out from his sides for emphasis. "These shoes cost only a little more than the pair we bought last year," he quickly added.

"How much more exactly?" Derek asked.

"Thirty-three dollars."

"Jake, you do realize that's about a fifty percent increase, don't you?"

"Yeah, but, come on! I've got my own money. Between my birthday money and my allowance, I have it covered. I really need 'em."

He saw the longing on Jake's face. There was no way he could tell him no. The fact was, he'd made all the correct arguments.

He was happy and a bit sad. His son was maturing and making good choices.

He stepped forward and put his arm around Jake's shoulders. "Come on, kiddo," he said as he hugged his son to him. "Let's go shoe shopping."

"Cleats, Dad, they're called cleats, not shoes."

He squeezed his shoulder. "Okay, Jake, let's go get those cleats. Where do we need to go?"

Jake didn't bother trying to answer. He didn't know either. They walked another fifty feet before they saw a directory sign.

"Okay, it looks like we need to go to the sixth floor," his dad said. The nearest elevator was just a little bit further along the walkway.

Wentley's was basically two eight-story buildings with a two-story walkway connecting them. The walkway was enclosed from the elements with windows all around. It gave a great feeling of openness while still affording the patrons the comfort of air conditioning. Shops and small concessions, like the coffee

Levels

shop they'd stopped at, were located in the center of the crossing sections.

The store they needed was on the sixth floor of the east building appropriately named East Wentley. To get to the elevator, they had to go into the clothing store on the second floor, which they were currently on.

Jake was getting frustrated. His dad was taking his time looking around the boy's section. He knew he didn't really need anything. They'd basically bought him a new wardrobe for the new school year. He had just shot up with a growth spurt over the summer, and he wasn't done with it yet. His feet had grown two sizes since July. Now that the back to school rush was over, there were some good deals on the discount displays, and he was taking his time, looking at every piece of clothing. He knew the real reason his dad was dragging his feet. It was too obvious. He was trying to give his mom time to catch up.

His dad tried to sneak a look at Jake. He was caught and judging by the look on his son's face, he was out of time. Derek stood up to his full height and let out a sigh. "Come on, kiddo. I just want to take a quick look at a pair of jeans for me before we go up."

Jake threw his hands in the air in exaggerated frustration.

"Don't worry, they're right by the elevator. I'll just be a minute."

After another ten minutes of stalling, and with a new pair of jeans in hand, Derek knew he was out of time.

"Come on, Jake. Let's go on up and get those cleats." He gave one last hopeful look at the entrance to the store before turning toward the elevator, which was to the right of the cash register where they were. The stainless-steel doors opened, discharging shoppers to continue their consumerism.

The doors closed, and the elevator departed before they reached it.

When they got to the elevator, Derek saw that the button with the up arrow was illuminated. A woman was already there waiting on the elevator to return. She was watching the floor indicator at the top of the elevator doors. An arrow pointed to the number five which was illuminated orange. The numbers were arranged in a half circle with the arrow in the center tracking the location of the elevator. He liked the look. It was a cool meeting of the old and new.

"Is there anything else we need to get while we are up there?"

Levels

Jake thought it over for a minute before answering. "I could use a new mouth guard. Oh, some soccer socks too."

He saw some color creep into Jake's cheeks as his eyes cut over to the woman. She was tall, about five ten or eleven with a strong build. She was wearing cream-colored slacks and an emerald green silk blouse. The blouse was sleeveless and showed off her well-toned arms and rich brown skin. Her thick black hair was cut to shoulder length. She stood with her hands clasped easily in front of her. Her purse, which hung off her left shoulder, was protectively held against her body by her elbow. Derek had the impression that she was a strong and steady person.

"Is there anything else?" he asked. He had a feeling Jake needed a new cup but wasn't about to say that in front of the woman.

"I'll let you know if I think of anything else."

Derek looked out of the store, back along the walkway one more time to see if he could spot her.

"She knows what we're here for. She can find us," said Jake. "We'll probably finish and find her still on the phone."

Derek looked at Jake's face. It didn't look like he was upset about that. It was just something he'd come to expect from his mom.

"You know her. She's always taking care of business. It's what she's good at."

Jake smiled up at him.

Other people joined them as they waited for the elevator to arrive. A group of three teenage girls was talking about the jeans they were going to buy. The two blondes were talking with each other while the brunette, who looked to be more Jake's age, stood to the side and watched them.

A mother was trying to keep her two young children in line and hold a conversation with her father. Somehow, she was managing to pull it off.

"Mom's birthday is almost here, Dad. You should get her something nice this year. It's her sixtieth after all—Jimmy! Stay still. Mommy's talking with Grampa."

"I told you, she could use a new vacuum," her father replied.

"Dad, please be serious. She deserves to be spoiled. You need to show her how much you love her. Anna, we'll get you an ice cream for dessert, after you eat your lunch, if you behave and let Mommy and Grampa get the shopping done. Plus, Dad, she's put up with you all these years. For that alone, she deserves it,"

Levels

she said a bit too harshly as she exhaled a pent-up breath of frustration.

"I've been putting up with her too, mind you," he said, stubbornly staring a hole in the elevator doors.

"Stop being a grump," she said, laughing a little. "Jimmy! Stop fidgeting."

Jake kept his eyes forward and watched the drama play out in his peripheral vision. He was looking at the brunette. He didn't think she went to his school. He was sure he would remember her. He forced his eyes to look straight ahead. He didn't want to get caught checking her out.

The floor indicator showed that the car was still stopped at the fifth floor. As Jake watched, it changed to the fourth floor and stopped there.

A guy in his early twenties joined the small crowd. He stood back from the teens and off to the side. He wore glasses with round lenses, which he absentmindedly pushed back up on his nose. He looked like one of the kids from the local university. *Probably a liberal arts major*, Derek thought to himself. He was wearing jeans that ended at his ankles and no socks. He even had on a corduroy sports jacket, the kind with patches on the elbows in spite of the heat outside.

15

Jake always thought his dad would look good in a jacket like that. He was a writer, and he thought all writers needed to have one. Last year, he'd told his mom that he wanted to give him one for his dad's birthday. She said that it was way too cliché for a writer to actually dress like that. Still, he liked the look.

Jake took a step back. He let his eyes wander over the racks of clothing, looking for a jacket with patches on the sleeves. *It would be nice to know if they had them here*, he reasoned.

The light blinked off from the fourth floor. The arrow tracked the progress. The number three briefly flashed then finally the number two lit up. A chime sounded its arrival at their floor.

The brushed aluminum doors weren't even open all the way when a man in a brown suit bumped into his dad in his haste to depart the car.

"Excuse me," he mumbled hurrying along his way. He was a smallish man. He probably wasn't any bigger than five-two and slight of build. He was clearly in a hurry to get to wherever he was going.

Jake looked up and saw that his dad's attention was riveted on the feather sticking up from the band of the man's fedora. He watched it bob jauntily along as the man rushed off toward the exit of the store.

Levels

A few seconds passed while the rest of the passengers disembarked the elevator car. They flowed past him and the other people waiting to board. The last of the passengers cleared the car, and now, it was their turn to board.

"Come on, Dad," said Jake, nudging his side.

They followed the other passengers and boarded the car. Jake looked for the man with the hat before the doors closed, but he was gone.

They joined a group of older ladies who had stayed inside the car. The women were engaged in a conversation about, of all things, flower gardens. There were also two women in their thirties already onboard the car. They were talking about their young children.

Jake couldn't help but notice how beautiful the woman with the red hair was. Her friend was pretty, but there was something about the redhead that was very beautiful. Her skin was pale. What people called milky white. Her's wasn't pasty white, though. It was more like alabaster. It looked strong and yet still pliable. Her thick, wavy hair was anything but smooth like a model on TV. It was coarse and strong, the color of copper. It may have been the light shining down from the ceiling of the elevator car that made her hair glisten. Whatever it was, it looked beautiful. Their conversation was about their experience at a recent parent-teacher conference. From the sound of it, neither woman was pleased with the way the teachers were educating their offspring.

His dad ended up standing next to the control panel, so he asked, "Which floor, folks?" He'd already pressed the button for six. The mother said, "five, please." One of the teens said, "four."

The other passengers must have been satisfied with the selections as they didn't add any further destinations to the itinerary.

The doors began to slide closed.

"Hold the door, please," called out a male voice.

Derek pushed the button to reopen the doors. They continued to slide closed. He confirmed that he had pushed the right button. Sure enough, it had been the one with the arrows pointed toward each other. Satisfied that his selection was now correct, he stabbed it in rapid succession. The antiquated doors finally got the message and reversed their progress.

"Thank you," said the man as he stepped aboard. He was easily in his sixties, maybe even in his seventies. It was hard to tell. He was about five-six and of average build. He wore a goatee on his dark-skinned face and was dressed in khaki pants and a

Levels

polo shirt with a blue blazer. The smile he flashed his dad revealed a set of very white teeth.

"No problem, sir," he replied.

The doors stayed in the open position for another twenty seconds or so before cycling to close again. Jake observed the other passengers. The teen girls were still actively engaged in their conversation. The subject had changed from jeans to shoes. Undoubtedly, this was a dramatic shift in their world but only a minuscule shift for everyone else. The mother was making suggestions to her father on what would make a good present for his loving wife. The rest of the passengers were doing what passengers who don't know each other do when in such a confined space. They were looking anywhere but at each other. Most of the people, Jake could see, were looking at the floor indicator above the doors.

Finishing the path of their cycle, the doors closed with a dull *thunk*. Five seconds turned to ten, but there was no discernable movement. He looked down to make sure the light for the fourth floor had been pushed. The button was still lit up.

Another few seconds went by, but still, there was no change. He saw a few of the other passengers looking at the floor buttons, as he had done. Finally, the doors began to slide open again. They were still at two.

The mother stepped out of the elevator, still involved in her conversation with her dad.

"Ma'am," said Jake to get her attention. "I think we're still on the second floor."

They looked around and saw that it all looked the same.

"I guess I wasn't paying attention," she said laughing as she re-boarded the car.

His dad pressed the button to close the doors again. Everyone watched as they proceeded on their track. The same reassuring *thunk* sounded when they met. The same awkward amount of time passed before the doors opened again. This time they had all been watching the floor indicator and noted that no change had occurred. Things outside of the car looked the same.

"Well, that's odd," said the young college student.

His dad pushed the button for the doors to close again.

Odd is the right word. Something was troubling Jake. He couldn't quite place it, but something was off. He reached over and held his dad's hand. The doors were almost closed when his gaze fell on the young woman that had operated the register when his dad paid for his jeans. She was pregnant. Obviously pregnant

Levels

too, at least seven or eight months along. He could have sworn
she hadn't been when she'd sold him the jeans.

The same sound of the doors meeting and the same pause
after they closed. He felt the added gravity pushing down on him.
The elevator was finally moving. They looked at each other,
exchanging relieved smiles. The kind that said: I wasn't worried;
even though we know I kind of was.

The floor indicator bar went out for two, and the three lit
up. The car slowed, easing to a stop. Derek saw some of his
fellow passengers looked at the control panel. The button for the
third floor wasn't lit. He hadn't pushed it.

Chapter 2

Jake gripped his dad's hand tightly.

Derek squeezed his hand back and leaned down toward him. It wasn't like he had far to go. He marveled at how quickly his little boy was growing up. *Fourteen already! Where have the years gone?*

"It's just a little delay, kiddo. We'll get you those shoes in no time."

Jake looked up at him. Derek was surprised to see fear on his young face. He leaned in a little closer.

"What's wrong, son?"

"I don't know. Something feels bad."

Derek's mind cast back to another time. Jake was six and had wanted to see the dolphins. He was interested in animals, all kinds of animals. They'd already seen most of the exhibits. He'd really enjoyed watching the alligators being fed. They were really slow until the food was thrown, in then they went crazy, thrashing around and rolling over each other to get at the food. The show they'd really gone to see was going to start in about 15 minutes. They were below the seating level looking into the big tank. The

Levels

dolphins were already performing. They were swimming by the glass performing for their audience.

School was out because of a teacher administrative day. A day for the teachers to catch up on their admin meant a day for the kids to have some fun.

They'd been watching the dolphins for a little over five minutes. He'd felt good standing there holding his little boy's hand. As much as he'd wanted the moment to last, he knew it couldn't. He'd checked his watch. He didn't want to rush to find a seat for the show. He figured they had another five minutes. He was surprised Jake hadn't gotten bored yet. Six-year-old boys didn't usually have much of an attention span. Something caught Jake's attention. He'd turned from the tank, trying to look everywhere at once it seemed. He was squeezing Derek's hand tightly.

"What is it, son?"

"I don't know dad. Something feels bad."

"Do you need to go to the bathroom?"

"No, not that. Something feels weird," Jake said, scrunching up his shoulders.

A woman was standing to their left. She was struggling to keep her little boy and girl from fighting. Derek could hear in her voice how much of a challenge it was for her to keep her patience. Derek had to give her credit. He sometimes felt stressed looking after Jake. He couldn't imagine trying to take care of three kids at the same time. She was handling the situation well, managing two toddler's temperaments and handling the needs of an infant in a stroller.

The mother's attention was fully focused on the little girl. She was throwing a fit, claiming the boy had pinched her arm. That was when the baby in the stroller tossed her toy onto the ground.

Wanting to help his fellow parent, Derek had reached down to retrieve it for the tired mother.

"Thank you," she'd said.

He could tell by her expression that she'd appreciated the small act of kindness. More than that he could see she appreciated that someone else understood how difficult her day was.

"It's really no problem, ma'am," he had assured her.

Jake was gone. He'd just let go of his hand for a second.

Derek had frantically looked around. He couldn't have gone far. The crowd was light. There were less than ten people standing around. He hadn't seen his son anywhere. Jake was wearing a red jacket. He should have been able to spot him right

Levels

away. Derek had hurried around the exhibit, not quite running. *Maybe he wandered around the side to get a better look*, he thought. *Oh, God help me. Where are you, Jake?*

Derek hadn't see him anywhere. His fear had threatened to overwhelm him. He was breathing fast. Derek doubled back to the side of the enclosure they'd been standing at.

Jake wasn't there. He'd forced himself to scan the area slowly, trying to make sure he wouldn't miss anything. It hadn't helped that the lights were dimmed so you could see inside the tank better.

He'd checked the area as thoroughly as he could.

No Jake.

The sharp teeth of panic had gnawed on his senses. He was breathing fast. His eyes darted everywhere, trying to catch a glimpse of his son. *This can't be happening. He can't be gone. Not my Jake.*

He'd felt sick. Sweat beaded on his upper lip. His throat had clamped down to a tiny opening. He couldn't take a deep breath. He'd felt sure he was going to vomit. He had to find Jake.

"Have you seen a little boy? He has blond hair. He's wearing a red jacket with a hood and jeans." He'd asked anyone he could.

He'd seen an employee and ran over to her.

"Excuse me, ma'am. I can't find my son. He was standing right there with me," he'd said, pointing to where Jake had been. "He was there, holding my hand and then he was just gone."

"I'm sure he's fine, sir," she'd replied confidently. "I'm going to call this in." She'd unclipped the radio from her belt. "Maybe he's already been found by another employee and is sitting safe and sound in one of our offices," she'd said trying to reassure him.

"What does he look like, sir?"

Derek had given her Jake's description.

"Central, this is Shirley, we have a report of a lost boy. His father reports that the child is six years old, blond hair, wearing jeans and a red hooded jacket. The boy's name is Jacob."

"He goes by Jake."

"Central, the boy goes by Jake."

"Roger that, Shirley. We'll let you know when we find him."

"Okay, sir, we have his description, and every employee is going to be looking out for him. We're actually pretty good at this," she'd said reassuringly. "It happens more often than you think. Kids are curious. Sometimes they wander off, chasing

Levels

something that caught their interest. I'm sure we'll find him in no time."

Derek had nodded his head. He'd felt numb all over. He couldn't think clearly. All he could think about was that he had to find Jake. Nothing else mattered.

"Sir, would you like to come with me? You can wait in the administrative offices," she'd said with genuine concern. "That way, as soon as any word about your son comes in, we can let you know." She'd noted the lost look on his face. She'd seen that look enough times in the two years she'd been working there. In almost every case, they'd been successful in reuniting the family.

"No, thank you, I need to stay here. He could come back looking for me."

The woman looked at him kindly. She reached up and squeezed his shoulder. "We'll find him, sir," she'd said reassuringly.

Derek had thanked her and walked back over to stand in front of the tank. The dolphins had stopped swimming around. They were staying still. It looked like they were watching Derek. The only movement they'd made was to move their heads from side to side.

One of the larger dolphins turned to the side and moved closer to the glass. He was right in front of Derek. They looked at each other eye to eye.

Derek had been transfixed. He'd felt like he was being pulled into that intelligent gaze. He'd had no sense of time passing. Even his anxiety over Jake had subsided for a moment.

Derek marveled at how much intelligence he felt looking back at him. He'd felt like he was being analyzed. The dolphin looked like he'd been in deep thought as if he was puzzling over something. Maybe he was. Maybe he'd been thinking about why the people were there.

He'd stood there, lost, for a while, looking back at the big male staring at him. He'd felt completely lost. He didn't know what else he could do. He couldn't think straight. He'd replayed in his mind what had happened over and over again. He'd tried in vain to see what had happened. How he could have been separated from Jake.

He'd picked up a subtle change in the animal's expression a split second before it broke contact and looked down.

Something had slammed into the side of his leg. The force of the impact had almost knocked him off his feet.

Levels

He'd stumbled a couple of shuffling steps to the left pinwheeling his arms to catch his balance. He'd been stunned to see the top of Jake's head. His little face had been pressed so hard against Derek's thigh, arms wrapped around his legs, holding tight.

Derek had kneeled down and wrapped Jake in his arms.

"Where were you?" Jake had choked out the question between his panicked sobs.

"Where did you go, Daddy? I was so scared. Why'd you leave me?"

Derek had gently pushed his son back, so he could see his face. Tears streamed down his chubby cheeks. His whole body was wracked with the force of his sobbing.

"I didn't leave you. I've been right here. Where did you go?" Derek had asked, confused.

"I didn't go anywhere, Daddy. I stayed right here. I felt you let go of my hand and then you were gone. Where did you go? I was so scared. I didn't move. Just like you said. I didn't move. I stayed right here and waited for you to find me. Why did you leave me? Everybody was gone, Daddy. Where did everybody go?"

Derek had been confused. He didn't understand what had just happened. The only thing he knew, the only thing that mattered, was that Jake was okay. He'd picked him up and hugged him tight to his chest.

"It's okay now, son. Everything's going to be okay."

Derek had held onto him tightly. He'd looked back at the tank. The dolphins had gone away.

Derek had never found out what had happened that day. He'd written it off to Jake being scared and disoriented. He'd been grateful that nothing worse had happened.

Derek's senses were on high alert. The memory of that day kicked his protective instincts into high gear.

The elevator was not quick. It took a few seconds for the door to open onto the third floor. A sign hanging from the ceiling directed patrons to the sections they were interested in. An arrow for bedding and linens pointed straight ahead. Bathroom and other household items were to the left. Draperies and blinds to the right. Derek saw the bedding displays. The section was in the center of the store. The aisle went around the central circle. Inside, draperies were hung from false walls hanging to the side of simulated windows. Pictures were mounted, tastefully accentuating the display. It was all designed to give the

Levels

impression of what your bedroom could look like if you bought the ensemble, the whole ensemble.

To the left, towels and bath rugs were on display. Farther along, sheets and bedding ensembles were prominently positioned on the shelves lining the aisles. To the right, pots and pans adorned the stove tops of simulated kitchens.

All along the back of the floor, furthest from the elevator, living room furniture was showcased. Couches, lamps, and end tables were set up to simulate the living room you wanted to come home to. Warm light bathed the staged room. He saw one display that had a picture of a football game on the TV set prominently in the center of the room.

A young man was standing in front of the open elevator doors, waiting to board. He was dressed in a pair of gray slacks, a white shirt, and a simple gray tie. He had on plain black shoes. His hair was neatly combed to the side. He looked to be about Jake's age. It was kind of odd, Derek thought, for a boy of his age to be dressed that way, especially on a Saturday morning. He looked so proper. It was in stark contrast to the ongoing trend of sagging.

The passengers already on the elevator stepped back to make room for the boy. Derek noticed the boy looking at the

31

other passengers, especially the teenage girls. When his eyes found Jake, Derek saw the questioning look on his face.

Derek's attention went back to the scene outside of the now closing elevator doors. He noticed that the shoppers were dressed like the new passenger. The ladies were wearing knee-length skirts, and the men were in dress slacks or suits. Even the children were dressed that way.

The doors eased closed and made the now familiar *thunk* sound.

He turned his attention to the new passenger, looking at him out of the corner of his eye. The boy stood as close to the door as he could, as far away from the other passengers as possible. His hands held rigidly down by his sides, not in his pockets. His whole demeanor was stiff. His discomfort was palpable.

Derek's imagination was hard at work trying to figure out what was going on. What could be the reason this boy was dressed like he was? Why would the other shoppers on the third floor be dressed the same way? Sure, some of them could be expected to be dressed up for different reasons. The adults anyway. They could be working on a Saturday or maybe they just normally dressed that way. Some of the kids could be explained

Levels

in the same way. Maybe their parents just dressed them that way. It wasn't so easy to understand why all of them would be dressed like that though. *Maybe they just came from a wedding?* He thought. *No*, he rejected that scenario. *It was too early in the day for that. Maybe they were all going to a dance recital.* The performing arts theater wasn't far away. *Maybe they were putting on a noon performance.* That was possible, except he knew that at least some of the people would have been wearing jeans.

As hard as he tried, he couldn't fit what he saw with any solid explanation. It wasn't that it was strange for people to dress that way. It was just strange that so many of them would be dressed the same way. It was almost like pictures he had seen from the fifties and sixties.

The car rose on its cable. "Here we go, Jake," he said, giving his hand a gentle squeeze. The floor indicator changed to four. Derek turned his shoulder, preparing to step out once the doors opened. He moved behind Jake and put his hands on his shoulders, ready to follow him.

The elevator didn't slow. The indicator light for four went out. Derek looked down at the control panel and saw that the light there was still glowing its dirty yellow light. He looked over at the other passengers. Some of them were obviously dismayed as well.

Jake looked up at him. He was scared.

Derek couldn't tell if he was feeling spooked by his son's fear or if he was feeling something ominous as well. In the end, it didn't matter. He needed to keep Jake safe. If that meant calming his fears, okay. If it meant protecting him from something else, then that was what he would do.

The ascent of the car changed, slowing as it approached the fifth floor. The indicator above the door illuminated the number five. Derek unconsciously tensed his muscles in anticipation of what might happen.

The car came to a halt, and the doors slowly slid open onto the women's department. Prominently on display in the center of the floor were the jewelry and perfume display cases. The area was bathed in clean white light. Customers were scattered around the glass cases browsing the items on display.

The area to the left was the section for makeup products. Customers were sitting on stools while employees in white smocks danced around them with brushes in hand working their art on the canvas of their faces.

Levels

Derek saw a few men standing nearby trying to look interested in the process. Some of them had given up the effort and were focused on their phones instead.

Everything looked normal here. The woman with her father and children got off the elevator and made their way toward the center counter. *It looks like Grandma's going to get either jewelry or some perfume.*

Nobody was waiting to board the elevator, so Derek took the opportunity to poke his head out and look around. Nothing looked out of the ordinary. Everyone was dressed and acting as he expected. It looked, for lack of a better word, normal.

He stepped back into the elevator and looked around at the other passengers. "Nobody else?" he asked. No one wanted to get off, so he pushed the button to close the doors. He reached down and took Jake's hand in his again. He figured the car would go up to the sixth floor next. He wanted to get the cleats for Jake and get back to Julie.

The button for five hadn't been pressed and was still not lit up. It made sense the car would continue in the same direction it had been going. In this case, to continue going up before going back down again.

The doors went through their cycle again, including the solid *thunk* when they met. He waited for the feeling of the car rising up the cable. The seconds ticked by. Ten seconds went by with nothing happening. Ten seconds normally is not a long time, but when you are in an enclosed space, looking at a set of closed doors, and waiting for something to happen, time stretches out.

Finally, something happened. The doors began to open again. His eyes, as well as most of the other passengers, went up to the floor indicator, even though he knew they hadn't moved. Sure enough, it still said they were on five.

The passengers looked around at each other. Most were smiling a little. The elevators were old. Even though the buildings had been completely refurbished during the last upgrade, they had kept the original elevator cars. They wanted to keep as much of the historic buildings as possible. Everyone understood that sometimes glitches happened. It was the price to pay for patching the past and present together.

Again, there wasn't anyone waiting on the car. That would have explained it. If someone had pushed the call button, then it might have opened for them. But there wasn't anyone there.

Derek took a step out of the elevator and looked to each side. He didn't see anything to explain why the elevator hadn't

Levels

moved. He shrugged his shoulders and stepped back into the car then pushed the button to close the doors again. They went through their cycle, and again, they didn't go anywhere. The doors opened to the same scene.

The woman in the emerald green blouse stepped forward. "I don't know about you guys, but this isn't normal."

"What are you going to do?" asked the man with the goatee.

"I'm going to ask one of the employees if there's something wrong with the elevator." She had a confident, purposeful stride. Her heels clicked on the tile flooring as she walked to the jewelry counter at the center of the floor.

Derek decided to follow her. "Come on, Jake," he said, gently pushing him forward by the shoulders.

Jake was looking around at the displays lining the aisle they were walking down. Box sets of men's and women's perfumes and bath products lined both sides of the aisle. Down the center, prominently displayed, were fragrances endorsed by celebrities. Banners with their perfect faces hung suspended over the products.

Derek recognized a few of them. He wasn't one to keep up with the tabloids, so he wasn't surprised that there were some he didn't know.

Muted footfalls caught Jake's attention, so he turned and glanced over his shoulder. The fellow with the goatee was following close behind them.

"Might as well try and find out what's going on," the man said with a small shrug of his shoulders.

Derek recognized the mother with her father and children. She was talking with one of the sales representatives over on the far side of the jewelry cases. From the look of things, she wasn't having much success convincing her dad.

The woman in the emerald green blouse had arrived at the counter and was waiting to speak with a store employee. They were all busy with customers.

Derek took advantage of the situation and engaged her in conversation.

"Ma'am, excuse me," he said to get her attention.

"Oh, hi," she responded.

"What do you think is going on?"

Levels

"It's probably just what it seems to be, probably nothing more than old equipment that's been in service too long," she said with a little smile.

That sounded reasonable. Except why was she going to talk with an employee if it was that simple?

She answered as if she had been reading his mind.

"I just think there's a small chance that this could be the start of a problem with the elevator. If they know about it, maybe they can get it fixed before someone gets stuck between floors. Trust me, that's no fun."

"How long were you stuck there?" Jake asked her.

"It wasn't very long, sweetie," she said looking down at him with a smile. "They were able to get the car moving again in no time."

She probably has a son too, thought Derek. She had effortlessly eased any possible anxiety Jake may have had about getting back on an elevator.

The look she gave Derek confirmed his suspicion. She'd been stuck in that elevator much longer than she had liked. She was trying to do something to avoid it from happening to someone else.

Seeing one of the clerks finishing up, Derek raised his hand and waved to get her attention.

"How can I help you?" she asked stepping closer to them.

Derek inclined his head toward the businesswoman. She took his cue.

"We were just on the elevator, and it's acting a bit strange."

The woman sighed. "I'm sorry about that. Those old cars are always having issues. What happened?" she asked.

They told her what had happened, and the clerk nodded her head in understanding. "I'm sorry to say, but that is pretty normal. They're safe to use. Fortunately, they don't break down on us too often. When they have broken down, they usually come right back up." She flashed them a smile that was meant to be reassuring. Unfortunately, it conveyed too much of how tired she was of talking about the elevator. She stood a little straighter and tried to inject more sincerity into her voice. "I appreciate you letting us know. I'll call maintenance, so they can look into it. Is there anything else I can help you with?" she asked with a small smile.

"No, thank you."

Levels

"Okay, you all have a nice time and thank you for shopping at Wentley's."

They turned and walked a couple of steps away from the counter. The businesswoman slowed to a stop.

Curious, Derek did as well. "What is it?"

"I'm not sure," she said. "It's probably nothing."

Derek just looked at her and waited. The gentleman with the goatee was also standing off to the side, waiting for her response.

"Did you see the perfume displays?"

Each of the guys nodded their head and turned to look over at the displays.

"Maybe you didn't notice, but one was a contestant on one of those singing reality shows. The thing is, she shouldn't be on that display. She didn't win. In fact, she didn't even place in the top ten. She wasn't very good, and her attitude was terrible. There's no way she got that endorsement. It's just wrong."

Once she explained who the woman on the display was, Derek recognized her. He'd watched a few episodes and agreed with the woman's assessment. He also thought that she looked pretty plain. She wasn't ugly, but she wasn't pretty enough to overcome the points the woman made against her being on that display. He chose to keep his thoughts to himself.

The guy with the goatee was nodding his head. "That does sound odd. Did you notice the clothes our young friend is wearing? The one that's about your age, young man," he said looking at Jake.

"Yeah," answered Derek. The woman was also nodding her head.

"Did you also notice how the other shoppers were dressed on the floor when he got on with us?"

"I thought that was weird too," answered the woman. "Why would they all be dressed that way?"

"Did you notice the small man in the brown suit and fedora?" Derek asked.

"What's odd about that?" asked the goateed gentleman. "I wear a fedora myself from time to time."

"Yeah, I understand," he answered. "I don't know; it just felt a little strange is all. I don't know how to say it any better than that."

The woman was looking over Derek's shoulder, back toward the elevator. He turned and looked too. The doors were

Levels

still open. Most of the other passengers were still inside the car. A few people had gathered just inside the store.

"Okay, that's strange. Maybe it's broken down now," she said. "I'm going to go find the stairs." She turned on her sensibly heeled tan shoes and walked off.

"You know, Jake, that sounds like a good idea. Let's look around for a little bit while we're here."

"Do you mind if I follow along?" asked the man.

"Sure, I'm Derek, and this is my son Jake," he said, reaching out his hand to shake the other man's.

"Pleased to meet you. My name is Khalid."

"Okay, so, she said that the display for that perfume was wrong. What if we go around and see if anything else looks, well, off?"

Khalid and Jake both nodded their heads that they agreed. Since the woman had gone to the left, they decided to go to the right to see what they could find, if anything.

"Stay close to me, Jake."

They roamed around the store, looking at the different merchandise. Derek admitted to himself that he was at a disadvantage. He had never been the guy that was interested in colognes and perfumes.

At the back of the store, a section was set aside for the display of crystal bowls and decanters, Faberge eggs, and other gift type items. Derek stopped to examine a display for some interestingly designed cat figurines.

Julie had started a collection a few years back. Her favorite artist was Stromzin. Derek was happy to see that several of the items on display were ones she didn't have yet. He was kind of surprised because he'd been buying them for her and thought he recognized the whole catalog. Maybe these were a new collection. He turned the figurine over and looked at the label on the bottom. He almost dropped it in his surprise. *This must be a mistake. There's no way that this costs eight hundred and forty-five dollars.* The last time he bought one, it was only forty-seven, fifty. Curious, he looked at the other pieces and saw that they were similarly priced. *Maybe this is a limited edition or something. There's no way I'm spending that much.* He carefully put it back down.

Jake was looking at a display of miniature antique car replicas. "See anything you like?" Derek asked him.

"Look at this, Dad." Jake handed him a white car with teal trim.

Levels

Derek knew enough to know that it was an early 1950s model. He was good at recognizing the cars from this timeframe. He didn't recognize this one, though. He looked closer at the plaque: 1953 Atwood Airstream. He was puzzled. He'd never heard of a company called Atwood. He looked around and saw Khalid a few feet away. He brought the car over to him.

"Hey, have you ever heard of an Atwood Airstream?" he asked him, handing the car over.

Khalid shook his head as he looked over the model. "It looks like a Buick, but not quite. The fins are too flared at the back and look here," he said pointing at the grill. "I have never seen a car with a symbol like this, $\mathcal{A}$. Are these supposed to be models of real cars?" he asked.

Jake led him back to the display. Khalid took a few minutes looking over the other models without saying anything. After a couple of minutes had gone by, he stood back up to his full height.

"There are a few that I don't recognize at all. Some, I recognize, but there are a few things about them that are a little bit different, though. There's something off about them. Look here," he said, pointing to a 1964 Cadillac Convertible. "The hood is flat. It's supposed to be curved with a scoop on it. There're more models like the Atwood. Models I don't recognize as ever being produced. There's a chance these are foreign cars. Not much of one, though. I know a lot about the cars of this time. I have a Bellaire that I restored and show at car shows. It's a hobby of mine. Now that I'm retired I have learned a lot about these cars."

"So, what do you think it means?" Derek asked.

"I don't know," Khalid answered, shaking his head slowly.

Derek liked this man. He felt that he could trust him. He sounded like a serious man that wasn't prone to fantasy.

"I think we should keep looking around. That woman went to go find the stairs. Maybe we should do the same," Khalid suggested as he cast his eyes to the other side of the store.

That sounded like a good idea to Derek. As good an idea as any at this point anyway. Things definitely felt strange, but thankfully, he didn't think that they were in any immediate danger.

He looked back to the elevator. It was still there, doors standing wide open. The young scholar and the boy in the tie were standing inside the car talking with each other. The two

Levels

older women were just outside, to the right of the car. The other passengers must have wandered off.

Derek looked around and spotted the three teenage girls over by the Sofe' display. The mother and father were looking over another selection of perfumes. Her children were looking into the display cases as only children do. They had their little noses pressed right on the glass. Derek couldn't suppress his smile as they walked past the kids. Jake used to do the same thing when he was little.

On their way across the store, they saw the woman in the emerald green blouse looking out the window. Curious, Derek decided to go and see what she was looking at.

When they were still a good ten feet away, she turned and watched them approach.

"Hello again," said Derek in greeting.

"Have you seen anything interesting?" asked Khalid.

"Well, for starters, the stairwell isn't accessible. They are doing work on the fire main, or so the sign says. There's scaffolding blocking the door from opening so we can't use the stairs."

"That's very strange," said Khalid. "That's a major fire code violation."

She nodded her head. "My thought exactly. You can also forget the windows. They don't open," she said pointing to the place the glass met the frame.

Derek tapped his finger on the glass. The tone sounded strange.

"You guessed it," she said. "Some type of plastic."

He leaned in closer and looked at the pane. "It's one of those energy efficient windows, there are actually three panes inside," he said.

"They must have put them in during the renovation," said Khalid.

He looked at the woman and reached out his hand to her. "I'm Khalid."

She shook his hand. "Nancy," she replied.

"I'm Derek, and this is my son, Jake," he said.

Khalid filled her in on the things they had observed.

While he was talking, Derek let his eyes wander to the scene outside the window.

Traffic was flowing by, both on the road and on the sidewalks. He stepped closer to the window and looked down to get a good look at the pedestrians on this side of the road. He didn't know what he had expected. Maybe a blurred line that

Levels

separated the building from the rest of the world. Something that looked strange that would explain why they were different in here. Maybe even a film crew. Things were weird enough, maybe they'd stepped into a reality show and would all sign waivers and release forms.

There was no blurred line, no TV crew, no visible explanation to put this all on.

He let his eyes wander over the scene below. From this height, it all looked like something out of a movie. Everything was orderly and neat. There wasn't any trash in the gutters. There weren't any bums looking for handouts. He didn't see any graffiti marking the walls. He was looking to his right when he saw two men walking side by side. What had drawn his attention to them was that they were wearing identical black uniforms with tall black boots. Each of the men had a black beret, tilted to the side, on his head. The crowds of people flowed around them as water in a stream flows past a boulder. No one came closer to them than a few feet. He didn't know what to make of the two men.

He noticed that Nancy had moved next to him. "I see our friends are back again."

"Who are they?" asked Derek.

"I'm not sure, but they act like beat cops," she replied.

"I've never seen any police uniforms like that," said Derek.

"Me either," agreed Khalid. He had his face pressed so close to the window that his breath was fogging it up when he exhaled.

They watched the pair of men as they continued on their way. Across the street, a bus pulled away from its stop. On the side of the enclosure, a sign caught Derek's attention: Curfew Strictly Enforced. Under those words, an official-looking badge, like a police badge, was displayed.

Derek had seen enough. Whatever was going on was not confined to this building. It didn't matter if they found a way down or not. Things were not the same.

"What in the hell is going on?" he muttered.

Jake looked up at him. It wasn't like his dad to use that kind of language.

"I don't know about you, but I'm going to go back to the elevator and try to get out of here," said Nancy.

"I don't think that's going to make any difference," said Khalid. "Things aren't normal outside. I don't know about you guys, but when I came into the store we didn't have a curfew, and

Levels

I know we didn't have men in all black uniforms and jackboots patrolling the streets."

"Okay then, what do you propose we do?" she asked.

"While I stick to what I said, I don't think it's going to make any difference, but I don't have any better ideas. Nancy, I think your idea is the best one we have," said Khalid.

Derek agreed. He didn't see any better options. Staying here was only continuing with this strange reality they were in.

"Hey, Dad ..."

"It'll be okay, son. We'll figure this out."

"The elevator's gone."

They all looked across the store at the shiny metal doors. No one was standing near them.

Derek looked at Nancy and Khalid. He didn't see fear on their faces, but it wasn't far away, he thought.

"I don't know about you, but I think it's time for us to go," she said as she set off walking.

The rest of the group fell in stride behind her. Derek looked around for any of the people they had arrived with. He didn't know how he would go about explaining things to them, but he knew he didn't want to leave anyone behind.

The family that had been shopping for a gift was nowhere to be seen. Derek looked around as they made their way past the jewelry counter and proceeded to close the distance to the elevator. There were parts of the store they couldn't see because of the way the displays were set up. He didn't feel like wasting time looking around. As much as he didn't want to leave any of the other passengers behind, his priority was Jake and he felt a sense of urgency. He felt the need to get away from there as soon as possible.

They were still a good thirty or so feet away from the elevator when Derek saw that the floor indicator wasn't lit. *Maybe it's in between floors.* He kept his eyes on the display while they closed the distance. The small group slowed as they arrived at the elevator. The lights above the doors remained dark. No one said anything. They just stood there looking up. After what felt like a long time the indicator for five lit up, and the doors began to open. Their fellow passengers were still inside the car. Everyone except the mother with her children and father.

The little old lady in the dress with the yellow flowers spoke up. "This elevator is not working well at all," she said to her friend. "We should take the stairs."

Levels

"You know we can't do that, dear. My hip simply will not allow me to."

"Well, this elevator isn't getting us anywhere. Look, we're right back on five again. If we don't hurry and get our shopping done, we'll be late for tea."

"I'm sure we still have plenty of time," her friend reassured her.

They made room for Derek's group to re-board the car. The college kid was now standing next to the control panel.

Jake looked at it and saw that the lights for seven and eight were lit in addition to six. Two and one had also been pushed. *Okay, which will it be? Up or down?* The doors slowly closed. *And what will we find when we get there?*

Chapter 3

The car began to rise.

"It's about time," said the blonde girl with the short hair.

"I don't even have a signal inside this piece of junk," complained her friend with long blonde hair as she stared at her phone in frustration. "I can't believe Billy hasn't answered me yet."

"I don't have a signal either," said the shorter haired blond. She lowered the phone and exhaled in frustration. "Can't this old piece of junk hurry up already?"

The younger girl, the brunette with her hair pulled back in a ponytail, looked at Jake and gave him a little smile.

He responded with one of his own then quickly looked away. After a few seconds, he stole another glance. She caught him looking. He could've seen her grin if he hadn't looked away so fast.

The car slowed its ascent, and the light for six above the doors lit up. It slowed even more as it eased to a stop. Derek saw the other passengers were eager to arrive. The doors began their opening cycle.

Levels

As soon as there was enough room for her to slide through, the long-haired girl stepped off the car, her cell phone leading the way. "I can't believe it, Angie. I still don't have a signal for this piece of crap. What, are we in a dead zone?"

Her friend with the shorter hair was right on her heels with her phone in hand. She waved it around as if that would help her find the elusive signal. They were so focused on their phones that they didn't notice the younger girl lagged behind them.

"Aren't you going to go with your friends," asked Jake.

"They're not my friends," she responded. "The one with the short hair's my sister. They're so preoccupied with texting their boyfriends that they barely realize I'm here. Besides, I know where they're going anyway."

"I'm Jake, by the way."

"Clare."

"Do you go to Brookston?"

"No, Saint Catherine's," she answered him.

"Well, that explains why I didn't recognize you," he said hoping that she couldn't tell how nervous he was. "How do you like it there? I heard it's pretty small."

"That's one of the things I like about it. The teachers are engaged, and they push us to know the subjects. I have friends that go to public schools, and they tell me how some of the teachers don't even teach the lessons. They just tell the kids what to read and then give them tests. One of my friends, Linda, asked her teacher to explain something she got wrong on a test. I couldn't believe it. She said that the teacher told her that it was okay, not everybody's bright enough to get it. She then told her that some people weren't destined for higher education. This was a teacher telling a freshman that." She shook her head in disgust.

Derek saw the look on her face go from indignation to a dawning of embarrassment as she realized Jake went to a school like that.

Jake knew what she was thinking. "I'm glad I don't have anybody like that. So far, all my teachers are good. I can't believe a teacher would say something like that."

Unfortunately, Derek didn't have such a hard time believing it. It wasn't so long ago that some people had a much narrower view of who should go on to college. They thought that a girl's place was in the home. There was no need for her to get an education beyond how to take care of the house and her family. Then there was the other mindset of only those that came from the upper social classes should pursue a higher education. That wasn't even talking about how terribly minorities were

Levels

looked down on and actively denied opportunities. He thought that those prejudices had been left in the past. Sadly, it would seem that some of the lessons had managed to stay alive to interfere with the futures of this generation as well.

"Hey, isn't this the sixth floor?"

"Yeah, why?" said Clare.

Jake looked back at his dad. "We came here to buy soccer cleats. The directory said they were on the sixth floor. This doesn't look right," he said looking around.

The entrance was blocked off for security. Two turnstiles were on each side for entering the store and four in the center for exiting. On the side of each exit were panels to detect if the anti-theft devices had been removed or not.

He looked up at the ceiling and saw what he expected to see. All throughout the store black globes hung from the ceiling. He looked behind him and sure enough, two cameras, not hidden inside the black globes, were aimed at the exit stalls. The point they made was blatantly clear. In fact, the sign between them spelled it out for the less astute. In bold black letters: Shoplifters will be prosecuted.

To the right, printers were lined up on display. On the left side of the main aisle, another turnstile controlled access into the gaming area. A full third of the store had been partitioned off for the display of the latest systems. Sony had a large section devoted to their products as did Nintendo and a few other brands he didn't recognize. The area was busy with people of all ages playing the games.

"Dad, what do you think?"

"We might as well look around while we're here," he said reluctantly. "Please stay where I can see you though."

Jake nodded his head then turned back to Clare. They walked down the center aisle, heading toward the center kiosk of cell phones. Along the back wall of the store, giant screen TVs were on display. To the right of them were the home theater systems and then the audio section picked up. Sections had been enclosed for serious audiophiles to hear the capabilities of the systems. The brand names Bose, Polk, and Klipsch announced the merchandise within.

Jake and Clare wandered over to a display for discounted movies, rifling through the box of Blu-Rays. Derek saw that Clare's focus was on her sister who was with her friend at the cell phone counter, browsing the phone covers. The friend of Clare's sister was busy sending a text, so she must have found a signal. Everything looked normal.

Levels

Jake's eyes wandered to the back of the store. To the left of the biggest TV he'd ever seen and the partition for the gaming section along the back wall, he noticed a sign above an entryway announcing the presence of a returns section. He let his eyes wander over the TVs from halfway across the store. *How big of a living room do you need to be able to see a TV that size?* He watched a bit of the football game airing on the giant screen TV. *It must be at least an eighty-inch screen.*

Jake was randomly flipping through the movies, not really paying attention. He hadn't even heard of most of them. He kept stealing looks at Clare. She was on the other side of the display flipping through the cases. She didn't look like she was any more focused on the movies than him. She was watching her sister.

"So, what gives?" he asked her. "Are you grounded and getting stuck with your sister's your punishment?"

"No, she wanted to come here and hang out with Melissa. The only way my mom would say yes is if I came along."

Jake didn't say anything. He didn't know what to say. All the lines he ran through his head sounded lame.

"I don't go out much. My mom thinks I need to make more friends," she said. "What position do you play?"

"What?"

"You said you were here for some new soccer cleats. What position do you play," she asked him?

"Striker. You?"

"Midfielder," she said.

"I just finished the PDP program. I'm trying to get into the Olympic Development Program," said Jake.

"Me too," she said. "The problem is, my school's not very good."

Jake was nodding his head. "That's why I did the Player Development Program Richmond. The coaches were great," he said.

Clare looked back at her sister, who was walking toward the elevator. "I guess we're leaving," she said looking back at Jake.

He quickly caught up with her.

"You going to get those cleats?" she asked. She picked up her pace as they cut across the store, trying to catch up with her sister.

"Yeah," he said.

"Do you think you just read the sign wrong?"

"I must have," he told her. He knew he hadn't.

Levels

She picked up the pace. She was wondering why Angie was walking so quickly.

"They're probably on seven," he said. He waved to his dad to meet him at the elevator.

Derek and Nancy caught up with them as the elevator arrived.

They stood to the side to allow the passengers to leave the car. Standing in the back was a familiar face. Recognizing the group, Khalid smiled at them.

"I was wondering if we would meet again," he said. "I am happy it is so."

Derek found himself next to the control panel again. Seven and eight were already lit. They waited for the doors to close.

An awkward amount of time passed, and nothing happened. Derek smiled at the rest of the group then pressed the button to close the doors. Still nothing.

Movement from the returns room caught his attention. Two men dressed in black and wearing berets walked purposefully down the center aisle toward the elevator. Their boots sounded a heavy tattoo from their purposeful strides.

"You two need to come with us," said the bigger of the two. The men reached out their hands to isolate the girls not quite putting their hands on them. Their intent was clear.

"What's going on?" asked Derek.

"This is none of your concern, sir," said the smaller of the two men.

"My niece isn't going anywhere with you until you tell me what this is about."

The guard looked at him and quickly sized him up. "We have some questions for these young ladies," he explained. "They are going up to our offices. You are welcome to come along."

"Not until you say why first. This isn't a police state. You don't just say march, and people fall in line. The last time I checked this is America, and we have something called due process."

"They are being detained for suspicion of shoplifting."

"Let's go, ladies," said the larger of the two. It was clear he meant business.

Angie, Clare's sister, looked really scared. She looked to Derek for help.

Levels

"It's going to be okay. We'll get to the bottom of this. There's obviously been a misunderstanding. We'll get it sorted out," he reassured her.

By this time, they were walking back to the returns room. Clare started to follow Angie.

"Clare don't!" Jake warned her. He grabbed her arm to hold her back.

She turned and looked at him. "She's my sister, Jake."

She tried pulling her arm free to go after her sister when everything around her changed.

Chapter 4

A bright light washed out everything around her, and a loud buzzing sound invaded her head. She felt like she was floating, without any sense of up or down. It was like she had become untethered. Her throat tightened up. She felt like she needed to puke, it was all she could do to take small sips of air. She flailed her arms for balance, not sure if she was going to pass out or not, and only then realized that Jake was still holding her arm. She spun around and grabbed onto him with her other hand. The nausea and weightlessness eased up.

She risked opening her eyes just a little bit. It was too bright to see anything clearly. Jake was a dark blur. She quickly closed her eyes again and took a couple of quick breaths to steady herself. They were shallow because it was all she could manage. The buzzing in her head receded to a dull roar. Feeling more in control of herself, she opened her eyes for another look.

The bright lights of the electronic displays were gone. In their place, she found herself looking at rows of mostly empty shelves. A thick coating of dust covered everything.

Levels

She froze in place, unaware that she was holding her breath, and looked around. The only other person there was Jake. The amazed look on his face must be a match to the one on hers, she thought.

"What just happened?" she asked him.

"I'm not sure."

She shook her head, trying to shake herself out of this, this … whatever *this* was.

"Jake, do you see what I'm seeing?"

"Yeah, I think so."

"Okay, but please tell me what you see anyway. I think I may have just lost my mind."

"Empty store, nobody else here, everything covered in dust. Is that what you see?"

She nodded her head. A fascinated, not quite scared yet, look on her face. It was too much to believe. It wasn't real yet.

Jake turned around. There weren't any footprints on the floor, other than the ones they had just made. He realized he was still holding onto Clare's arm and let it go.

She didn't say anything, but she took a step closer to him.

"What do you think happened?"

"I'm not sure. Listen, do you hear that," he asked.

They both listened intently for a few seconds.

"I don't hear anything. What is it?"

"Exactly! I don't hear anything either. That's really weird."

He turned and walked toward the windows. Dust puffed up from where their footfalls disturbed it. The coating was thick.

Jake kept looking from side to side as he made his way to the window. All he saw was more of the same. Most of the merchandise was gone. Only a few things remained. Some of the shelving had been tipped over and lay broken on the floor. The only place where light came through the windows was on the side where the audio displays had been. The rooms had been torn down and the merchandise was gone. All that remained to mark what had been there were some of the pictures displayed on the back wall. One side of a display banner had come loose and was lying mostly torn from the wall. That was where the light from the outside was coming in.

They both looked out from the dirty pane. The view was to the south, looking back up the street toward the other part of the department store. The other tower stood at the far end of the block. In between them was the promenade where he'd left his mom talking on the phone. This was not the same promenade.

Levels

The windows were covered in dirt, many of them broken out. As he watched, a bird flew out of a broken pane. No traffic moved on the road. No cars. No people. Nothing. The only thing that moved was trash blowing in the breeze and that one bird.

The store windows on the other side of the road were broken out as well. Graffiti was painted all over the place. One painting in particular, stood out. It was a crude rendition of a person hanging from a noose with the phrase "White Lives Don't Matter" written in red under the gallows.

Jake looked at her. Maybe it was just an effect of the light coming in through the dirty window, but she looked pale. Without thinking, he reached down and held her hand. They stood there for a few minutes, taking in the scene. No one appeared from around the corner. No car crossed a side street. The street lights didn't change either. The power must be turned off too. They didn't hear any sounds through the window. The breeze had even quit. The trash wasn't blowing around.

She walked to the side of the window. Through a gap in the buildings, she was able to see the river. There wasn't anyone out on the rocks. Normally, on a day as hot as this one was, people would be out on the rocks, swimming in the pools they made. It didn't look like anyone was on Belles Isle either. The fence with barbed wire at the top probably had something to do with it. It cut off access to the river from the city.

"What do you think we should do?" she asked him without turning from the window.

"Come on." He started walking back the way they'd come. Without thinking about it, he kept holding her hand. He didn't know where to go. He only knew that they needed to do something. Over to the right, about halfway to the middle of the store, he noticed light coming in. The sign that announced the area for returns was still in place.

The area was lit more brightly than the main floor area. Along the back of the room, at the top of the wall, windows let light in through their dirty panes.

To the left were three doors. Two were clearly the bathrooms, and the third was a door marked "Employees only." It had a strange looking lock and a window with wire mesh in it.

To the right, the room opened up to the returns area. A U-shaped counter was the central feature of the space. The cash registers, where the workers had processed the returns, had all been removed. The lifeless cables they had been attached to were sprawled on the counter and in a couple of cases on the floor. The display that usually indicated the number for the next customer to

Levels

be served was as dead as the clock next to it; its hands were frozen at 10:42.

He stopped walking suddenly.

"Oh, sorry," she said after bumping into him.

Jake was looking over at the bathrooms. More specifically, he was looking at the floor by the bathrooms.

"What is it?"

He stood still a moment longer. Something had triggered him to look back toward the bathrooms. He let his eyes slowly scan the area. There didn't seem to be an immediate threat. He looked back the way they had come. There wasn't anything that drew his attention. He shifted his focus further out over the deserted space. Everything still looked as it had since they'd arrived. Apart from their footprints in the dust, it didn't look like anything had changed. The doors of the elevator were still closed. He darted his eyes to where he knew the stairs were. That door was closed too. As much as he could tell, nobody had come in from there either.

Satisfied that they were still safe, he let his eyes wander for a little bit longer. Something had caught his attention.

Clare was busy looking around behind the return counter. She was opening drawers and rifling through the detritus of items that had been cast off to see what she could find.

Jake brought his gaze back to the bathroom doors. That was what had caught his attention. The dust in front of the door for the women's bathroom was disturbed. The small tracks in the dust led from the employee's door to the bathroom. Someone had been here. Someone with small feet from the look of the prints. His eyes went back to the employee's door. The tracks didn't go anywhere else. The person must have gone back through that door he thought.

"Hey, Clare."

"Yeah."

"Did you find anything?"

"No, just some junk. How 'bout you?"

"Maybe, come here a second."

When she got close, he pointed out the tracks in the dust.

"Do you think they're in there?" she asked him.

"If they are they had to have already heard us. I don't think the tracks are fresh."

He looked at the way she was smiling at him.

"What?"

Levels

"Are you a tracker?" she asked him playfully.

He blushed a little. "No, but that's the way it looks." He felt heat rise in his cheeks.

"Okay, Gale, should we continue tracking our prey?"

She was met with a blank look.

"Seriously?"

He shrugged his shoulders.

"*Hunger Games*, dude. Ever hear of it?"

"Of course," he said. "I just don't recognize the name. Which one was he?"

"Just the one she should have ended up with. Do you remember her friend she went hunting with in the beginning?"

He slowly nodded his head.

"Okay, that was him." She waited. Nothing. She threw up her hands, exasperated. "He was a tracker in the movie. He went out into the forest with Katniss to get food for their families. You really don't remember any of this?"

He did. He just liked the way she was getting worked up over a movie. His grin must have given him away.

She smiled because she realized he was teasing her.

"Seriously, I think we need to see what's in there," she said waving her arm toward the door.

"Yeah, me too. Let's go." He stepped up to the door, stood to the side, and reached out his hand to grab hold of the metal handle. He hoped it didn't start shaking. He took a deep breath and slowly let it out. He looked over at Clare. She nodded her head that she was ready. He didn't want to hesitate and show her how scared he really was. *Just do it already.* He slowly eased it open.

"Thank you, sir," said Clare as she walked past him boldly into the dark.

Jake quickly went in after her.

"No," she said turning back to him and thrusting her arm out toward the door. "You need to keep it open, so we can see," she said a little too loudly.

He realized she was right. The light from the return area was being cut off by the closing door. He caught it before it closed all the way.

"There's nobody here, Jake." Her voice came from the back of the room.

The bathroom was shrouded in darkness. The meager light coming in from the door wasn't enough to reach the back of the room. All he could make out were shadows and darker shadows. Her's moved among the stationary ones.

Levels

"This place has been empty for a long time."

He believed her. He used his foot to brace the door open and leaned as far into the room as he could to keep an eye on her.

Clare had barely enough light for her to see what she needed to do. It was dark, but her eyes were slowly adjusting. She looked around as quickly as she could. She would never admit to Jake how scared she was. All she wanted to do was to turn and run. Instead, she forced herself to take a quick look around. Seeing nothing of interest, she made herself walk slowly and calmly back out of the dark.

"You do not want to go into that second stall," she said fanning her hand in front of her face. "There's nothing important in there."

Satisfied they were alone, they went back to the returns area.

"Do you think we should check the men's bathroom?"

"No, there aren't any prints. I don't think anyone's been in there, at least not in a very long time," he said.

"Maybe you should look around anyway."

He looked at her to see if she was just messing with him. She wasn't.

He grudgingly agreed.

They went through the same process except, this time, Clare held the door open for him.

Jake took a tentative step into the dark space. The meager light did little to illuminate the room. To his left were two sinks with what was left of a mirror above them. The one on the right had been broken, and the jagged pieces of porcelain crunched underfoot. To the right, three urinals, two of them also broken, lined the wall. Further back and deeper in shadow, was a mess of what had been two toilet stalls. The stalls and toilets had been destroyed and lay in pieces. In the far back corner, a pile of what may have been clothing or blankets, or maybe something else, lay in the darkness. Jake had no plans to investigate that far back. He ventured as far in as the first toilet stall.

"What are you doing? Taking a nap?"

The sound of her voice nearly made him jump out of his skin. He tried to calm down his breathing and get his heart out of his throat and back down to where it was supposed to be.

He took a gulp of air. "There may be something here. Hang on a second. Can you open the door a little more," he asked?

The door banged loudly against the wall causing him to jump. He was immediately embarrassed.

Levels

"Sorry, Jake."

He took a deep breath and tried to calm his racing heart. He could see a little better. It still wasn't a lot of light, but it was enough for him to see what had caught his attention.

He idly moved some debris aside with his foot. A giant rat reared up on its hind legs and squealed at him before scampering away. He let out a high-pitched scream that echoed off the tile.

"Go! Go! Go!" he yelled as he pushed Clare out the door. He stumbled and tripped over his feet as they tangled up in hers.

They fell in a heap on the dusty floor just clear of the bathroom door.

"What is it?"

"It's nothing," he said breathing hard.

"What did you see?"

"A rat! I hate rats."

"A rat? That was some scream for a rat," she said jokingly. "Are you sure it wasn't a mouse?"

"I hate rats," he grumbled. He shivered involuntarily at the thought of the rat.

She relaxed and lay down on the floor next to him, her head resting on Jake's arm.

"Do you want me to go in there and take care of it for you?"

He turned his head to her and cut his eyes in response. When he saw the smile turning up the corners of her mouth, he couldn't help but smile too. The smile soon turned into a fit of giggles and erupted into uncontrolled laughter.

"We should go in there and check it out," he said pointing to the employee's door and hopefully changing the subject.

Letting the rat episode drop, she nodded her head.

They stood up and brushed their clothes off as good as they could. Clouds of dust billowed around them.

A tall counter to the left of the entrance divided the area. A huge safe door stood open on the back wall. Beyond were what looked like metal shelves. Jake could make out what looked like big TV boxes and other smaller boxes cast haphazardly aside. He couldn't see far into the dark space. It must have been a large room. He couldn't see to the back. It didn't look like anything of value remained. Whatever was left wasn't enough to make him want to brave the dark again.

About ten feet back and to the left of the counter, a set of wooden stairs rose to the next level. A little light came down from above.

Levels

The prints on the steps were small. They looked like they belonged to the same person that had gone into the bathroom. He looked back at Clare. She must have been thinking the same as him because she nodded her head. He nodded back and put his hand on the wooden handrail. A small puff of dust rose into the still air. He quietly began to ascend the staircase. His senses were on high alert. He didn't know what he was expecting, but he was scared. This whole thing that was happening was beyond strange.

He focused on making his steps as quiet as possible. He feared at any moment a random squeak from a step would betray their presence.

They made it to the top without incident. A landing turned to the right, opening up to a large open area. It looked like it had been the administrative area for the department store. The carpet on the floor still looked like it was in good shape even through the layer of dust. The place had been cleared out. What was left was a mishmash of broken and discarded items. The bottom pedestal for a desk chair, one of the wheels broken from it, was the first thing Jake focused on. A telephone cord, still attached to a handset, lay about three feet from it.

Someone had been here. An area was cleared of junk and some effort had been made to clean it up. There was less dust on the floor. Whoever they had been, they used some metal shelves to light a fire on. Charred paper and half burned books littered the shelf. Judging by the amount of ash, the person, or persons, had been here for a while. Jake thought there had been only one. A single black leather office chair sat near the charred remains. If there had been more than one there probably would have been more chairs close to the comforting fire, he reasoned. Several potential candidates were scattered around the open floor.

They wandered around, just looking at what they could find. Offices lined the side of the floor, their glass walls still intact. The names and titles on the doors announced who had once worked here: Mary Tillerson, Director of Sales; Michael Mitchell, Director of Marketing; and so on.

Eventually, they made their way to the back of the room. A section had been closed off from the rest. Even the offices were temporary compared to this section. The door had a silver metal lock of some kind above the pull handle of the same material. The lock had six buttons numbered one through six. They didn't need to bother with figuring it out. The door wasn't locked. He looked at Clare to see if she wanted to go in. She shrugged her shoulders in response.

He pulled the door open, surprised at how heavy it was.

Levels

"Hang on a second, Jake," she said. They'd learned their lesson at the bathrooms. "Let's find something to prop the door open with."

They used one of the partitions to wedge it open.

"Hey, check it out," she said, pointing to the painting on the wall. "Security Enforcers" was written above a badge. Across the top of the badge, in sweeping letters that kind of looked like the wings of a bird in flight, it was repeated. Going down the sides of the badge, in a V shape, were the words "sempre fortis sempre vigilis."

There were two cells in the back. They weren't prison cells; they were much smaller. There was only room to pace three or four steps to either side of the small metal bench that was bolted to the floor. The bench was barely big enough to sit on.

The doors of the cells were open. Everything had been cleared out. All that remained was a layer of dust. They saw more footprints in the dust. Others had been interested in this room as well.

They left and continued checking out the rest of the floor. Jake was a couple of offices away from Clare, rifling through the drawers of a desk. He was haphazardly going through some of the files in the bottom left drawer out of curiosity. They were just boring transaction reports and invoices. The label on the door said that Julia Martinez was the head of clothing sales. He hadn't found anything useful, just an empty bottle of vodka in the back of the bottom drawer. There was nothing else of interest in the room.

"Hey, come here."

Jake looked up and saw her through the dirty office window. She was waving her hand excitedly for him to come to her. He hurried over to see what she'd found. He stopped just inside the doorway.

Clare had her back to him. She was standing behind a big wooden desk in the center of the room looking down at something. The carpet on the floor, unlike the other areas, had been cleaned up some.

She looked up and turned to him. "Check it out, this diary was just sitting here on the desk," she said, raising the book for him to see.

He stepped closer to the desk for a better look. The book, a journal or diary, had hearts, bows, and kittens on the cover. He noticed a sleeping bag lying on the floor behind the desk. There was a Hello Kitty backpack next to the pillow at the head of the sleeping bag. He walked around the desk and sat on the sleeping

Levels

bag. He put the backpack on his lap and began rummaging through it to see if there was anything interesting inside.

"Listen to this," she said. "I read a few of the entries already. Her name is Kimberly, and she's a pretty resourceful and lonely girl." Clare leaned back against the desk and started reading out loud from the journal.

The sun is warm today. It feels good just lying here with my eyes closed, feeling the heat on my face. I'm able to forget where I'm at, even if it's just for a little while.

Jake went back to looking through the backpack while he listened to Clare. He didn't see anything interesting. There were a couple of books, a few bottles of water, some canned chicken, and cans of fruit and vegetables, some clothes, and a few other odds and ends.

Clare continued reading.

Yesterday was a close one. By the time, I made it back here, I was so tired, I fell right to sleep. Okay, this is my journal, and I promised to be honest. I cried myself to sleep again.

I had to go down for more food and water this morning. The store is almost empty now. I know I'm lucky that it's right

81

here. I tried the Walmart a couple of days ago. I left before the sun came up. It had been raining all night, so I thought the dark and rain would keep anyone left inside. I was really careful and made it there without any problems. I've become very good at sneaking around.

There wasn't any more water on the shelves. Of course not, right? What's the first thing to go when the world falls apart? It must be water and anything worth eating! The grocery section was small, not much to pick from. There wasn't anything useful left.

I ran when I heard some other people. The sun was up by then. It was still raining, not hard, but it was coming down steady. I ran as hard as I could, still trying to be silent. I turned down a small road and kept going straight. After a block, the road ended, and a brick paved walkway began.

I was sure someone was following me. I kept looking back, but I never saw anyone. A beautiful compass was designed into the brick walkway at the next intersection. I didn't have time to slow down and look at it.

Levels

"I know where that's at," said Jake. "It's a few blocks from here at the University. Yeah, right by that big Catholic church."

"That's by Monroe Park, right?"

Jake nodded his head.

Clare went back to reading.

The person sounded like they were getting closer. I poured on the speed even more. I saw a big wooden door cracked open in the big building on the right. I squeezed through the gap. The second set of doors opened easily, and I fell/stumbled in. I was in a big church. I ran up the center aisle and then hid under a pew on the right. I hid under that pew, shivering for a long time, waiting for the sound of the door opening.

I don't know how long I was there. At some point, I fell asleep. When I woke up, the sun had come out and was shining through the stained-glass windows, at least the ones that weren't broken out. I crawled out from my hiding place then walked right up the center aisle to the front of the church.

The sound of clapping made me duck down and hide under the closest pew. A split second later I realized what the sound was; a bird was flying around. I looked up and saw it was a pigeon.

My knees went weak at the beauty above me. At the top of the roof, a gold dove flew among the rays of the sun with waves of water rippling out from it. I looked at it so long my neck got sore.

I hid in the church until it got dark then made my way back here. A big storm woke me up that night. Lightning lit up the sky. It was beautiful until it became scary. I think the store was struck a few times. The thunder was so loud the building shook.

I'm so thirsty!

I went down to the grocery store on the ground floor this morning.

All I found were a couple cans of cherries, some peas, and corn. Well, at least I can drink the juice.

There's almost nothing left. Each time I come back, there is less and less. I guess I'm not the only one scavenging away like a mouse.

Levels

I went into the stockroom at the back. I was careful like I always am. I stood outside the door, listening. I waited there for like five minutes. I didn't hear anything, so I thought it was safe to try. It was dark back there. Once the door closed, I couldn't see anything. I stood in the dark trying to breathe slowly so I could hear if there was anyone or anything in there with me. I was just as afraid of a person as I was a pack of hungry dogs or whatever they call a lot of hungry rats. My eyes adjusted to what little light there was and since I was still alive and hadn't been eaten, I figured I was safe enough.

I browsed around. This area had been picked clean too. Plastic wrapping and cardboard were everywhere. It looked like someone or ones had stayed here for a while. A big flashlight and some blankets were back in the farthest corner. Surprise, surprise, the flashlight didn't work.

I kicked my foot through a pile of trash out of frustration and hit something hard. It really hurt my toe. Part of my mind already knew what it was before I got past the pain and focused on what had happened. I followed the path that it sounded like it had gone and was rewarded with a can of chicken. Not chicken of the sea mind you. Yuck! How can anyone eat canned tuna? No, this was chicken chunks.

My toe was throbbing, but it was worth it. Yes! Meat!

I went back to the pile of trash and found a couple more cans of chicken and two bottles of water. Well, one and a half. I wasn't complaining. Just to be safe though I opened the unopened bottle and took a drink. I'd save the other one for later. You never know, right?

The sun was starting to come up. A sliver of light lit up the floor. It was coming in from under the big doors that the trucks backed up to. It wasn't much, but it was enough to light up the room a little.

I was lucky that I'd been looking at the light coming in under the door. I saw their shadows as they crossed on the other side of the door. At least two people walked by. I didn't hear them make any sound.

I knew, from scouting out the area before, that the only way in was the door on the right side of the dock. If I stayed where I was, I'd be caught. I didn't want to be caught. They

Levels

could be just regular people like me, just trying to get by, or they could be the other ones, the ones dressed all in black.

I wasn't going to wait around to find out. As quietly as I could, I went back to the door that I'd come in through and poked my head up to the small window. I needed to know if anyone was waiting for me on the other side.

I didn't see or hear anything, so I cracked the door open a little. Still nothing. Knowing my time was running out, I took the only chance I had and quickly left the stockroom.

I don't know how they knew I was there. Maybe I let the door swing closed too much. Maybe they heard me leaving the store. I just don't know. I hurried as quietly as possible, not running, not walking, sort of an in-between shuffle.

The sound of running feet broke the silence. I looked around and didn't see anyone. It sounded like they were running after me. I couldn't be sure. The sound could be coming from the side. I just didn't know. There wasn't anywhere safe to hide.

Every part of me was screaming to run, so I did the opposite. Hopefully, they would think like my instincts and think I was running as fast as I could away from them. Instead, I doubled back and hid under the checkout counter for aisle seven. It was off to the side but not all the way down at the end. It was completely random. I hoped it was random enough to be overlooked.

The sound of running boots was getting closer. It sounded like there were two of them. The closer they got, the harder I was breathing. The sound of my heartbeat was roaring in my ears. I thought for sure they were going to find me. They had to hear how much noise I was making just to breathe. I tried to calm down, but it didn't do any good. I thought for sure I was caught.

The men in their black clothes and their little hats on their heads were going to find me, pull me out from my hiding spot, and beat me with their clubs. That was what they'd done to that woman. They chased her down in the road and then just beat her. Even after she was on the ground and not moving anymore, they just kept hitting her.

Levels

A truck finally came, and they tossed her in the back. They tossed her like she was a bag of trash. She was the last person I saw. The last person that wasn't an Enforcer.

She looked over at Jake. She was sure that she looked as shocked as he did.

What the heck? This can't be real. As soon as she thought it she rejected it. Of course, it was real. All she had to do was look around her to know it was true.

She went back to reading.

Where was everybody? I still don't understand those stories I found. Why would they do that? Why would anybody do that? Why would they get rid of everybody?

I didn't understand at first what they were talking about when they kept talking about the 'White problem.' I saw the graffiti of 'White Lives Matter' on the bus stop from the window. I thought someone was just taking the other side of 'Black Lives Matter.'

Everything is different here. Wherever or whenever or whatever here is. I still don't know how I got here.

Okay, so about those stories, after the sounds of the boots faded away I stayed hidden. I don't know how long I stayed there. I looked around my hiding spot and was surprised to see that tucked way up under the counter was a purse. Most of the stuff inside it was boring, normal junk. A billfold with pictures of an average looking white family. She had the same kind of junk that my mom has in her purse. She also had a tablet. I didn't want to risk turning it on right then. It was probably dead, but I wasn't going to risk turning it on and having the operating system music tell the world where I was hiding.

Clare looked over at Jake and was happy to see him holding the tablet in his hand.

"It needs a password. I don't want to guess too many times and get locked out," he said.

Clare nodded her head that she understood and went back to reading from the journal.

I made it to the stairs without any problems. It took forever to get there. I kept against the wall. My imagination was getting the best of me. I kept thinking that I could hear

Levels

someone. I was sure I was going to get caught. I kept thinking that someone was in the frozen yogurt stand just waiting for me to walk by and then they would grab me.

I ran past it as fast as I could and took the stairs two at a time. I didn't stop until I was at the top.

I know, stupid right? What if there had been someone up there?

I realized my mistake as soon as I got to the top. I almost tripped over the last step when I thought about it. I dashed to the side and hit the locked metal cage barring entrance into the store. It rattled so loud, I was sure someone heard it. I ran as fast as I could away. I just knew they had to be right behind me. My legs were burning. I was getting tired fast. I was going to take the stairs and then changed my mind. They would catch me for sure. There was no way I could make it all the way to the top without stopping. Besides, they could be waiting for me there.

I looked over and saw that the elevator doors were open a little. I thought I could hide in there. I was sure the elevator was on the ground floor. Where else would it be after the power went off?

I planned to hang out on top of it and wait for the coast to clear while I caught my breath. Just goes to show you what I know about elevators. It wasn't down on the ground floor. I looked up at the bottom of the car.

Okay, no need to panic. It's still a good plan. I would just hide inside the elevator shaft and wait for it to get dark. By then whoever they were would have left, I thought.

As it turned out, I didn't need to wait. A ladder painted yellow was attached to the wall. The air felt thick. The smell of oil and hydraulic fluid hung on the stale air.

I decided to modify my plan and climb the ladder to the top of the elevator and then wait there. At least until my legs stopped burning.

It was a tight squeeze, but I was just able to make it. By sticking my elbows and knees way out to the side and squeeze my body as close to the ladder as possible I was just able to make it. I'd never been so happy to be a string bean of a girl, like my aunt always called me.

Levels

I made it to the top of the car. I leaned back and looked up the dark shaft. Enough light was coming in from a couple of the doors that were open. Way up at the top, it looked like it was a thousand feet up, the door was open some. I was overwhelmed. I sat down on top of the elevator and just stared up at that distant light. I was already breathing hard, and my muscles were burning.

I don't know how long it took me to get to the top, but eventually, I did. My arms and legs were shaking. I hadn't planned my escape all the way through. The ladder was on the side wall. The door was on the wall to the left of it. The thing was there was a span of open air between the two. I don't know what I would have done if the door closest to the ladder wasn't open. As it was, I had to make a move that would have made Spider-Man proud.

I fell out of the elevator shaft and onto the floor. I just lay there, happy to be alive. Pretty stupid that I didn't look around to make sure I was safe. I was too exhausted and happy that I hadn't plunged to my death to concern myself with those small details.

It took me a couple of minutes of rest before I could think clearly. I sat up and looked around, panic making my heart race again. I realized I could still be in danger.

I took another deep breath and calmed myself with the thought that if nothing had happened yet, it was fairly safe to assume that I was safe for the time being.

It's not easy to tell what time it is. The buildings block where the sun is. All I knew was that it was way too bright, and I felt way too exposed. I drank some water and stayed back from the windows far enough that I could see out, but hopefully, the tint wouldn't let anyone see me. I watched out of the windows for a long time, scanning for any movement on the streets. After a while, I felt pretty sure that they weren't conducting a major sweep and had called in the re-enforcements.

I sat down on the carpet and pulled the purse into my lap. I dumped everything out onto the floor, looking for anything useful that I may have missed before. The only thing I found interesting was a half-eaten roll of mints and the tablet.

Levels

I was surprised when the tablet turned right on. The screen was password protected. I thought for a minute then went with the most obvious choice. It was way too easy. I mean, who uses '1234' as a password? Only a grown-up would do that. What do they do when they need to change it, use 'password' as the password?"

Clare looked over at Jake. "1234—Got it?"

"I'm in," he said.

She went back to reading while Jake worked his way around the tablet.

The background picture was of her family. He clicked on the pictures folder. She had a lot of pictures of her family, like over two thousand. They looked like they were happy. Her husband was a big guy, not muscular big. He wasn't fat either. He was just big. It was kind of funny because she was so skinny.

He clicked on a folder named "News." The last file modified, was about the president signing something.

"I can't believe it! I thought Hitler was the worst person in history. It seems that there are people here that are just as bad," said Clare, shaking her head in disbelief. "Why would they round up all the white people? All of any type of people for that matter? That's just nuts."

"They brought them to what they called 'safe places.' They put up big walls around Detroit, Chicago, and New York to keep the white people there. That was phase one. Phase two included Richmond."

"I'm in the middle of the solution to the White problem!" she said shaking her head some more.

"I found that file," Jake said, stepping closer to her. He set the tablet down on the desk and clicked play. "I'm not sure how long the battery will last. It says there's fourteen percent left, but …"

The video started. Two news correspondents were sitting behind a familiar looking news desk. Behind them the station logo ANN was displayed, under that, in smaller letters: All News Network.

The male anchor spoke in a deep and powerful voice. His colleague, a beautiful woman with very black skin, dazzled with her subdued smile.

"This is Janiqua Am'Bate', and I'm Marquis Wilson, and here is the news at the top of the hour. It's eight a.m.

Levels

on this beautiful eighteenth of July," he said in a resonating baritone voice.

"Today's top story: President Morris to sign the Baker Security Act into law. He is scheduled to address the nation from the Oval Office as a prelude to signing it into law."

"President Morris outlined his reasons for this highly controversial decision at a press conference last night. Chief among them was the refusal of the radical group White Lives Matter to abide by the cease and desist order issued last week."

"Marquis, I'm being told that the president is ready to address the nation."

The picture changed to the White House and then to the scene inside the Oval Office.

Jake and Clare looked at each other.

"Do you recognize him?"

She shrugged her shoulders and shook her head.

The camera zoomed in on the president's somber face. His dark brown eyes looked straight into the camera.

"Good morning, my fellow Americans. I do not take this action lightly. Our great nation has been attacked, yet again. As you all know, these terrorists refuse to abide by the civilized rules of our great nation. Too many lives have been lost to their radical measures. Over the past three years, they have carried out over six thousand bombings. Hundreds of lives have been lost and billions of dollars of damage to buildings and vehicles.

"The cowardly act in Richmond last week was the final straw."

The president sat forward in his big leather chair, and the stern set of his jaw conveyed his determination.

"Our brave Enforcers were cut down in the line of duty. Forty-five men and women were slain when they responded to a report of a group of WLM leadership gathering in a populated area of downtown. They were enforcing the law and trying to apprehend the leaders of this terrorist organization when, at nine, twenty-seven yesterday morning, a bomb detonated on the fourth floor of the Montgomery building. The powerful blast took the lives of six members of the elite Pacifier unit. The survivors secured the floor, then fell back to tend to the wounded.

"The cowardly terrorists waited until reinforcements arrived on the scene before unleashing more destruction.

Levels

Three more blasts cut through the gathered troops. During the chaos, terrorist snipers in surrounding buildings fired down on the exposed officers. The ensuing battle lasted five hours. Thirty-eight brave officers were pronounced dead at the scene and seven more succumbed to their injuries at the hospital. Three more are in critical condition fighting for their lives. In addition to the loss of the brave men and women of the Enforcers, there were also twenty-seven innocent civilian lives lost.

"Forty-three members of the terrorist group were killed, and six were captured. I'm told that some of those captured include senior leadership of the movement. They are being held in a secure location and are being questioned.

"My fellow Americans, this situation is grave. We all need to realize how much of a threat these terrorists are to our way of life. No, to our very lives.

"We have rounded up local sympathizers and moved them to the Fan Detention Center in Richmond. I do not take this action lightly. I know the gravity of these actions. I regret that we must undertake such severe measures, but sadly we must. We must stop these senseless attacks.

"We are continuing this active investigation and are aggressively rooting out this poison.

"It is with a heavy heart that I sign this Act into law.

"When I came into this office, it was my sincere hope that I could lead this country into a new future. A future where we could get past our racial differences. A future where we could all realize our potential. I remain hopeful that one day that may be able to happen."

He paused for a moment before continuing.

"Today is not that day. Today is the day that I say, 'Enough is enough!'

"I will not let the whites tear this great country of ours apart.

"Once they are safely and humanely relocated to the exclusion sites, we can return to our peaceful existence."

"My fellow Americans, it is your duty to help us find all the radical sympathizers, so we can put them where they can't cause any more harm. No more kidnappings. No more assassinations. No more bombings.

"I long for the day where children can play in their own yards without fear.

Levels

"The whites say they want peace. They say they want equality. Today we give them what they want. They will have peace and equality among themselves, in the secured exclusion sites.

"To those Americans that are being forcefully relocated, I am sorry."

"This is a national emergency, and your sacrifices will not be forgotten. You will be moved to a home of equal size and value in a safe city. A city that is no longer threatened by whites. Richmond, Hartford, Philadelphia, Atlanta, St. Louis, Detroit, Louisville, Phoenix, Reno, San Diego, San Francisco, and Seattle are now designated as exclusion sites. The walls are almost complete."

"The whites will have complete autonomy to govern themselves how they wish, inside the walls. We will not abandon them, though. We will ensure that this is a peaceful transition. Our brave Enforcers will patrol these sites. They will ensure order is maintained and the kind of violence we have witnessed is held in check. I truly wish that we could have reached a peaceful resolution, but these people have nothing but violence and hatred in them. Historically, all we have offered them is a better life. We brought them out of their tribal and clan lives and into the enlightened ways of a cultured society. They have proven that they cannot evolve past their violent ways."

"We are ushering in a new day. A day of peace and prosperity our country has been held back from realizing."

"We are pure, and we are proud."

"God bless America."

With a bold stroke of his pen, he signed the document. Those gathered around clapped their approval.

The camera panned back to focus on the presidential seal before shifting back to the two commentators at the ANN news desk.

"The president met with Emperor Umboto earlier in the week at the palace in Cape Town. The exact nature of the meeting was not disclosed, but the emperor has stated publicly his concern for the civil disturbance caused by the non-pure."

The female correspondent put her hand up to her ear while her male counterpart went on discussing the emperor's views.

She raised her right hand, and the man let her smoothly take over the conversation.

Levels

"Thank you, Marquis. This just in. I'm being told that European Chancellor Gotthard and Russian President Stalin have both denounced the signing of the Act by President Morris."

"President Stalin reiterated his warning of military action if the humanitarian violations of minorities in America, especially Whites, did not cease."

"Secretary of State Robinson is scheduled to meet with members of the World Alliance to discuss the attempts by Russia and Europe to meddle in the affairs of America at the summit in Berlin this weekend."

That was the end of the video.

"So, where are all the people?" asked Clare. She was visibly shaken. "He said they were moved to exclusion zones, and they were going to police themselves. Why isn't there anyone here?"

All Jake could do was shake his head. "Maybe they moved them to another city. Maybe they decided that they didn't need to have as many zones." It struck him how easily he had fallen into talking about this... this what? This crazy impossible reality? Whites rounded up and placed into exclusion zones?

He remembered reading about soldiers rounding up Japanese Americans and putting them into camps during World War II. People were scared at the time because Japan had just attacked Pearl Harbor, and they didn't know who they could trust. This was like that but bigger.

"Let's see if there's anything more we can learn from the journal," suggested Clare. She resumed her reading.

Anyway, back to my great escape. Obviously, they didn't find me. If they had, I wouldn't be telling my story to you, whoever you are. I don't even know why I keep on writing in this stupid book. It's not like anybody's ever going to read it.

Okay, I feel better now. I don't know why I cry so much. I'm turning into a real crybaby. I miss my mom. I even miss my stupid aunt.

"This is the last entry, Jake."

I haven't gone back out again. I'm okay on food and water. I can probably make it a few more days on the water. I've seen more of the Enforcers. They are increasing their patrols. I have even heard helicopters flying around. One must have flown right over the top of the building. I felt it shake. I stand back from the window when I can't take it anymore. I figure

Levels

I'm safer that way and I can at least see the street a couple of blocks away. At night, I can see better. There haven't been many clouds, so I can see pretty good. There aren't any lights, of course. This place is dead.

A patrol passed by. It was the biggest I've seen yet. There were ten of them. Instead of the sticks they usually carry, they had guns. I don't know where they went. I wish I could look down on the street.

I just can't risk it. I thought I saw movement in the building across the street. It could have only been the reflection of a bird flying by or probably just my imagination.

I'm getting so tired of canned chicken. It doesn't even taste like chicken anymore, not like it ever really did. It tastes like a mouthful of nothing now. And don't get me started on how nasty cold canned peas taste. Yuck!!!

They're in the building. I hear them slamming things around. I don't know what floor they're on, but they sound like they're getting closer. I've looked around, and there's not any good place to hide. I thought about the bathroom downstairs, but they'll find me for sure there. I'm really scared. I'm going to look around again. Maybe there's a way for me to get into a ventilation shaft or something. They do it all the time in the movies. There's got to be someplace! Well, this may be . . .

A helicopter just flew by the window. They are really active. I didn't find any way to get into the ventilation shaft. I had another idea, though. I'm going to hide in the elevator shaft. How did I get here? I just want this to be over.

I just heard what sounded like a door bang open. It had to have been the one on the next floor down. I hear their voices. If I don't

Clare looked up. "That's it. That poor girl. She was so scared and all alone."

Jake held his tongue. *If we don't get out of here, they may come looking for us too.* He looked at Clare. She was holding the book tightly to her chest. Tears were running freely down her face.

He went to her. He didn't know what to do. He wanted to comfort her but felt awkward about hugging her. What if she didn't want him to touch her? He didn't want to make her feel uncomfortable.

Levels

She closed the distance between them and put her head on his shoulder. She was still clutching the journal to her chest.

Jake awkwardly patted her shoulder. He didn't know what to say. He couldn't tell her everything would be okay. He had no idea if anything was ever going to be okay again. He put his other hand on her forearm.

A wave of dizziness hit him so hard his grip tightened on her. A deafening buzz filled his head. It felt like it was cutting into his brain. Clare had her eyes squeezed tightly shut, her face was all scrunched up from the strain she was obviously under. She had grabbed onto him reflexively seeking support from the onslaught on her senses. They clung to each other for support.

His eyes blurred even more as they began to water. A wave of nausea hit him. His guts clenched up tight. A metallic taste filled his mouth. He felt his throat tighten up. He was sure that he was seconds away from puking. The light faded then brightened around them. It became so bright that dots danced in his vision. A room full of electronic gadgets with their lights flashing swept by. Another jolt of dizziness rocked him. His guts clenched so tight he was afraid he was going to mess himself. It passed as quickly as it had started. He squeezed Clare tighter without realizing it.

107

Suddenly, they were standing in front of a man with white hair. He was sitting behind a large desk, phone held to his ear, stabbing his finger down on something on his desk. The man stopped his pointing and looked up at them. The startled look on his face probably matched the ones on Jake's and Clare's.

"What are you kids doing in my office?"

They didn't hear what the man said to them. Their ears were still ringing.

They both quickly looked around at the office. It was the same room they'd been in, except now it was occupied. It was a real office. Books lined the shelves behind the man. Pictures of what Jake assumed were his family lined his desk.

Jake looked behind the man. The sleeping bag was gone. He looked back at Clare. She was still holding tightly to the journal. Her tears had left tracks on her dirty cheeks. He hadn't realized they were dirty. Under the bright light of the overhead fluorescent's, she looked very upset.

"I'm not going to ask again, what are you kids doing in my office?"

Thinking quickly on his feet Jake answered. "We're looking for our dad. Have you seen him? He said he was coming up here for an interview. My sister's not feeling good," Jake said.

Levels

"We need to find him, so we can go home. I guess we're in the wrong office, sorry."

"The HR office is two doors to the right. Are you okay, young lady?"

"Yes, sir, I just need to get home," she said giving him a small smile. "Sorry to bother you, sir." They both turned and left the office.

The floor was busy. People were talking on their phones, hard at work in their orderly cubicles. A couple of guys were talking by a printer about a football game.

"Man, the Lightning should have won that game."

"Are you kidding?" asked his friend. "The Cowboys had their number from the kickoff to the end."

Jake and Clare made their way past the men. They gave the kids only a cursory glance while they continued their conversation. Jake was holding her by the hand now, leading her toward the staircase they had come up. Realizing that the Hello Kitty backpack was dangling from his arm, he slung it over his shoulder.

"What are we going to do?"

"We're going to find your sister and my dad."

"What if they're not here?"

"We'll find them," he reassured her.

"No, Jake. I mean what if they're not here or there? Like, I don't know, we're in another timeline or something?"

"I don't know if this is another alternate reality or if we're back where we belong. The only thing I know is that I need to find my dad and then my mom. The best way I can figure to do that is to go back to where I last saw my dad and start from there."

They turned to the right. Jake remembered that this was the way back to the elevator. At the end of the hall was the big door that led back into the Enforcer's security area. A right turn there would lead to the elevator.

"What's going on?"

"I wish I knew," he said shaking his head. "But I do know that just happened. We didn't imagine it. I don't know what it was, but I don't think it's over yet."

Levels

Chapter 5

"Move it!" barked the man behind Angie.

He marched her out of the elevator while the smaller Enforcer escorted Melissa.

"It'll be okay, girls. We'll get to the bottom of this," said Derek.

"These gentlemen have a few questions for you. Tell them the truth, and we'll get this sorted out." They fell in step behind the security guards.

The group turned to the right and made their way along the hallway. Workers were going about their business and only gave the group a passing glance as they went past.

A large, imposing metal door was at the end of the hallway. A sign identified what was inside. "Security Enforcers" was emblazoned in bold gold font over the same badge they had seen at the bus stop. There wasn't any glass in the heavy-duty security door, just a metal handle to pull it open with. A numerical keypad was mounted on the wall. The taller of the two guards entered a code into the numerical keypad. A heavy metallic *thunk* sounded as the security bars retracted from the reinforced frame.

"All right go on up to the desk to the left," he said as he held the door open with his meaty arm.

Derek looked at the security camera mounted up in the corner, before walking in. It had a clear view of the hallway; a matching camera looked off to the left. *So, even the employees are watched here.*

The desk to the left was manned by a man and a woman. Both were dressed in the same black uniform. Even inside they wore black berets on their heads. The company logo was displayed on the wall behind them. It was the same as the sign on the outside of the door, but this one was more polished. "Security Enforcers" was written in big gold letters, and "We Enforce and Protect" was directly under that. A larger version of the badge was below. Across the top of the badge, in sweeping letters that looked like the wings of a bird in flight, was "Security Enforcers." Going down the sides of the badge, in a V shape, were the words "Enforce" and "Protect" on each side. In the center of the badge, a dove had a length of chain clasped in its feet.

Levels

Derek looked to the left of the security desk. A large screen TV was mounted to the wall. Images of security camera footage were on display. The eight separate images were in two lines with two of the images enlarged. These large images rotated every few seconds. Derek recognized the top left feed as the hallway leading to the elevator.

Off to the right side of the room, a sofa and two chairs made up a waiting area. A coffee table in the center had various magazines spread out on it.

The shorter of the two security guards that had escorted them addressed the woman behind the counter. "These two young ladies are accused of three violations of code 723."

The woman behind the counter recorded the information in her desk log.

"What's a 723 violation?" asked Derek.

"Identification ladies?" she said with a bored put-upon inflection. She didn't bother to look up.

"They took our purses," said the taller of the two girls, with an attitude in her voice.

The biggest of the two security guards deposited their purses on the counter with more force than was necessary.

"Hey, watch it!" complained Angie.

The security guard behind the counter looked up at the girls. Her green eyes were even more stunning as they contrasted with her black skin.

"Id's, ladies," she said with enough ice in her tone to frost even the hottest of disdain. "Do not make me repeat myself," she advised the adolescents.

While the girls retrieved their driver's licenses, Derek spoke up.

"Ma'am, I'm sure this is some kind of mistake. My niece is a good girl. I'm sure this is all just a misunderstanding," he said.

The woman didn't even acknowledge that he had said anything. She finished logging in the information from their Id's before speaking. "Follow Enforcer Green, ladies."

The man behind the counter stood up. "Come this way," he said without waiting for them to respond. The girls obediently followed.

Derek and Nancy turned to follow the girls.

"You can wait out here," said the woman behind the counter.

Levels

"Thank you, but I'll be going with my niece," responded Derek with a little heat of his own in his tone, "and what the hell is a 723 violation."

"No, sir, you will not," she said firmly.

"Ma'am, my niece is a minor and you will not have her alone in a room for interrogation."

The woman looked down the hall the girls had just walked down. Seeing that they were in the rooms and safely out of earshot, she turned back to Derek. A violation of code 723 is shoplifting. We saw them on camera stealing two articles of lipstick and an eyeliner."

She watched the set of his face soften as the reality of the situation set in. "Listen, sir, I understand what you're saying. We're not going to question the girls like this. We need to screen our records to make sure that they aren't repeat offenders." She saw that he was about to protest, so she held up her hands. "Whoa, I know you said your niece is a good girl. I'm sure she's going to come up clean. If that's the case, then all we're going to do is let them sweat for a little bit, let the lesson sink in. If we do need to question them, then you can be in there with her."

"Please have a seat until they're done being processed," she said in a more reasonable tone of voice.

Derek could see there wasn't anything more he could do. He took a deep breath and shrugged his shoulders back to ease the tension he was fighting to contain and resigned himself to wait it out.

He took the chair and sat down across from Nancy, the coffee table was between them. He looked over the assortment of magazines and chose a copy of *Time* in favor of the selection of *Guns & Ammo*.

"Derek, come and look at this," said Nancy. She was looking at something on her phone.

He moved over to the edge of the couch and leaned over to see.

"I'm looking into our friends in black," she said cutting her eyes in the direction of the security desk. The search had come back with some useful information.

The company, Security Enforcers, Inc., was a major player in the defense contracting industry. They had performed on contracts for the military around the globe providing base level security for the Army and the Air Force throughout Europe. They had also conducted force protection for vessels transiting hazardous shipping lanes around Somalia, the horn of Africa, and

Levels

the Philippines. They were also contracted for maintaining security at U.S. embassies and consulates.

The third hit was a news release about another major contract they had just been awarded.

Stock in Security Enforcers, Inc. soared in early morning trading after news of their award of a major contract. We were able to get a statement from the company president and founder James Smith.

"We are honored that we have been chosen for the performance of this very crucial task. We demonstrated our capabilities when we were asked to augment the police forces during the riots in New York and our nation's capital. We were called on again when the unrest in Fergusson boiled over. When rioting broke out in L.A., Atlanta, Shreveport, and Richmond, we were there to assist the men and women in blue. This contract formalizes what we have already been doing. We are there where and when we are needed. Our worldwide network of security experts is on site, highly trained, and ready to answer the call."

Mr. Smith went on to say that they planned to grow the company by thirty percent over the next five years. "We plan to bring on another fifteen hundred employees. We actively recruit our nation's veterans. You already know how to fight and win.

Come, join our team, and help us to enforce our nation's security."

Nancy looked up from her phone to Derek's face.

"They sure are a big company," he said.

"Yeah, real big," she agreed.

Nancy clicked back to the search results and quickly ran her eyes down the listing. About halfway down her eyes stopped, the cursor hovering over the words: "Protest turns violent."

Three confirmed dead and eleven wounded at a planned protest in Richmond, Virginia. A planned protest by the group Black Lives Matter was met by a group of between three and four hundred carrying signs and chanting "All Lives Matter." Initially, both groups kept to their sides exchanging nothing more than their voices. Tragically, this didn't last. Things escalated and quickly turned violent. The reports aren't clear, but we have eye witness statements that someone raised a sign stating, "Only WHITE Lives Matter." Some witnesses we spoke with say that the person was dressed like a member of the KKK. What is clear is that things quickly became physical. Law enforcement was on the scene and did their best to keep the two groups apart, but they were quickly overrun by the incensed protesters.

Levels

People on both sides died. Six people are in critical condition with what authorities are stating are stab wounds. One of the victims died from severe trauma to the head. Reports state that a man repeatedly slammed the victims head to the road. He only stopped when police officers used their Tasers. That man is in custody.

Things were restored to an uneasy order when members of Security Enforcers, Inc. arrived to augment the local police. "Thirty-two people have been arrested, and the investigation is ongoing," said Chief Dansen of the Richmond PD. "We aren't ruling anything out. We are conducting interviews with protesters and witnesses. We are also reviewing security cameras from around the area. If anyone has footage of the events on their cell phones, please come in. You never know what is important."

The chief went on to say that they were also looking into whether there had been instigators in the crowd, specifically with the intent of escalating the situation. The chief made an appeal to the public. "Peaceful protests are your right. We support you and your right to be heard. We will be there to keep the peace. To those of you that think of this as an opportunity to instigate violence, vandalize our city, steal from and damage our businesses, I have a message for you too. You will be caught, and you will be prosecuted to the fullest extent of the law."

Nancy and Derek looked at each other. It wasn't hard to imagine how easily things could go from the problems they were reading about to out of control enforcement. All it would take is more fear. Politicians were running on immigration control platforms. The racial and cultural divisions were straining under the pressure of terrorist threats and police shootings. It wasn't hard at all to imagine a different reality than the one they faced today.

"Sir," said the female security officer.

They both stood and walked back over to the desk.

The woman looked up from her desk and looked meaningfully at each of them before speaking. "We didn't find anything in our records that would indicate any previous incidents of theft. They are free to go unless you want them to cool their heels a while longer."

Derek looked at Nancy.

"I don't think that'll be necessary," said Nancy. "I think the girls have learned their lesson, don't you?"

Levels

The girls were led out from the back. They stood forlornly in front of the counter. Their chatty, indignant attitudes were gone. They seemed to be just scared kids.

"You both need to understand that we are remanding you to the custody of your aunt and uncle," said the woman with the piercing green eyes. She used them to full effect, letting them work on intimidating the girls, driving home the severity of the situation. "If your Aunt and Uncle weren't here, we would be turning you over to the police. Do you understand, ladies?"

"Yes, ma'am," answered Angie. Her friend simply nodded her head.

"You both are prohibited from these premises for a period not less than six months from today. Do you both understand?"

To that, both girls nodded their heads.

"If you violate this instruction, you will be apprehended for trespassing."

The girls' heads snapped up, and they looked at the woman. She stared right back at them. Her intense gaze conveyed how serious she was.

She continued, "If you are caught shoplifting elsewhere, they will discover your criminal activity today, and you could be prosecuted for both incidents. Do you understand?" She raised the volume of her voice.

Both girls visibly winced before saying that they did.

"Okay, you're free to leave. By that, I mean that you will directly leave the store. Do not loiter around. Do not linger in the mezzanine area. In case you don't know, that is the area between the two main buildings where the restaurants are located.

"In case you have a crazy idea that you can get away with it," she paused as she clicked some buttons behind the counter. Images throughout the department store were displayed on the TV screen. She focused them in on the escalators then rose her gaze back to the girls. "I'll be watching." She turned her attention to Derek. "Now, sir, if you'll sign here, that you are assuming custody of these two, then we'll be done here."

Derek stepped up and took the offered pen. He quickly signed the book next to the girl's names.

"Thank you, ma'am," he said.

"Yes, sir," she responded. She closed the book firmly and turned her attention to the desk in front of her. They had been dismissed.

Levels

Derek turned and ushered the group to the door. As soon as his hand gripped the handle of the formidable barrier he heard the locks *thunk* as they retracted into the reinforced frame.

The group walked back to the elevator in silence, each focused on their own thoughts.

"Jake!"

He nearly jumped out of his skin. He'd been looking at the numbers at the top of the car thinking about how he was going to find his dad when there he was with the rest of the group walking toward him.

"Keep it down," cautioned Nancy. People were looking to see what the commotion was about.

They closed the distance between them. Derek held his arms out, and Jake went into them, giving his dad a big hug.

"Are you guys okay?" asked Derek looking up at the rest of the group.

"Yeah, we're good," Jake said looking over at Clare.

"I thought you were following us. What happened?"

Jake looked around. Some people were still watching. "I'll tell you about it on the way down," he said.

They stood awkwardly in front of the brushed steel doors waiting for the car to arrive.

They didn't have long to wait as it only needed to go up two floors. Derek was happy to see the car was empty when it arrived.

The doors closed, and the car began to descend. Angie and her friend visibly relaxed and leaned against the walls.

Angie looked at Derek. "Thank you, sir, I appreciate you getting us out of that."

He didn't like the sound of that. "You are not out of it. You and your friend are very much still in it."

Melissa buried her face in her hands and started to cry. Nancy stepped up to her and put her arm around the girl's shoulder to comfort her.

"I know," she said. "Thank you for not calling our parents."

Realizing that she wasn't completely in the clear, Angie looked at Clare. She held her gaze for a while without saying anything. She must have seen something that satisfied her or maybe she felt that she had gotten her unspoken point across. She finally broke contact. Neither one of them said anything more about it.

Levels

The car slowed its descent. It looked like they were going to delay their departure for a little longer, at least long enough to board some additional passengers, it would seem.

Chapter 6

The car eased to a halt on the fourth floor. They waited for the doors to open.

Derek put his hand on Jake's shoulder and gave it a reassuring squeeze. His boyish face looked up to his dad. Derek forced a smile and nodded his head confidently. He hoped he was conveying a reassuring demeanor. He wasn't completely sure if he was. The truth was, he felt very rattled. Not only were things not as they were supposed to be, but he was also feeling an ominous threat getting nearer. His senses were on high alert. In spite of all that, he wanted to show Jake that things were going to be okay. He wanted to look confident, even if he didn't feel that way himself.

Finally, the doors began to slide open. He didn't think he imagined it, but they seemed to be taking longer and longer to open.

"See, son, nothing to worry about," he said. As soon as he got the words out, they began to close again. They hadn't even opened halfway.

"What in the world is going on?" asked Angie.

Levels

When no one said anything, she looked around at them then shook her head in frustration her short blond hair twirling around her head. "Am I the only one who thinks this is weird? They're supposed to keep elevators working, right?" Her voice was getting louder and higher in pitch the more upset she became.

"It's going to be okay," Jake assured her. "These elevators are a little old is all."

"Are you okay?" asked Clare.

Jake clutched his hands to his stomach. "Yeah, I'm fine. I just felt a little strange," he said. That was an understatement. He felt like he was floating for a few seconds before he was thrust back to the ground. His insides felt like they had been twisted up and then let go again. Whatever it was it had passed quickly. He saw his dad looking at him, so he stood up straighter.

"I'm okay, Dad." The look on his dad's face was less than convinced. "Really, I'm okay."

Jake looked at the others and wondered, and not for the first time, why they weren't telling them what they knew. Why were they keeping it to themselves? It was more than them not wanting to worry the girls more than they already were. Why worry them about something that they didn't have an answer to?

The light for the first floor was no longer illuminated, so Derek pushed the button again. Nothing happened. They didn't move. The doors stayed closed. He counted to ten and then when nothing happened, he pressed it again. He started counting to himself again. He made it to eight when something changed. They didn't continue down to the first floor, but at least something happened. The doors began their opening cycle once more. They didn't make it all the way open before they began to cycle closed again. Derek decided to try something. He stuck his foot in between the closing doors. When they didn't immediately change direction, he began to worry for his foot. He reached through the decreasing gap and waved his arm up and down, hoping to trigger a sensor. When nothing changed, he quickly pulled it back out but stubbornly left his foot in place. Would they sense his foot or close completely? He gritted his teeth and left it in place, determined to follow it through.

The heavy metal doors closed. His foot was squeezed on both sides by the black cushions that ran down the middle of the doors. The sides of his foot bent uncomfortably from the pressure. The doors halted their advance and abruptly opened back up. He quickly pulled his foot back and flexed his affronted appendage.

Levels

He was pleased to discover that he had escaped without any damage.

The doors made it to the halfway point and then froze in place.

"Well, that didn't exactly work as planned," Derek said after nothing further happened.

"I'm outta here," declared Melissa. She walked through the gap in the doors and out to a wonderland of toys.

An arch made to look like a tree branch spanned the entrance to the floor. A monkey hung from the left side swinging back and forth from a pair of vines. On the right side of the arch, a very realistic snake had its tail wrapped around the branch. Its head wandered back and forth, changing direction and height, all the while its tongue flickered out of its mouth. The eyes caught glints of light from the nearby bulbs giving the snake the impression of looking at you as if sizing you up for a snack. On top of the arch, a lion paced back and forth. Its large, hairy, head swinging majestically from side to side as it walked the length of the arch. When it stopped at either end, before making its turn, it raised its head, surveyed its kingdom, and then gave a mighty roar. The King of the Beasts was on the prowl, keeping a watchful eye on his domain.

The sounds of the jungle greeted the newcomers. On the other side of the arch, lights danced along the floor, moving away from the entrance. Jake watched as some kids ran off, trying to catch the lights, laughing gleefully as their parents struggled to keep up with them. The lights led the eager tots deeper into the wonderland. He saw that the designers knew what they were doing. The lights led the tots to their section of the store. They were just far enough ahead of their parents for them to get their hands on the things they just had to have. By the time the adults caught up, the sale was all but over.

Jake paused to take the place in. To the right of the entrance, there was a section for little kids to play. Wooden trains were assembled on tables and on the floor. Children were gathered around, happily pushing them along their tracks. Puzzles and other games were available for them to play with as well. A track was set up for older kids to race cars around.

Benches were placed around the attractions for tired parents to rest on while their tireless tots tested out the merchandise. Toys of all kinds adorned the shelves. There was everything from the latest electronic educational toys to the tried and true Tonka trucks. Further back there was a section for reading and story time. All around this area a dividing wall was

Levels

decorated with familiar characters. It ensured that the wee ones didn't wander off once their attention wandered.

Next to this section was a child drop-off center. Parents were able to look in on their little ones through the plexiglass windows any time they wanted to drop by. There was only one way in or out of the controlled area. The gates were controlled at the main desk. The desk was about chest high and ten feet long. Behind the counter were cubicles of different colors to store the kids' shoes and other belongings in. To the right of the counter were the gates. Parents entered with their children through the first one and signed them in. The parent and the child were issued matching wrist bands. Once they were in place, the children proceeded through the chute to the next gate. It was made of clear plastic inside a metal frame. It was a pretty heavy-duty gate for keeping the little ones in. It was more for keeping unauthorized adults out. About ten kids were playing inside the kid safe area.

A large Lego display stood next to a Barbie wonderland. There were completed X-Wing fighters, a miniature White House and Eifel Tower competing for the attention from Barbie's Dream House and her battery-powered convertible. Next to Barbie was the rest of the doll section including dollhouses and costumes. They had just about everything you could imagine.

There was a section for the battery-powered cars and jeeps, the kind the kids sit in and drive, set up inside a track. A couple of them were navigating the course, their faces intent on keeping the toy on the track.

The section for puzzles of all kinds was next to the model section. Completed aircraft hung from the ceiling, suspended in various stages of flight. A large aircraft carrier was prominently on display inside a case with bright accent lights focused on it.

Next to the models was an area marked yesteryear. This area was for retro-style toys that were still somewhat in fashion. It was also where collector's pieces were to be found.

To the left of the entrance, a large area had been cordoned off for remote-control toys. This was stating it lightly. A full-scale off-road course, complete with water hazards, fallen trees, staircases, and sand dunes had been created. There was also a race track, a very large race track, that looked like it belonged in Monaco, complete with buildings, trees, sidewalks, and pedestrians. In the middle of the two tracks, boats and submarines were operating in the pond.

Above all of this, quadcopter drones and helicopters were buzzing and swooping around. Video feeds from their high

Levels

definition cameras were displayed in real time on large screens along the back wall.

In the center of the store, a snack bar was available for recharging the human batteries. It really was a bar in the shape of eccentric ellipses with stools on all sides of it and booths circling it in an outer ring. Suspended above the bar was the mascot of the place, a big, friendly looking Labrador Retriever named "Woofus." He was leaning against a sign that said "Meeting Point" with arrows pointing at it from all directions.

Jake felt his pulse race as he looked around. This was a wonderland. Even though he wasn't a little kid anymore, he couldn't help being excited.

Angie and Melissa were at the snack bar talking with the girl behind the counter. Clare had held back with Jake. Derek and Nancy stood off to the side of the elevator, on the other side of the arch. The rest of the passengers had dispersed. The elevator now stood empty, its doors still half open.

Jake walked back to his dad, Clare following a few steps behind.

"I don't know, Derek. Things look okay for now."

Derek was nodding his head in agreement with what Nancy had said. "I just have a bad feeling about this place. I don't like how that elevator is acting up." He saw the look that came over her face, so he quickly held up his hands to forestall her protests. "I don't know, alright? Something just doesn't feel right. I wish I could define it better than that."

"I don't know about you, Dad, but this place is pretty awesome," Jake said excitedly. "Have you looked around?"

"It does look cool, son." Derek lowered his voice and lowered his head, so Jake could hear him over the din that was generated from this place. "I'd appreciate it if you stay where you can see me. Something doesn't feel right," he said.

They all looked the place over again. Derek's attention was drawn to the center of the floor and up to the meeting point sign. Above Woofus, a nest of security cameras pointed out to the four points of the room. He looked back at the archway spanning the entrance and saw a camera looking down on them with its ever-vigilant gaze. He let his eyes wander the floor, looking for the security guards in the black uniforms. He found what he was looking for. Over by the remote-control demonstration area, two men were posted. These were huge men. They stood a good foot taller than the people around them. They weren't just tall either. They were massive. Well, he reasoned, in their line of work it was normal for strong men to be hired. Still, though, they were big.

Levels

He continued looking around and saw more of the Enforcers standing by the child drop-off area, a tall woman and three much smaller women Enforcers. He was surprised by the number of security personnel on the floor, but he was also equally surprised by the size of these Enforcers. The tall woman was at least six foot two, but her fellow women Enforcers didn't look to be over five feet tall. Of course, from this distance, his perspective could be way off. Still, though, there was a big difference in their sizes. He looked over the rest of the store and didn't see anything that stood out to him. Angie and Melissa were still sitting at the snack bar talking with the girl behind the counter. They had a couple of glasses in front of them with what looked like shakes in them. Clare and Jake were walking over to join them.

"What do you think, Derek?" asked Nancy.

"I think there's quite a bit of security around."

"Yeah, and did you see the size of them?"

A family of shoppers was approaching them, so he responded by nodding his head. The family was small. The husband and wife were both less than five foot tall. The wife might have been four eight if she stretched tall. It was impossible for Derek to guess at how old the kids were. The boy looked to be in his early teens, but his size left him wondering.

The family passed them by. Derek didn't fail to notice that they had intentionally avoided making eye contact. *They must be used to getting looked at all the time for being different*, he reasoned.

The family was standing in front of the elevator. The doors of the car were still frozen open. The father reached out and pressed the call button a couple of times.

"It malfunctioned when we arrived," Derek said to them. "I'm going to tell someone about it, so they can get maintenance working on it."

The little man had turned toward Derek as he was talking to him. "Thank you," he said with a small bow of his head before turning crisply back toward the elevator. He wrapped his arms behind the backs of his wife and children and ushered them back through the arch and off to the left of the store. Derek presumed he was searching out the stairwell.

"Come on, Nancy," he said. "I think they're looking for the stairs."

She followed along a couple of steps behind him.

Levels

The family was quickly walking away. The father kept glancing nervously over his shoulder.

Derek slowed down. He didn't want to make the man any more uncomfortable than he already was.

The family had moved away from the main aisle. Derek soon lost sight of them among the shelves. The fact was that he couldn't see them over the shelves.

"Come on, over here," he said walking quickly to where he had last seen them.

Nancy had fallen a few steps behind. She was trying to keep an eye on the drones as they buzzed around while still keeping Derek in her peripheral vision. She ducked her head reflexively feeling the wind from the blades of a drone as it buzzed by her.

The sound of laughter brought a smile to her face before she had the time to raise her head again. She saw the young boy that had given her a fly-by. He was still laughing.

She was surprised to see how young he looked. He couldn't have been more than four or five. That couldn't be right. He was too good at flying that quadcopter to be that young. *Maybe he spent a lot of time flying them*, she reasoned. It didn't feel right, though. Most kids that age wouldn't have the nerve to fly so close to an adult.

She looked back at Derek in time to see him turn to the left at the end of the RC zone. He looked back over his shoulder and seeing that she saw where he was going, continued on. When Nancy turned to follow him, she saw that he was almost at the door to the stairwell. There was no scaffolding blocking the way and no warning signs posted. There was also no sign of the family they'd been following.

Derek stopped at the door and waited for Nancy to catch up to him.

"What happened back there?" he asked.

"A boy thought it would be funny to give me a scare. He flew his drone close to my head. He got a real laugh out of it," she told him. What she didn't say was her feeling that he was older than how he looked.

"Are you okay?"

"Yeah, I'm fine. Just boys being boys."

Satisfied, he turned back to the door and pushed the bar to open it. No alarms sounded. The door swung freely on its hinges. He stepped onto the landing and looked around. Nancy held the door open. She wasn't taking any chances of being locked out.

Levels

A large orange number four inside a blue circle indicated what floor they were on. Beside the four, a sign advised that in the case of an emergency to stay calm and exit in an orderly fashion. Above the four, a set of emergency lights were mounted. A small red light flashed indicating it was standing by if needed. A speaker was mounted on the wall, next to the lights. Presumably, directions would be given in case of an emergency.

The stairwell was clean and looked like it had recently been painted. Derek looked at the red pipes running down the wall. He assumed these were the water lines for the sprinkler system.

"This place looks pretty good," said Nancy.

Derek nodded his head in agreement. He felt good about the stairwell, but he still had that feeling of foreboding. He couldn't shake it.

"What do you say if we get the others and get out of here," he asked her.

"Okay," she said, stepping back into the store. She led the way over to the snack bar.

Angie and Melissa were still sitting there. They were both busy with their phones. Melissa's thumbs were flying as she sent a message.

"Do you guys know where Clare and Jake are?" asked Nancy.

Angie kept swiping through whatever she was looking at and only shook her head in response.

Even if she wasn't her daughter, Nancy wasn't going to put up with that. "Angela," she said in a no-nonsense tone. It was enough to get the girl to look up at her. "I asked you a question."

"I said no," Angie answered, rolling her eyes, making sure Melissa saw what she was doing.

"No, you didn't. You shook your head. It's polite to answer someone when they talk to you. Especially when that someone has recently helped you out. Drop the attitude," she said it in such a way that there was no question she meant it. Seeing Angie immediately sit up straighter, she continued. "Now, do you know where your sister is?"

"They were walking that way," she said, pointing toward the reading section of the store. It was on the other side of the snack bar area and was just visible from where they were talking. Nancy didn't see either of them.

"Listen, girls, I'm going to go find them, then we're getting out of here."

Levels

"Is the elevator working again?" asked Melissa, looking back at it. The doors were still stuck open. A small crowd of people had gathered around it.

"It doesn't look like it," said Derek. "We found the stairs. You girls stay here. Once we find Clare and Jake, we'll meet back here and then we're going to leave. Okay?"

Both girls nodded their heads. Angie realized her mistake when she saw the look that came over Nancy. She sat up and said, "Yes, sir."

"Okay, we'll be back in a minute." Nancy walked to where Angie said they went.

Chapter 7

The reading area was next to the child drop-off area. Bookshelves lined the aisles. They effectively blocked off the area from the rest of the store. You could enter from either side. Once in, the aisles were laid out in sections appropriate for the different stages of reading development. At the end of each stage, the aisles opened up to a reading nook. Couches, chairs, bean bags, pillows, and even nooks on the shelves themselves afforded the reader a comfortable setting to go on a journey.

"Did you ever get into reading the *Goosebumps* series?"

"No, but I watched them on TV."

"I remember reading them back in third grade. They were really scary but cool," Jake said. When she didn't say anything, he kept going with his thought. "This doesn't feel cool."

She looked at him for a minute before nodding her head.

He didn't have anything more to add, so he went back to browsing the titles on display. After a few minutes had passed, he looked to see what she was doing. She was looking through a very thick book.

"In the mood for some light reading?" he asked her jokingly.

Levels

"Very funny," she said. "Did you ever see *Twilight*?"

"Yeah, it wasn't bad. Too much romance for my taste, but the action was pretty good."

"I started reading it a couple of days ago. It's really good," she said.

"I don't know. I don't think vampires should sparkle. I like the classics, the kind that stalks you in the night. Vampires aren't supposed to be cuddly."

"You're such a boy. Vampires are romantic. They hypnotize you and make you fall in love with them."

Jake wrapped his arm in front of his mouth and theatrically high stepped toward her. "I'm going to . . ."

"Hey! That's my backpack."

Startled, Jake turned toward the voice and stumbled over his feet. He shot out his arm and grabbed hold of the bookshelf for balance. A thin, dirty-faced girl was sitting on one of the couches.

"Where'd you find it?" she asked him as she sprang from the couch and quickly closed the distance to him.

"What's your name?" asked Clare.

"Why?"

Clare answered her by taking the backpack off Jake's shoulder and pointing to the tag between the shoulder straps.

"Kimberly."

Written clearly in black marker was the name "Kimberly Winston."

"Just making sure it's really yours."

Kimberly looked at them for a minute before saying anything more. Jake could tell she was sizing them up, judging whether she could trust them. Having reached her decision, she righted her head, which she'd been unconsciously tilting to the right as she pondered their trustworthiness.

She tentatively asked her question. "Where'd you find it?"

"Right where you left it, in that unused office up on the eighth floor," Jake told her.

"Did you find my journal?"

"It's in there," said Jake as he handed the backpack over to her.

Kimberly reached in and rummaged her hand around until she found it. Satisfied, she pulled it out. Now that she had it safely in her hands, she raised her eyes to look at Jake and Clare. "How'd you find it?"

Clare looked to Jake to answer.

Levels

"I guess, the same way you went there and left it behind," he said carefully.

Kimberly looked around. Not seeing anyone paying them any attention, she lowered her voice to little more than a whisper. "What was it like over there?"

"Deserted, everything was covered in dust," said Jake.

She took a step closer to him clutching the journal to her chest protectively.

Jake could see how scared she was just thinking about that place.

"Did you see them?" Her quavering voice was little more than a whisper.

He didn't need to ask who "they" were. "Yeah, a group of them were searching the building. We barely got away."

"Me too, I heard them on the floor below me. I was so scared. There was no place to go. Then things got quiet. I was hoping they'd left. The door to the stairs banged open. It sounded like there were a lot of them. There was nowhere to go. I was trapped. I was hiding under the desk. I could see my backpack. I wanted to grab it. I needed it, but I couldn't risk grabbing it." She looked at them. "I knew that once they saw it and the sleeping bag, they'd know I was there. All I could think about was going away. I kept saying it over and over in my head. I've gotta get outta here. I've gotta get outta here."

They waited for her to say more. She was looking at the floor, rocking back and forth.

"Kimberly," Clare said gently. "What happened then?"

She looked at Clare. "I was in an office. It was a real office. Not abandoned like over there. It was night, but there were some lights on. I looked around for a while. I found some food people had in their desks. I guess that's stealing, but I was so hungry."

She looked at each of them hoping to see that they understood. A tear fell down her cheek.

"I'm so scared," she said to Clare. "I don't know where this is. I don't know how to get home." She sobbed and snorted at the same time.

Clare stepped up to her and gave her a hug. She gently led her back to the couch she'd been sleeping on. They sat there until Kimberly calmed back down.

Jake sat on the other side of her. When she was ready to talk some more, she sat up and wiped her nose on the back of her hand.

"How long have you been here?" Jake asked her.

Levels

"Like I told you, it was dark, and nobody was around. I didn't pay attention to the time. I was trying to figure out where I was and if I was safe. You were there. You must know what it was like."

Clare squeezed her hand. "We do. We barely made it out too. We read your journal. Thank you. It helped us get a better idea of what was going on. We also found the tablet you found in the grocery store."

Kimberly nodded her head. "I don't know what time it was, but after not seeing anyone for a while, I got sleepy. I don't know how long I was asleep, but here we are," she said shrugging her shoulders and smiling a little.

"Do you know how you were able to get out of there?" Jake asked her quietly.

She shook her head. "I was so scared. All I could think of was getting away from them. I saw what they did to that woman. I just knew they were going to hurt me, but there was no place to go. I remember that I felt my stomach tie up in knots. You know, like you really have to go to the bathroom, but you have to hold it? Then my head started to tingle. You know, I thought that was because of how scared I was, but now I remember it was how I felt when I went there too."

Jake and Clare looked at each other.

"Do you remember what you were doing when you went there, Kimberly?" asked Clare.

She leaned back so far into the cushions of the couch, she was almost lost in them. She pulled her feet up on the couch and wrapped her arms around her bony knees. She looked so small, so defeated. She took a deep breath and turned her head and looked at Clare.

In a quiet voice, she answered her, "I was in my room. Debbie and Mark were fighting again. They always fight. As usual, it was about money. Mark doesn't work. He hurt his back at work a few years ago. I guess he gets some money for that, but Debbie doesn't think it's enough. She's a waitress. She had worked a double shift then stopped at a bar before coming home. She's been drinking a lot lately. As soon as she got home, she started yelling at him. She's always on him about keeping the house clean. He's a good guy, but cleaning the house is not his thing. He likes to play video games. He gets lost in the games and doesn't realize what time it is. Anyway, they're yelling at each other, calling each other names like usual, but Debbie loses it. She starts hitting him."

"Is she your mom?"

Levels

"No, my mom died when I was little. Debbie's my aunt. She took me in. She tries, but she gets so mad. Anyway, so she's hitting him, and he's yelling louder and louder for her to stop. She starts saying: 'What are you going to do about it?' You know, really pushing him. I was so scared something really bad was going to happen. All I wanted was for it to stop. I didn't want to hear them fight anymore. I remember now that I had the same feeling in my tummy and the same tingling in my head. The next thing I knew I was over there."

"How long were you there?"

They'd only been there for a little while, and that was too long.

"Eight days."

"Eight days?" Jake asked in disbelief. "How'd you get by for that long?"

"I didn't see anybody at first. I wandered around. You know, checking the place out. I liked it at first. It was exciting. I was like an explorer discovering things. It was quiet. There wasn't any sound except for the wind blowing the trash around. Then it became too quiet. It was creepy being in a city without any noise from traffic. It felt so empty. I knew I needed to find food and water, someplace to sleep. I saw Wentley's in the distance. I remembered the grocery store and all of the cool things, especially the camping section, so I came here."

"Wait a minute," said Jake. "You weren't here at Wentley's when you crossed over?"

Kimberly shook her head. "I was home, in my room. I opened my eyes when all the yelling stopped. I thought that they went out. I didn't think anything about it except I was glad I could go to sleep. The next morning when I woke up, they weren't home. No big deal. I went downstairs to make breakfast. That's when I found out things were different. Everything was dirty, dusty. I opened the fridge and found out the power was off. It had been off for a long time. What was left inside had gone bad a long time ago. I had some stale cereal then looked around the house. I was afraid I was going to find Debbie and Mark's bodies like some horror movie. I didn't. I don't know what happened to them.

"I went outside to see what had happened. Everybody was gone. Even the neighbor, Mr. Anderson, who never leaves his house was gone. I knocked on his door to see if he could help. The door was already open. Nobody was home. Nobody was home anywhere. I wandered around the neighborhood for a while. Finally, I looked down the street and like I said, I saw Wentley's.

Levels

"I stayed in my house that night. I made sure the doors were locked. I don't know how many times I checked them to make sure they were really locked. I even locked the door to my bedroom." She didn't want to tell them that she hid under her covers like a baby. She'd been so alone and afraid. The smallest sound startled her out of her shallow slumber. She'd left the house as the sun was just beginning to light the day.

"You said in the journal that you saw what happened to a woman in the street."

Kimberly nodded her head a little. "I was up on the eighth floor. There wasn't anything I could do." She looked back and forth between Jake and Clare. "Even if I was right there, there wasn't anything I could have done to stop it. I would have just been taken too."

They nodded their heads sympathetically that they understood.

"There were a few people still around. They never talked to me. I never got too close to them. They were hiding, like me. The only ones that weren't hiding were the guys in black."

"Here, they're called Enforcers. They have an office on the eighth floor. They handle the security for the store," Jake told her.

Kimberly whipped her head around, frantically looking for the men in black. She was scared and ready to run at the first sign of that uniform.

"Relax," said Clare with her hands out in a calm down gesture. "They aren't rounding up people here. At least not like in your journal."

Kimberly obviously wasn't convinced. She kept jerking her glance from place to place.

"Kimberly," said Clare. When the girl didn't respond, she said her name again, this time a little louder, "Kimberly."

She jerked her head around to look at Clare.

"It's going to be okay," she reassured her. "You aren't alone anymore."

She looked from Clare over to Jake. He nodded his head in agreement.

"We're in this together, and we'll get out of it together," he said.

He could see that she wanted to believe him but still wasn't convinced. That was fair, he thought. He wasn't fully convinced either. He didn't even know what was going on, let alone how to get out of it. He was starting to get some ideas, though.

Levels

"Can you tell me again about what happened when you crossed over the first time?" he asked Kimberly.

"I already told you," she said.

"No, I mean the first time you remember crossing over." He went on and told them the story of what happened when he was at the aquarium with his dad, back when he was little.

Chapter 8

Derek and Nancy walked across the store to find them. He kept scanning the store for any glimpse of Jake. He was looking for the green shirt he was wearing. It was the Richmond Kickers 25th-anniversary jersey. Jake just had to have it when they were at the game last weekend. Jake not only played soccer, he loved the game, he lived it. He was always watching a match. If there wasn't one on TV, he'd watch an international match live streaming on his computer. For some reason, his favorite team was the Tottenham Hotspurs.

Because of his passion for the sport, they had a family season pass. At first, Julie had gone to the games with them. She had always been more competitive than Derek. Jake got that from her. They both enjoyed feeding off the energy of the crowd. They would be the first to jump out of their seats and yell at a play or a call by the refs. Derek was always happy just to sit back and enjoy the show. The best part for him was watching how happy his family was.

That lasted for a few games into the second season. Julie started working more overtime and weekends and said she couldn't take the time to go with them. But she was still interested

Levels

in hearing about the match play by play. For that, Jake took the lead. He loved telling her all the details, and she loved hearing about it too.

Time went by, and she made an effort to go with them less and less. By the third season, it was just the boys. This was the fourth season, and they didn't even bother asking if she wanted to go anymore. There wasn't any need to. If she wasn't already at the office, then she was hard at work on the phone in her office at home.

A flash of green by the entrance caught Derek's attention. It was a false alarm. A woman in a green dress was walking out with a toddler on each side holding her hands. He looked over at the remote-control area and, not seeing Jake, let his eyes wander back to where they had been heading. He hadn't realized that he'd stopped walking until Nancy asked him if everything was okay.

"Yeah, I just thought I saw him walking toward the exit. It wasn't him. Come on," he said to her as he turned back toward the book section.

He was hit from behind so hard he stumbled forward a few steps before he could catch his balance.

A man in a long black raincoat continued to hurry on his way as if nothing had happened.

The guy didn't apologize. He didn't say anything. He looked back over his shoulder at Derek and continued on his way. The man had a white pasty complexion. His face was set in a rigid mask, void of any emotion. It was his eyes that made Derek's gut clench tight. They were two dark, empty pits.

"What the hell, man," demanded Nancy in a loud voice.

Derek reached his hand out and clasped it around her forearm. "Nancy, don't," he said very quietly.

"He can't just go. . ."

She stopped when she felt the pressure of Derek's firm grip on her arm. Surprised, she shifted her focus from the guy in the black coat to Derek's face.

He gave a small shake of his head and nudged her to the side of the aisle, letting other shoppers walk past them. He wanted to keep an eye on the guy, so he picked up a book at random and tried to make it look like he was interested in it.

"What gives?" Nancy asked him.

"I'm not sure, but that guy is not right."

They watched as the man proceeded past the child drop-off area and veered over to the left side of the store. They lost sight of him behind the snack bar. Derek knew it was time for

Levels

them to go. He gave one more look back at the snack bar to see if he could see the guy. No luck.

He craned his head to the left and was just able to see that Angie was still sitting at the same spot at the counter. He couldn't see her friend from his angle but knew that where there was one, the other was close at hand. He didn't feel comfortable knowing that the guy was close to them, but he knew his best course of action was to find Jake and the girl and get out of here. His instincts were screaming at him.

He put the book back on the shelf and led Nancy into the reading area.

"How much longer do we need to wait already," whined Melissa. "I need to get home. David could've already stopped by. If I miss him, I'm going to go nuclear," she fumed. She leaned forward and took a long pull on her straw, slurping the last bit of shake loudly from the bottom of the glass for effect.

The young girl behind the counter came back. "You want another one?"

Melissa said no, but the look on her face said that she really did. She'd been a chubby girl until last year, always in a fight between her appetite and her figure. Angie was lucky that way. Not only did she not put on any extra weight when she did indulge a bit, but she also didn't crave sweets or junk food like Melissa did. She wasn't a vegan or anything. She just liked a good variety and was just as content with a salad as a serving of chili fries.

"Come on," Angie said standing up from the stool. She turned to her right angling between the booths.

Three loud bangs followed by five more cut through the air. Angie reflexively ducked her head and crouched down. A shrill scream pierced the air. It was loud enough that it was clearly heard over the din of the competing toys and the roar of the lion.

Angie looked around to see what was happening. Everything was confusing. People were running everywhere and yelling.

"What's happening?" she asked. When Melissa didn't answer her, she looked over at her. She was shocked to see that her friend was still standing up.

Angie grabbed her by the arm and jerked down hard, dragging her to the floor with her. "Stay down! Someone's shooting. Did you see where they are?" she asked.

Levels

"There's a black woman under the arch," Melissa said. "She looks like that guy from the *Matrix*."

People were running past them in all directions. Some were even running toward the exit to the store and the elevator. *Didn't they know it wasn't working? Don't they know that woman was shooting a gun?*

"Melissa! Come on! Follow me," she said pointing toward the reading section. She had to find Clare and then get the hell out of there. Melissa nodded her head that she understood.

Angie looked around to make sure she was clear to go across the aisle. A series of rapid pops from the direction of the elevator arrested her attention. A tall woman dressed all in black complete with a long black coat was shooting people. Movement from her right caught Angie's attention. Two large security guards were running toward the entrance. They went by her so fast she felt the wind of their passage. The larger of the two, the one on the right stumbled. His body jerked like he was getting punched. Whatever it was scored a knockout blow. He fell to the left. The other guard was making the same jerky movements before his head snapped back so far he was looking up at the ceiling, a pink mist colored the air behind him. The mist hung in the air. The security guard did not. He fell on his back with two

159

ugly red holes in his face. They'd been running toward where the woman in black was. As Angie watched, the woman shot three more security guards, this time they were the little ones. The woman was smiling. Her bright white teeth were in stark contrast to her ebony skin and black clothes.

Angie dropped down, taking cover behind the booth.

"Melissa! Get down! She's shooting people!" Angie looked over and saw Melissa lying on the floor.

She looked back across the aisle. It seemed clear, so she crept forward, looking both ways for any sign of danger. She made it to the edge of the snack bar area and risked a quick look both ways. She didn't see anyone.

"Only the pure shall rule! The good book says man shall rule over the earth," a deep baritone voice sounded clearly over the bedlam.

"He shall have dominion over all beasts and plants on land and in the seas. Man Shall have Do-min-ion!" he bellowed. "Trolls and Hobbits are nothing more than animals."

She'd heard enough. It was time to go. She waved her hand, telling Melissa to come up next to her. She didn't want to say anything for fear of being discovered. After a few seconds

Levels

and Melissa not coming up next to her, she looked back to see where she was.

"Come on," she whispered to her. Still nothing. Angie crawled across the space between them. She reached out and lightly slapped Melissa's hand. It moved a little. Other than that, there was no response.

"Hey, we need to go, now."

Melissa was staring under the booth, looking out at the aisle in front of the Lego Display. Angie followed her line of sight. She didn't see any feet walking past. Shots were still being fired from the left, by the entrance. Somebody else was shooting. It sounded like they were over by the RC toy course.

She tracked the sound of running feet and screams fleeing from the source. It sounded like they were trying to get as far away from the two crazies as possible. That would put most of the people on the back side of the child drop-off area.

Angie put her hand on the back of her friend's head. "I know you're scared. I'm scared too, but we need to get out of here, and I'm not leaving without Clare." She rubbed Melissa's head reassuringly. Something felt strange… wet. She pulled her hand away. Her breath froze in her throat. It was covered in Melissa's blood.

She scooted away from her quickly, scuttling across the floor in a bumbling backward crab crawl before bumping into a booth. She started to breathe again, too fast. She couldn't catch her breath. She couldn't make sense of what was happening. No rational thought fired through her panicked mind.

A barrage of gunfire brought her back. More people were screaming. Feet pounded the tile floor as they ran past her, trying to flee deeper into the store. Angie turned and quickly crawled back to the edge of the snack bar. She checked to make sure the aisle was clear. Keeping low, she ran across the open space and into the reading area. She had to find Clare, and they had to get out of there.

She kept going along the winding aisle. Parents were huddled with children their backs pressed up against the bookshelves, stark fear plainly written on their faces. She rushed past them. She wasn't stopping until she found her little sister.

She'd already gone through two of the reading areas. She was expecting the third one to be the same. She rounded the corner and saw where it was opening. She ducked her head down out of instinct. Something flew over her head as soon she crossed into the space. Her legs were taken out from under her, and she was tackled, hard. Her head bounced off of one of the

Levels

bookshelves! Her vision shrank down to what was right in front of her. Bright pinpricks of light flitted along the black backdrop that had been the rest of her vision. She was completely disoriented. A crushing weight fell on her back, knocking the wind out of her.

"I've got her," called out Nancy. "Does anyone have the gun?"

Derek fell in on the other side of the body grabbing the flailing arm. "No gun on this side."

"I don't have a gun," Angie tried to say. Nothing came out. She only said it in her head. Her fall had knocked the wind from her lungs, and she was desperately gasping for air.

"Let her go! It's Angie. It's my sister!" Clare yelled once she recognized who the crazed interloper was.

Nancy watched Clare fall to her knees by her sister. She looked over at Derek and nodded her head. As soon as Clare said it was Angie they recognized the clothes and hair matched. They both eased up.

"Sorry about that, sweetie. Are you okay?" Nancy asked as she rolled Angie over onto her back. She helped her to sit up. Seeing that she was gasping for air, she took her arms by the elbows and raised them up, trying to open her diaphragm a little.

"Take little breaths, sweetie. It'll be okay," she reassured her. Nancy's body jerked as another volley of shots rang out.

"Sub-humans are nothing but animals," the deep voice announced.

"We have dominion over you. It's our duty to put you back in your place. You think you are as good as us. You think you have rights. You are nothing more than animals, and you deserve to be slaughtered."

"Shoot me, but don't kill my kids. Please don't kill my babies," a small voice called out.

"Oh, I'm going to shoot you," the shooter said in his deep voice. "But, first you get to watch this."

"Noooooooo!" The voice wailed with such despair, it was punctuated by the sharp report of gunfire as the children were butchered.

"Now it's your turn." The wails of the mother were cut off as the report of the fourth shot cut the air.

The group looked at each other. They were all terrified.

Jake made a snap decision. He knew if they stayed here they would soon be discovered. They only had one possible way out. He took Kimberly by the hand, and after making eye contact

Levels

with his dad, led the way out of the reading area and further along the aisle.

Nancy and Derek helped Angie to her feet. She was breathing, but only in little gasps. She couldn't take a full breath yet, and she was still disoriented. Thankfully, the book Derek threw had gone over her head. He'd aimed for a six-foot-tall man, not a five foot four or so girl. He had picked a collection of Grimm's illustrated fairy tales as his weapon of choice. It was thick and heavy and would probably have caused serious brain damage had his aim been true. Her head had hit the book shelf as she was falling. Luckily, it was a glancing blow.

She was wobbly, but at least she was standing. Derek had his arm wrapped around her waist, supporting her in case she started to fall. They followed Jake and the girl toward the exit from the reading area, Clare and Nancy close behind.

They passed through two other reading areas on their way. In the first one, a little boy was sitting on the floor all by himself. He had his knees pulled in tight to his chest, and his hands were covering his face. He was shaking all over.

Derek checked Angie again. A little color was coming back into her face. Since he was closer to the boy, he knelt in front of him.

Nancy put her arms on Angie's shoulders to support her.

"Are you okay?" Derek whispered.

The boy peeked between his fingers.

Derek put his finger to his lips and made a shushing sound, signaling the boy to be quiet.

"Come with us. It's not safe here," he said. The boy looked around, and when he saw Nancy and Angie, he put his arms down around his knees. His face was wet from crying. His lip was still trembling.

Again, Derek quietly shushed past his finger.

The little boy nodded his head that he understood.

"We're going to get out of here," Derek said. "You need to come with us."

The boy nodded again.

Derek held his arms out, and the little boy jumped into them. Derek arched back and shot his other hand behind him to stop from tumbling over.

He recovered quickly and stood up with the boy in his arms. "What's your name?"

"Tommy," the boy said quietly.

Levels

Derek squeezed him in a quick hug. "My name's Derek. My son Jake went that way. Let's go get him." He set the boy down and, holding his hand, led the way toward Jake.

He hadn't taken three steps before the little boy pulled away from him. "No, that way, mister," he said pointing back to the way they'd just come from.

"We just came from there. Your mom or dad isn't back there," he said.

Tommy was shaking his head.

"We'll find them, I promise. Right now, we have to get out of here, *quietly*," he added for emphasis.

"No," Tommy said more forcefully. "We have to go that way." His little hand was pointing to the row that went straight out to the aisle. "It's the only way out."

Derek was confused. He looked to Nancy for understanding. The look on her face told him that she didn't understand it any better than he did.

In spite of the warnings of the boy, or because of them, he took a couple of steps toward Jake. He had to see that he was okay.

Angie lunged forward and grabbed onto the back of his shirt. She pulled him back. Derek had caught a fleeting look at

Jake. He was at the end of the aisle standing to the left side of the last set of shelves, looking toward the back of the store. Kimberly had taken a position on the other side and was looking toward the front of the store.

"What is it, Angie?" he asked.

"That woman is coming this way, the woman in black," she managed to get out in a voice barely louder than a whisper.

She saw the confused look on his face.

"The woman with the gun…" She inhaled a burning sip of air and continued, "that's killing people."

People were gathered at the back of the store, on the other side of the child drop-off center. Some people were still trying to hide.

Jake watched a young woman crawling out from under a display that had fallen over. She slowly stood then ran toward the other side of the store.

A short burst of automatic fire cut her down. Jake felt lucky he couldn't see her face. He couldn't tear her eyes from her left foot. Her shoe had fallen off at some point. He watched her foot twitch spasmodically. After a few seconds, it fell still. He'd

Levels

been so focused on that foot that he had no idea where the woman with the gun was, or the man for that matter.

He turned to look at Clare when she roughly grabbed his arm and pulled him back from the aisle. She was pushing Kimberly ahead of her and dragging Jake behind her.

"What?" he hissed between clenched teeth.

Clare pushed him past her and forcefully shoved him into the reading area then continued to push him back the way they'd come, hissing in his ear, "*Move, move, move!*"

Bullets tore into the bookshelf where Clare had been standing.

The group needed no more convincing. They bolted back through the reading area. Nancy picked up the little boy and followed Angie who was leading the way the boy had pointed.

They paused in the middle of the reading section. It was the point where the different paths converged. Derek had taken up the rear guard as they made their escape. When he rounded the corner, he signaled with his hands for them to keep it down and whispered, "Nobody's following us. We're safe for now." Without realizing it, he looked at Tommy for confirmation. When the boy didn't protest, Derek let out the breath he'd been holding in.

They paused there for a minute to make sure it was clear and to catch their breath.

Nancy put her finger to her lips, motioning for Tommy to keep being quiet. He nodded his head that he would. His brown eyes were as big as saucers.

"Where's your friend?" Nancy asked Angie in a whisper.

She shook her head. "They shot her," she choked out.

"Are you okay?" Nancy asked, pointing to her hand.

Angie grimaced and frantically wiped her hand on her jeans. She nodded her head that she was okay. She couldn't bring herself to say that it was Melissa's blood on her hands.

Angie put her head on Nancy's chest and let her wrap her arms around her as she sobbed quietly.

"Kimberly, I don't know how, but we need to get out of here," said Jake to her in a tense whisper.

"How? If they come in here, we're trapped. That man is still coming. I'm sure of it," she said.

"Yeah, me too. What I meant is we need to cross over with everyone." He saw that she knew what he meant.

"I don't know how," she told him.

"Yeah, I know. I don't either. I do know that we have to, though."

Levels

He looked at the others. They'd taken up positions to try the ambush thing again.

"Remember that feeling you get in your stomach?"

She nodded her head. "It starts there, but then it spreads out."

"Yeah, that's it. And the buzzing sound when that tingling starts in your head."

"Then you feel like you're starting to float away," she went on. "Then your vision gets all blurry."

"Yeah, that's it exactly," said Jake, nodding his head. "I think if we focus on that feeling, we can do it."

"I don't want to go back there again, Jake."

He didn't need to ask her where she meant. "Neither do I, but I know if we stay here we're going to die."

She nodded her head that she understood. "Okay."

"We need to be touching them. I was able to bring Clare with me when I was touching her. I think if everyone is holding hands we might be able to do it."

Jake quickly walked over to his dad and told him their plan.

"Are you sure, Jake?" he asked him.

"No, but we have to try."

Derek didn't need to think about it. He knew their options were extremely limited. They couldn't defend the three entrances, and their defense was shaky at best. It was more a hope to catch the killer off guard.

Derek walked over to Nancy. "This is going to sound crazy, and I don't have time to go into all of the details, just trust me, okay," he said.

"What?" she asked.

"Everybody," Derek said as he motioned for them to gather around him. Once they were close, he took Nancy by the hand. She'd set the boy down but was still holding his hand.

"Everyone hold hands like you do in church," he said. He was surprised when nobody questioned him. He noted that Jake and Kimberly arranged themselves to be on opposite sides of their circle. He didn't know what to expect. To be honest, he feared what would happen if it worked. But he was more scared of what would happen if it didn't.

Jake and Kimberly closed their eyes tightly in concentration. Clare was looking at Jake and was holding tightly to his hand. Derek smiled and bowed his head to pray.

"Dear Lord, please give us the strength to face what's ahead of us. Help us to know what the right thing is for us to do.

Levels

Guide us so that we make the right choice." He continued with his prayer. In part, he was doing it to distract the others from what Jake and Kimberly were trying to do. There just wasn't enough time to convince them that what they were trying was even possible. If God decided to intervene and help them out that would be great. They needed all the help they could get.

Jake was concentrating so hard he heard his dad's voice like it was drifting to him from a distant shore. He felt the sensations coming over him just as he'd described them to Kimberly. He felt them getting stronger the more he focused on them. Somehow, he knew it wasn't going to be enough. It wasn't strong enough to move all of them. He focused on trying harder. He opened his eyes a little to look at Kimberly. She had her eyes squinted tightly shut. Her head was tilted forward as if she was looking down at the floor. Beads of sweat were dotting her forehead. He closed his eyes and tried even harder.

Another volley of shots splits the air. Jake's guts wrenched tight. The roaring in his head threatened to overwhelm him. He kept thinking one word over and over again: *Safe!*

Nothing happened. He closed his eyes and tried harder. He felt it stirring inside him. He focused on that point and strained to push it. He strained harder.

It was no good. He felt it slipping away. He opened his eyes. Kimberly was breathing hard. He saw the sweat on her brow. She shook her head in resignation.

A burst of gunfire broke their concentration for good. Everyone crouched down on the floor.

Derek looked around, desperately trying to decide what they should do. He looked to Nancy. She jerked her head to the right, toward the direction they'd entered the reading area in the beginning.

Tommy stood up and grabbed his hand, pulling him into the row in front of them. Derek knew that it ended at the aisle facing the other side of the store. The reading section had three ways in and out. If you were to look at it from above, it looked kind of like the letter "E" if the top was open and laying on its side.

"We have to go this way, come on," said Tommy.

Seeing no better option, Derek agreed. "Come on, let's go," he said to everyone.

Tommy led them to the end of the row and without slowing stepped out into the aisle.

Derek stopped at the end of the row, not willing to expose himself. He was holding Tommy by the hand, so when he stopped

Levels

he stopped Tommy too. He slipped his hand away from Derek's grasp. "Hurry, come on," he said waving for them to follow him. From the other side, he gestured wildly for the others to hurry across.

Derek didn't see anyone moving. He didn't see the two shooters either.

"Come on, let's go. Cross fast," he said as he dashed across the open space.

They took cover behind a bench seat at the snack bar. When everyone was together again, Derek moved to the front, ready to cross the other aisle. He didn't see any movement. He turned back to tell everyone to follow him when he felt Tommy grip his arm.

"Wait." The look on his little face was so sure, so confident that Derek didn't question why he was listening to a little boy.

They didn't have to wait long.

An amplified voice came from the front of the store. "There is no way out. We have the exits blocked off. So, since you can't get away and I get paid by the hour, what do you say we start by you telling me what you are doing here?"

A frantic look came over the boy's face. "Follow me," he said before dashing to the snack counter. He followed the curve of the counter around to the far side where there was an opening. He didn't hesitate. He dashed inside and quickly found a place to hide under the counter. The others followed his lead and did their best to hide as well.

They weren't all settled in before more shots rang out. It sounded like someone was punching a wooden board. Derek felt the counter shake from the impacts. The shooting ended as quickly as it had started.

The big voice again: "Stop shooting! If you fire another shot, we will have no choice but to respond with overwhelming force. We have the numbers already, and the police are on the way. They will be on the scene within three minutes. You can't escape. The only way out of here is for you to surrender. Why don't you just tell me why you are doing this?"

"Fuck you! Fuck all of you stupid animals. Humans are the superior race. You're nothing but beasts." His voice was getting louder the more aggravated he became.

"You demand equal rights? Fuck you! You aren't our equals. The good book says man shall have dominion over all. MAN SHALL HAVE DOMINION! It doesn't say trolls or

Levels

dwarfs shall have dominion. In fact, every time it does mention you trolls, you are slaves of man. As it should be. You are subservient. You are not equal. Of course, you dwarfs are inferior. Just look at you. You are small and weak. You have weak spirits too, always cowering and shuffling off to the side. You know you should be followers, but some of you and, I must say, some of my fellow humans felt the need to empower you to think you could rise above your station. THAT IS NOT THE NATURAL ORDER OF THINGS!" he bellowed. "You will know your place. We are not going to put up with it anymore."

The negotiator at the front of the store waited before saying anything. "Those are some big issues. You know we can't fix everything right now. It's going to take time to work this out. There are a lot of people in there with you. Why don't you let them go? Then we can talk about how to resolve this."

"You must think I'm really stupid. Listen, you big dumb troll. I'm done talking with you. If I hear your voice again, somebody dies. Just shut the fuck up and fuck off."

They heard the man barking orders to the group of people at the back of the store. He was separating them by type.

The man's deep voice called out, "Midnight, I need you back here." He saw the woman approach. "Ah, there you are. What took you so long?"

"You heard the man. No more shooting or they rush our little game, so I had to get more hands-on," she said flashing him her bright white smile. She turned it on the group of small folks. "I was taking care of the dwarfs more intimately."

"You need to keep the trolls in line," he told her. I'm taking the dwarfs and our hostages in there," he said tilting his head toward the kids' zone. He looked her full in the face. "You know the plan, Midnight. We're doing this for the human race." They both nodded their heads.

Derek had seen enough. Those two weren't planning on surviving this. He'd been able to see a little bit through the crack in the swinging door into the snack bar. Kimberly took over as lookout.

He crab-walked to the middle of the group. They crowded close to him, so they could hear what he had to say. He summarized what he'd seen. "We have to get out of here. These guys aren't going to wait very long. Either those security guys or the police are going to decide to come in force, or they will say something that'll set off our twin crazies. Either way, we're

Levels

caught in the middle. That isn't the place I want us to be when this goes down," he said. He'd been looking at each of their faces as he told his story. He decided they were as ready as they were going to be.

Kimberly was still trying to keep an eye on things through the small crack. She looked up when they got close to her. "Nothing new," was all she said.

Derek nodded his head that he understood.

"Okay, we need to go out from here, fast. Everyone grab onto the person in front of you. Don't let go. Remember, fast is good." He looked them over. They were scared but ready.

"Okay, Kimberly, you lead the way," he said to her. She was the logical choice. She was the closest one to the exit.

"Tommy," he said looking at the little boy. "You follow, Kimberly. Hold onto her shirt and don't let go, okay? Remember, we need to be fast and quiet." He looked at the rest of the group to make sure they understood and were ready.

He looked at Tommy one more time. *Funny*, he thought to himself *how quickly we adapt*. Tommy didn't show any signs of wanting to wait, so he nodded his head telling Kimberly to go ahead.

The plan was a good one. The problem was it didn't last for more than three steps out of the gate. Kimberly froze in place. Tommy ran right into her, and the rest of the line jammed up inside the snack bar. Nancy was right behind Tommy and had the presence of mind to re-direct him. She shoved him to the left, clear of Kimberly and pushed him toward the stairs. She stepped out of the line to see what was going on with Kimberly. She looked back at Clare who was next in line before Jake. "Go, go!" she urged her, pointing toward the stairs and at the fleeing back of Tommy.

Seeing that they were moving again, she turned her attention to Kimberly. She was staring at the guy in the black raincoat. He was standing behind the counter of the child drop-off area. He wasn't moving. He was staring back at them with a confused look on his face. It didn't last long. Anger fell down his face like darkness clawing down a craggy mountain.

Derek put his hand on her shoulder. "What is it?" he asked.

"I don't know," Nancy answered him. "But it's time to go." She grabbed Kimberly's hand and pulled her along as she ran after the rest of the group. She expected to be gunned down at any second.

Levels

When they were clear, Nancy pulled back on Kimberly's arm. "What was that about?" she asked. Her eyes were wide open with fear as she searched her face for an answer. Her voice sounded angry.

"I don't know," was all Kimberly could say with a dismayed look on her face. "I looked over there to make sure we could make it safely across the aisle. That's when I saw him. He looked right at me. At first, I felt so scared. More scared than I've ever felt in my life. I felt like I was being pulled into his black eyes. Then it just went away. I wasn't falling anymore. I couldn't stop staring at him. Something had a hold on me. Anger and hate like nothing I'd ever imagined were coming from him. I felt how much hate he felt for the big and small people, the ones he called trolls and dwarfs. All I could think about was how could someone hate someone else that much. Then I felt some of the hate slip away. Not a lot of it, but some. He started to feel sorry for what he'd done. Then I felt his heart close, like a big door closing tight. That was when you pulled me away."

"Who are you? What did you do to me?" The deep baritone voice thundered.

"What are you talking about, Snake?" asked the woman's voice.

"I'm going to find you little girl, and then we're going to have a talk about how you got into my head."

"I said open that door. I'm done waiting."

"Don't shoot, Snake. Remember, that stupid troll said they'd come in if they heard another shot."

"Fine," he said. He pulled out a long knife and pointed it at the girl cowering on the floor in front of him.

She was only seventeen, still a kid herself. She'd taken this job to save some money for a car. She liked working with the kids. It was easy, and she liked playing with the little ones. She didn't want to let the crazy guy into where they were, but she knew she had no choice. If she didn't do what he said, she had no doubt he'd just kill her and then push the button himself. With a trembling hand, she pushed the green button.

He smiled at her. His teeth were dark and broken, really messed up. She recoiled from him. Lucky for her he mistook her revulsion for fear of him. It made him feel good, powerful. It saved her life.

"You take care of the kids," he told her. "Keep them quiet and out of my way."

The rest of you get in there," he said to his hostages. He pointed the knife at them for emphasis, not that he needed to.

Levels

"Dad," said Jake, "I'm going to go and see if we can take the stairs." He looked around at their small group. "You guys stay here. I'll be right back." Before anyone could protest, he ran toward the aisle, dodging in and out of the displays of models. He was crouched down so that he wouldn't be seen. He was so focused on where he was going that he didn't notice Clare was right behind him.

He pulled up and slid behind the last display shelf. The aisle was still about ten feet away. The open area in front of him had tables where people could sit and put the puzzles together. Puzzles with big pieces were on the floor for beginning puzzlers to enjoy.

He was about to sprint across the open space to where the RC track was and then to the door when he had a strong sense that he wasn't alone. He jerked his head back, sure he was about to die and was startled to find Clare's pretty face looking back at him. His fearful anticipation made it hard to process the not unpleasant reality. He shook his head to clear it.

"What are you doing? I told you I'd be right back."

"Are we going to stay here and talk about it or are we going to check out the stairs?" she asked him with a little smirk on her face.

"Okay," he said, turning his focus back to what they needed to do. He didn't see any trouble. After a few seconds, he turned back to Clare. "The coast looks clear. Stay here and let me know if you see anyone coming." Before he even got the words out, Clare was shaking her head.

"No chance, Jake. I'm coming with you."

He let out an exasperated breath and checked one last time to make sure it was still clear. "Alright, let's go," he said, then sprinted to the door to the stairs. He tried to look everywhere at once, looking for any sign of the crazy people in black.

They made it to the door without being discovered. The door had the standard metal push-bar across the middle and a window of safety glass, the kind with the wires in it. What was different was the gray blocks of stuff on the side of the doorframe with wires attached to the door. It looked like it was rigged to explode if anyone opened the door. Jake looked closer at the glass. It was dark. *That's strange, the lights in the stairs are out. Maybe they're on a timer, and when someone enters motion detectors turn the lights on.* It was a good idea, and in fact, that was how the system worked. In this case, though, the security forces assembled in the stairwell had turned the lights out, so they wouldn't be seen before they were ready to move.

Levels

Jake was staring at the rigged door when Clare had an idea.

"I'll be right back," she said.

"Where are you going," he whispered.

She carefully made her way to the far side of the little pond. Jake could see that she was doing something but couldn't tell what it was. Suddenly, a buzzing sound cut through the still air rapidly increasing in pitch. He watched as a drone rose and quickly turned to fly over the middle of the model section. The feed from the drone's camera was being displayed in real time and in high definition on the back wall. A clear picture of the explosive-rigged door to the stairwell was in the center of the picture. Unfortunately, his startled face was also being displayed in high definition at the bottom of the frame. He quickly ran away, back to the display shelf.

He couldn't believe it. They had to have seen him. He was sure they were coming to kill him at any second. Unfortunately, he was right. The cold steel of the gun barrel pressed against his skull.

"Don't even think about it," said a cold gravelly voice. This wasn't the deep voice from before, and it for sure wasn't the woman he'd called Midnight. This was a new threat.

"Move!"

Jake felt the pressure increase against his head, pushing him to the right.

The high-pitched buzz increased rapidly. Jake felt the wind from the drone as it buzzed right by his head and dive-bombed the bad guy.

Something flashed past him. A tangle of legs and arms crashed into one of the tables scattering the pieces of the puzzle that had been on it up in the air. Jake's mind finally made sense out of what was going on. His dad was fighting the guy. He'd managed to get on top of him and was pummeling him in the face.

"Are you okay, Jake?" asked Clare.

Startled by her voice, he tore his eyes from the unreal scene of his dad beating a man. He'd never thought of his easy-going writer father as a fighter. As he turned to her, he saw the gun the guy had dropped on the floor. Without thinking about it, he lunged for it.

Standing, gun in hand, he turned toward his dad, pointing the gun at the bad guy.

His dad was getting up off the man. He was breathing hard but didn't look too bad, considering. Seeing his son holding a fully automatic rifle froze him in place.

Levels

"He's not going to be getting up for a while, son." He stood the rest of the way up and walked over to Jake and put his arm around his shoulder. "You should probably give that to me," he said.

Jake was happy to do so. He was surprised how light the rifle was. *How could something so lethal be so light?*

The whole group was together again. They'd followed Derek as he ran to Jake. Tommy had told him about the man sneaking up on Jake. As soon as he'd said it, Derek saw the man crossing the aisle to where Jake was standing. He reacted out of instinct to protect his son. He didn't think about anything more than the threat to his offspring.

A new voice came from the speakers. Jake hadn't realized the music had stopped until the voice took its place. "This is Lieutenant Janson of the Richmond Police. You are out of time. Release your hostages. You have ten seconds to comply. This is not a negotiation."

Derek looked at Nancy. It sounded serious. They were literally caught in the middle. When the police started their assault, he had no doubt there would be more shooting and killing.

The deep voice of the man from the kids' area called out. "Okay, we'll let some hostages go. We want to talk. We have some demands we want to be met before we surrender," he said.

Jake heard the woman called Midnight's voice. "Move! Walk, don't run. You are the lucky ones. You get to leave."

They heard the group move down the aisle over by the snack bar. When they passed by, they had their hands on their heads and were looking straight ahead. The woman must have been behind them.

"Go ahead," she said. "You are free."

Jake didn't like the way she sounded so happy when she said they were free. A couple of seconds passed before he found out why it was so wrong.

The woman opened fire on the hostages. She fired in fully automatic mode into their backs. The front of the group had been only feet away from the police when they were cut down. The police had been expecting this move and quickly returned fire. The tall ones they called trolls were caught in the crossfire.

The wailing of the injured was joined by the popping of smoke grenades.

Levels

"Move, move, move!" a voice commanded.

They were caught in a pinch. Jake and Kimberly put their arms around their group and concentrated as hard as they could.

Chapter 9

This time, their efforts immediately produced results. They were hurled away. Shadows flitted by faster than he could grasp what they were. He didn't know if they were visible or if he was seeing them in his mind. There wasn't any sense of motion, no physical sense of moving. No wind rushed past his face. No sensation of running or sliding on the ground. In fact, there wasn't any sensation of the ground. He forced his eyes to open wider. He was still holding onto Clare's hand. She looked like she was sleeping. Everyone else had the same look on their faces. Everyone except for Kimberly. Her face was scrunched in fierce concentration. She was breathing hard, her chest rising and falling fast from her efforts.

Jake concentrated on seeing what was flitting past. The more he focused on those fleeting images, the more it felt like they were slowing down. He began to make out individual shapes. They were blurry and distorted, but his mind began to distinguish individual things. The more he focused on the shapes, the more they slowed. He was able to see what looked like blurry people. He couldn't make out what they were doing. It was like there was a strobe light flashing. Everything looked like it was stuttering.

Levels

The more he focused on the shapes, the more he was able to make out and the longer it was between those stutters. People were sitting around the tables working on puzzles. Others were shopping among the shelves. Parents were walking by holding their kids by the hand.

Seeing what looked like normal, he changed his word from *Safe* to *Stop*. He hadn't even realized that he'd been saying safe over and over in his head until he decided to change it to stop. In time, they did.

It felt like he was punched in the gut, hard! He fell to his knees and vomited.

"Mommy, Mommy look," said a little boy excitedly. "Dey impeared from da air. Deyre magic Mommy," he said in awe.

The boy's mother looked up from the puzzle the little boy had been putting together. It was a wizard battling a dragon.

"Such active imaginations," said the mother.

"Are you okay?" she asked Jake.

He was still on his hands and knees trying to catch his breath. He wiped his hand across his mouth and rose onto his knees before turning his head to the woman. He nodded his head and took a deep breath. "Yes, ma'am. I guess ice cream and Red Bull didn't agree with my stomach today."

The woman looked from Jake back over to Nancy. Nancy had sat down on a chair in between the tables. She was holding Kimberly on her lap, stroking the girl's hair. Seeing the concern on the woman's face, Nancy knew she had to say something.

"She's always trying to show her brother that she can do everything he does," she said, shaking her head. "You know how it is; you turn your back for a minute and the next thing you know they've chugged a whole Red Bull and raced to see who could finish their ice cream the fastest."

Nancy leaned forward and looked at the woman's son. He was fascinated with what had just happened. "You see my kids? That's what happens when you do what your mom told you not to do."

The boy looked scared and fascinated at the same time. Nancy knew that the mom had bought her story, but the boy was still holding on to what he saw. Kids believed in the mystery.

Jake managed to shakily get to his feet. He looked around and saw the others looked disoriented, but at least they were still standing. Everyone except Kimberly. She was pretty out of it.

Levels

"Come on, Billy, we need to get going. We can read more of your story when we get home, okay," the mom said.

The little boy nodded his head. As he was walking past, he looked up at Khalid. "You're a wizard, aren't you?"

Khalid put his finger to his lips and shushed the boy to secrecy.

Billy's face lit up with exuberance once again. He nodded his head as his mom led him away by the hand. He was still looking back over his shoulder in fascination when they turned the corner and disappeared behind a display.

Jake took a deep breath and waited for the bright flashing dots to clear from his vision. "Is everyone okay?" he asked.

Kimberly woke up with a start. She looked around, panic evident on her young face. "No! No! No!" Kimberly tried to squirm off Nancy's lap, but she held her tight.

"It's okay, sweetie," Nancy said reassuringly.

"No, it's not. They're going to catch us."

Clare took her hand. "Listen to me." When the girl's eyes kept darting around, Clare knelt in front of her panic-stricken face. "Look around—we're not there."

Kimberly focused on Clare's face. Her breathing calmed a little. She looked around and took in the orderly shelves. The people were calmly working on the puzzles, giving them only curious glances. Then she looked around at the other members of the group. Reasoning started to come back to her.

"We need to look around," Nancy said, looking Kimberly directly in the eye. "We need to see what's going on *here*. Then we need to decide what we need to do." She was nodding her head while she was talking.

"Right," agreed Kimberly.

"Remember, Kimberly, you're not alone anymore," she said, giving her hand a reassuring squeeze before letting it go.

"I want my mommy," said Tommy. His lower lip started quivering. A single tear fell from his eye and ran down his chubby cheek.

Derek picked him up and held him close to his chest. "We'll find your mommy. It's going to be okay," he reassured him. Now that things had calmed down the little boy was acting his age again.

The ragtag group went the same way that the mother had gone with her son. Jake again led the way. Things appeared calm, but they weren't taking any unnecessary risks.

Derek moved closer to Khalid. "Where did you come from?"

Levels

"I saw that you guys had left, so I took the stairs," he said.

That answer so surprised Derek that he stopped in his tracks. Nancy bumped into him.

"What is it?" she asked him.

Khalid looked over his shoulder and smiled at them. "Come on; we need to move."

Jake again waited at the end of the row with Clare in position opposite him. They didn't see anything out of the ordinary. People were going about their business. They looked normal, at least their clothes and hairstyles did. After all that had happened, Jake was wondering what normal meant anymore. After about a minute or so, Jake looked back at his dad for direction.

Derek raised his eyebrow asking if he saw anything.

Jake responded by shaking his head a little. He then shrugged his shoulders and then gave him a small nod. He tilted his head to the side to indicate that he thought they should go ahead.

Derek responded with a nod of his own.

The group followed Jake out into the aisle. There weren't many shoppers moving about, making blending in easy. Jake had seen that the elevator was working, so he turned left and walked toward it. All he wanted was to get out of here and find his mom.

A small commotion caught his attention. Angie was walking across the puzzle area, angling back toward the snack bar. It had been Nancy's protests that had caught his attention. His dad was standing in the aisle holding the little boy in his arms. Derek was undecided whether to follow Angie or catch up with Jake. He made eye contact with Jake, and the decision was made. Jake had made it for him by walking back to him. Khalid was right behind Angie, so Derek stayed back with Jake.

Clare ran to catch up with her sister. She must have figured out what was going on. If so, she was probably the only one. Angie likely didn't know what she was going to do. She just knew that she had to see for herself.

By the time Clare caught up with her, Angie was standing still, looking down at the floor, the clean floor. Nancy stood next to her, rubbing her arm comfortingly. Khalid stood off to the side.

Angie wasn't crying. She wasn't talking. She was just standing there looking at where she'd seen her friend die. Looking at the spot that now showed no sign of what had happened. In her mind, she could see the dark red pool of blood

Levels

that was spreading around her friend's head. She could see her eyes staring toward the aisle, forever open and sightless. She saw this imposed over the clean floor that she was now looking at. It was all so real. Both versions were real.

Clare took hold of Angie's hand and led her to sit down in the closest booth. She sat across from her. Angie never took her eyes from that spot on the floor. They sat like that for a few minutes. Nobody said anything. There really wasn't anything that needed to be said. It was all too much to talk about yet.

One of the waitresses started to approach them. Khalid intercepted her. Whatever he told her worked. The waitress nodded her head and walked away. She didn't hide the troubled look that had come over her face though.

Clare reached across the table and took her sister's hands in hers. Angie tore her eyes away from the floor and looked up. She looked at her sister for a little while before turning her gaze to Nancy. "How is this possible?" she asked. "I know what I saw." She raised her hand up, palm out so Nancy could see. Melissa's blood was still caked in the creases of her palm. She turned her hand, so the others could see it too.

"It happened. I'm not crazy. She died right there," she said pointing to the floor with a trembling finger.

She looked back at Nancy. "Where is she?" she asked, her voice falling to little more than a whisper.

Nancy didn't know what to tell her. She didn't know the answer either.

Clare squeezed her sister's hand and took a deep breath. "This is going to be hard to believe. I'm not even sure what I believe." She paused for a minute as she thought about how to proceed. A composed look came over her face. "This is what I know. I don't know how, but Jake and Kimberly can somehow cross over to…" She searched for the right word to say. Not completely satisfied she went with what felt like the right answer. "to other realities." She paused to gauge Angie's reaction.

"What? Like time travel?"

"No. At least I don't think so. Things are mostly the same, but some things aren't." She went on to tell Angie about the cars and what Khalid had said about them. She then pointed out the really big and small security guards. "I'm not sure if this is what it was, but think about this: remember how that crazy guy called them trolls and dwarfs? He said that only the pure were good."

She saw that Angie was following her. "Well, bear with me now, what if in that reality other humans survived and

Levels

developed along with us? What if those really big ones were Neanderthals and the little ones were Flores Man."

She saw the confused look cross Angie's face. "I forget the scientific name, but they discovered skeletal remains on the island of Flores, Indonesia, that they believe identify a separate branch of human. They nicknamed them hobbits due to their small size. They were only about three and a half feet tall."

She could tell that she wasn't convinced.

"What if, in that reality, they didn't go extinct? What if we all developed together, but the prevalent ones were us? Think about it. Instead of the 'us and them' being white and black, what if it is us and the trolls and hobbits, or as he called them, dwarfs? The same prejudice, just a different target."

She let that sink in for a minute before she continued. She told her about the first time she crossed over with Jake. She made sure to tell her about the physical feelings she had during the crossing, the buzzing in her head, the cramping in her guts, the flashes in her vision. She saw that both Nancy and Angie were nodding their heads as she explained. She told them about what it was like in that deserted reality. How everything was so abandoned and dirty.

The guys had joined them by then. Deciding that they needed their space they'd gone over to the counter. Derek thought it would be a good idea to get something for them to eat while they were taking a breather from all the craziness.

He wasn't surprised to recognize the girl that had waited on Angie and Melissa earlier. Well, not her but what? Another version of her? It was all so confusing. Jake had caught him up on what had happened, but it seemed that Clare was going into more detail than Jake had.

Derek ordered a Coke for him and Nancy and got shakes for the kids. He didn't know what Angie or Clare liked, so he got chocolate and vanilla just to cover the bases. Khalid didn't want anything.

"That'll be twenty-seven, fifty-three," said the helpful waitress.

Derek gave her two twenties. The girl took one look at them and smiled back at him. "Are you sure you want to spend these? You know they're quite rare now."

Instead of revealing to her that he had no idea what she was talking about he went along with it. "No, that's okay. I've still got plenty of the old stuff."

Levels

"Okay, if you say so," she said before walking over to the register. She came back with his change.

He calmly put it in his pocket without looking at it. He feared that if there were differences, his confusion might show and lead to an awkward conversation.

They settled into the booth behind the one where the girls were seated. Tommy slurped hungrily at his shake. Derek and Jake placed the drinks in front of the girls and then settled back into their bench.

Clare had passed the story over to Kimberly after describing how they had found her backpack. Kimberly was just finishing up her story about how she had wandered through the department store before falling asleep on the couch where they had found her.

Nancy turned around so that she was facing Jake. "I'm glad you're here, Jake. Clare and Kimberly have just told us what they experienced. I won't pretend to understand half of it."

"Good, then you are about in the same place as me," he told her.

"Maybe we all can do it," suggested Angie.

"Has it ever happened to you before today?" Derek asked her.

"No," she said.

He looked over at Khalid. Khalid smiled back and turned and walked away.

Derek turned back to the group. "How about you, Clare?"

She shook her head that it hadn't. Derek looked at Nancy and got the same response.

"Me neither," he told them. "It's happened to Jake at least one other time that I know of. He was little. We were at the aquarium." He told them the story.

"Was that the only other time, Jake?" Nancy asked him when Derek had finished the story.

"I think so. I'm not sure, though." He was still for a little bit before he continued. "There were a couple of times it might have happened but nothing like this."

Nancy nodded her head then looked over at Kimberly. "How about you?"

"Yeah, maybe a few other times," said Kimberly.

Nobody said anything for a little bit. They sat there, each one thinking their own thoughts. In essence, they all boiled down to the same two things: What was happening, and how do we get back to how things were before it began?

Tommy spoke up for the first time. "We need to go."

Levels

Derek put his hand on the boys back. "We'll go in a minute. We are going to find your mommy. I'm sure she's looking everywhere for you."

"No, we need to go now." Tommy looked up at Derek, trying to make him understand.

"It'll be okay," said Derek.

Tommy didn't know why they needed to go. He just knew that every second they stayed that feeling to run away got stronger and stronger. He tugged on Derek's shirt sleeve to get his attention again.

"We really really need to go now, mister. Something bad's gonna happen."

That got Derek's attention. "What's going to happen, Tommy?"

Tommy shrugged his shoulders. "I don't know,"

Derek saw how scared he was. "Those bad people aren't here anymore. They can't hurt us."

Tommy shook his head. "No, not them. Something else. Something bad. We have to go now." He pushed Jake to get off the bench in his hurry to leave.

Derek had learned to trust Tommy's premonitions or advanced warnings or whatever they were. He quickly looked over at Nancy.

She shrugged her shoulders and then mouthed why not.

Seeing that, Derek nodded to Jake to go ahead and let Tommy get out from the bench. The rest of the group followed him.

Once they were out in the aisle, Tommy continued across into the puzzle area.

Jake turned to go left, headed to the elevator.

Tommy saw that he wasn't following and turned back. "No, this way. Follow me."

"Come on, Tommy, let's take the elevator," said Jake.

"No, Jake, that's bad. This way, follow me, quick." Tommy turned and started to run away. Derek was right behind him, quickly following the fleeing boy. Derek was afraid he would lose sight of him among the displays. Tommy was only about three feet tall.

The rest of the group rushed to keep up.

Jake didn't have any idea why Tommy didn't want to take the elevator. He'd seen people getting off from it. It was obviously working again. Maybe he thought he knew where to

Levels

find his mom. There was something about the way Tommy had said that going to the elevator was bad.

The more he thought about it, Jake started to have a bad feeling too. He tried to discount it. He was probably making too much out of it. No, he had a definite feeling that something bad was going to happen. He took another look at the elevator and stopped in his tracks. He turned to fully focus his attention on the elevator car. It was still at their floor, and the doors were open. What had caught his attention was the smoke coming out from around the door.

"Dad! Check it out!"

He looked over to where he had last seen his dad and the rest of the group. He caught a glimpse of Clare's dark hair right before it disappeared around a shelf.

"Hurry, Jake. We're heading to the stairs."

A piercing wail cut through the air, and bright white lights started flashing from the ceiling. Water gushed down from the overhead sprinkler system.

Jake turned away from the elevator and slipped on the wet floor. He scrambled for balance. Once his foot hit the carpeting on the side of the aisle, he took off after his dad and the rest of the group. He was halfway across the middle section, back to where the puzzles were when a large explosion shook the building. He reflexively crouched down and covered his head.

He looked around frantically. Seeing no immediate threat, he scrambled in the direction his dad had gone. When the world didn't immediately come down on his head, he stood up and looked around, trying to see what had happened. Debris was falling through the air. He looked at the big, ragged hole in the ceiling above the snack bar. The floor above was engulfed in flames. Debris rained down on what was left of the snack bar. Woofus, the loyal mascot, was on fire.

A wave of intense heat hit him. He knelt down, hoping the displays would shield him. He had to get out of there. He crawled as fast as he could in the direction he thought the stairs were. The sharp tone of the alarm and the flashing lights were very disorienting.

Heavy smoke billowed out from the blaze.

People were disoriented, going off in different directions.

He tried to get them to follow him to the stairs. Some listened to him. Most didn't.

He was sure he should have found the wall by now. His foot caught on something, and he tripped and fell, splashing into the artificial pond. The water was only a few inches deep, but it

Levels

felt great. He remembered that the door to the stairwell was to the left of the pond.

It was hard to breathe the hot, smoke-filled air. He couldn't get more than small breaths at a time. He kept low to the floor. He could breathe a little easier down there. He crawled along, keeping one hand out in front of him, waving around in front of him. After what seemed like forever he found the far wall. Visibility was down to practically nothing. He didn't know which way to go. He looked to his right and saw nothing more than dark shapes shifting in the roiling smoke. He looked to the left and saw lights of different colors. It looked like there was a brighter light off that way. It was hard to tell. Everything was diffused from the smoke and water coming down from the sprinkler system. He couldn't make out much of anything.

Wait, he strained his eyes. Something he had seen gave him pause. He couldn't make out what it was on a conscious level, but he knew he needed to go toward it.

The sound of sobbing caught his attention. It was coming from his right.

"Shhh, baby. It's going to be okay. The firemen are going to be here any second. Everything's going to be okay."

Jake wanted to go to the light and get out of there. Every instinct was screaming for him just to go. She was right, he rationalized. *The firefighters are probably going to be here any minute now. They were probably here already;* he thought to himself as he turned toward where the voices had come from. As much as he wanted, no needed, to leave, something stronger wouldn't let him leave them.

Staying low to the floor; he made his way to the sound of the sobbing.

"Ma'am, come to the sound of my voice," he said as he got closer to them. "I'll lead you to the stairs."

"I can't," she said. "My leg's caught under a shelf."

He found them back by the doll section. A display shelf had fallen on her leg and had it trapped her from the thigh down.

"It's going to be okay. I'll help you," he told them reassuringly.

"Take my baby and go," said the woman. "The firemen will be here soon to help me. Just get her to safety please," she said. "Mommy will be right behind you," she added for her daughter's benefit.

Jake moved over to the shelf and tried to lift it up. It moved a little but not enough for him to free her.

Levels

"I'll be right back," he said.

He went to the side of the shelf and worked his way down. As he'd feared, the other shelves had fallen over adding their weight to the last one in line, the one that had the woman's leg pinned.

Think! Think! An idea came to him. He wasn't sure if it would work, but it was all he had. "I'll be right back," he told the woman.

"Take my baby with you. Please don't leave her," she begged.

"I'm not going to ma'am. I'll be right back," he quickly scrambled away, searching for what he needed.

He was gone less than a minute and could already feel how much hotter it was.

"Move over here, okay," he said to the little girl.

He turned his attention back to the woman. "When I tell you, scoot back as fast as you can," he said. He slid the chair into the space under the edge of the shelf.

"Ready?" he asked, looking at the woman. She nodded her head that she was.

He lifted up on the chair. It was working! He pulled harder and fell forward as it slipped out. He lost his balance and landed on top of the shelf. The woman screamed from the pain of his fall on top of the shelf.

"I'm so sorry," he said to her as he scrambled off the shelf.

He looked at the shelf again and saw what he'd done wrong. He quickly went over to the other side of the woman. He didn't waste any time explaining what he was going to do. He rammed the chair in, seat back first, and lifted up with the chairs legs. The corner of the shelf rose enough for her to pull her leg out from under it.

"Okay, we're going to play a game," he said to the little girl. "Do you want to go for a pony ride?"

"That sounds fun," said the woman. "Go ahead, honey. It's okay; I'm right behind you."

Jake put the little girl on his back and scrambled on all fours toward the stairs. He didn't check on the progress of the woman. Once he got to the stairs, he told the little girl to sit down on the first step and wait for her mom there. He hurried back and was glad to see that the woman had made good progress. She was crawling along, dragging her injured leg behind her. She made it to the stairwell and positioned herself beside her daughter on the

Levels

first step. Her injured leg was straight in front of her, leading the way down the steps.

Jake looked at them from the doorway. He was still on his hands and knees, breathing in the relatively clean air. He was trying to think of a way to get the injured woman down the stairs when his head was slammed into the side of the doorframe. Jake felt dizzy. Bright dots danced in his vision. Everything was spinning. A man fell down on the landing of the stairwell before his momentum carried him tumbling down the stairs. He rolled over the woman's injured leg making her scream out.

Jake shook his head, trying to clear it. He stood up. An intense wave of dizziness washed over him. He reached out for something to hold onto. There was nothing there. He stumbled forward, his hand waving from side to side, searching for something to support him. Tears streamed from his eyes, further blurring his vision. He heard the muffled sound of footsteps pounding on the concrete stairs. Strong arms wrapped around him and his dad's voice was in his ear.

"I've got you, Jake. It's okay. I've got you."

Jake blinked his eyes quickly, trying to clear them.

"Angie," called Derek, "Can you give me a hand with Jake?"

"I'm okay," said Jake. "I was just a little dizzy."

Derek made sure that Angie had Jake and he wasn't going to tumble down the stairs. He'd seen the blood running down the woman's leg. He couldn't tell how bad she was hurt yet, but it was obvious she wasn't getting down the stairs on her own.

Derek went to help Khalid with the woman.

Kimberly had picked up the little girl and was carrying her down the stairs.

Jake looked back up the stairs, causing intense nausea to wash over him. Fortunately, it passed as quick as it came.

The woman was hopping down the steps with Derek and Khalid helping to support her weight. Kimberly had made it down to the next level and was holding the little girl on her hip.

At the first landing, a man was in the corner moaning while holding his arm across his body. Jake wasn't sure if it was the same man that bumped into him, but it could have been.

He stopped in his tracks. "Where's Clare?" he asked Angie.

"I thought she was with you."

Jake turned and scrambled as fast as he could back up the stairs. It wasn't very fast. It was more of a crab walk to the top.

Where are you going?" Derek shouted after him.

Levels

"Clare's still in there," he said before pulling the fire door open. The smoke and heat billowed into the stairwell. Jake looked back at his dad before he went back over.

He stayed low to the ground, trying to keep under the thick roiling cloud of smoke. He was confident that she wasn't to the left. He was sure he would have found her before if she had been. He decided to go straight ahead and then turn right to the RC area. *She couldn't have gone too far he thought—he hoped.*

His hand fell on a jean-clad leg. It didn't move from his touch. *I hope I didn't just touch a dead body.* He was horrified to think that the body in question could be Clare.

He had to find out. He scrambled up to look at the face. It was her. He recognized her even through the soot covering her face.

He didn't waste any time. He grabbed hold of her forearm and dragged her to the stairwell. He tried to stay as low as possible, and still, the heat was intense.

The heat and smoke made it nearly impossible to breathe. Tears streamed from his eyes.

One thought kept going through his mind: *Don't be dead; Don't be dead; Don't be dead.*

Every pull he said it over and over until he finally found his way back to the door. He didn't know he was there until his back hit the release bar on the door. The unexpected resistance followed by the open space caused him to lose his balance. He stumbled across the landing and hit the far wall. He fell into a heap with Clare in his lap. He wrapped his arms around her and held on. He had no idea how long he sat there like that.

When his head cleared enough to think again, he realized Angie and Nancy were there to help. They were saying something to him. He blinked his eyes, he couldn't understand them.

"Jake, let her go. We need to get out of here. Jake, can you hear me?" asked Nancy. "Jake!" She put her hand on the side of his face and made him look at her.

"She's alive, Jake. If she's going to stay that way, we need to go down. Come on, Jake."

"Angie, help me get Clare up," said Nancy. Between the two of them, they got her upright. Clare was starting to come around.

Angie put Clare's arm around her neck and held her wrist with her left hand. She put her right arm around her, holding onto the waist of her jeans. She made it down a few steps in a

Levels

leveraging shuffle before Clare began to support more of her own weight.

Nancy wasn't far behind with Jake. They made it down to the next landing before pausing to catch their breath.

Jake was bent over with his hands on his knees taking big gulps of air.

"How is she?" he asked.

Angie didn't answer. All of her focus was on her sister. She looked so lost.

"She's breathing easier. I think she's coming out of it," said Nancy.

Clare started a fit of sharp, painful, barking coughs.

Jake stumbled over to her. He didn't know what to do. He fell to his knees and put his hands on her cheeks. He gently tilted her face up so she could see him. She looked lost, without focus. He had an idea suddenly. He grabbed her hands and raised them over her head.

"Try to breathe. Take a breath," he told her. He could see how scared she was. She did what he said. She was able to catch a couple of shallow breaths before the fit took over again. She was looking right at Jake and forced herself to take breaths whenever she could.

The fit slowly subsided. Nancy and Angie were sitting beside her on the step. Nancy was rubbing her back to help calm her down. Jake was kneeling in front of her. Her arms weren't over her head anymore. They were lying loosely in her lap. Jake held her hands in his.

"We need to move, guys," said Nancy.

"I'm okay now," said Clare, shakily getting to her feet. Jake held onto her, afraid she was going to fall back down at any second. She wrapped her arm around his shoulder for support, and they made their way down the stairs.

At the next landing, a man was huddled in the corner holding his arm across his body.

"Come on, mister," Clare said to the man. Her voice was raspy. "You've got to move. You can't stay here."

"My arm, I think it's broken," he sobbed.

"They can fix that downstairs," she assured him. "You've got to get to them though. Come on," she said.

Angie reached out her hand to help him up.

He looked at her hopefully and took her hand. Jake reached helped to pull him up; he wasn't a small man.

Clare looked at him once he was standing. She took a wobbly step over to him and unbuttoned his shirt in the middle,

Levels

then stuffed his hand inside. "There you go, mister. A temporary sling."

He looked down at her creative solution. "Thank you," he said.

They went as quickly as they could down the next flight of stairs where they paused to catch their breath. Jake's head was clearing now that he could breathe smoke-free air. It was still throbbing, and his left ear was burning from being slammed against the doorframe. He didn't know it, but the left side of his face was covered in blood from a gash on the side of his forehead. His balance was back, so he was walking on his own. Clare stayed close by. They were supporting each other.

Angie and Kimberly were almost down to the first floor when Jake met Derek on the second-floor landing. The rest of the group were spread out on the stairs between them. Nancy was holding Tommy by the hand. She'd been carrying him, but her arms were tired, and they only had one flight of stairs left to go.

Derek saw Jake stop. He knew what he was thinking. "I know, son. Think about it, though. We don't even know if she's there. From what you said, we don't even know if this is the right reality line? Is that right?"

"I guess, Dad. But, you know we should look anyway. I have to know or at least try."

"Hold up, girls," said Nancy. "Derek is everything okay."

Derek gave Jake a long look and not seeing any wavering decided. "Yeah, we need to go to Patrini's café'," he said.

Nancy came back up the stairs and joined them.

"I have to find my mom," said Jake.

"It was where we left her. We were just going to get Jake a pair of soccer cleats," said Derek. It seemed like a lifetime ago, but he checked his watch, it had only been a little over an hour ago. *Would she even still be there?*

"We have to look," he said to her.

"Of course," she agreed.

Angie and Kimberly had come back up the stairs and joined them.

The fire alarms were still blaring. A loud commotion from below caught their attention. A group of firefighters came pounding up the stairs. They hurried past them without so much as a passing glance. They were obviously focused on their mission.

Once they'd gone past, he looked over at Jake and nodded his head. "We should check it out." He looked to the man with the

Levels

broken arm. "Can you help her down? You guys need to get medical help and shouldn't wait for us," he said looking at the woman with the injured leg.

"Yeah, I can do that." He looked at the woman. "Is your daughter okay," he asked.

"She'll be fine," she said. "Can you lead the way, Lisa?" The little girl started taking one step at a time. "That's mommy's big girl," she said. They made slow but steady progress.

Derek tried to pull the door open. It wouldn't budge. *Could it be locked because of the fire, he wondered?* He quickly discounted that idea. It didn't make any sense. *Why would they design it that way? People could be locked in. Then again*, he thought, *in a case like this where the fire was someplace else, they would want to limit people wandering into danger.*

He decided to give it another try. Jake grabbed the door and together they pulled back on it. The door moved a little in its frame. Strange, he thought as a flutter ran through his gut.

Jake felt it too. He had a feeling what it was, so he put both his hands on the door and prepared to pull with all his strength. He was surprised to feel a pair of hands on his back. He figured it was Clare trying to give him her support. It wasn't Clare.

Kimberly had felt the sensation as well and realized what it was. She was concentrating as hard as she could, trying to project whatever power it was to Jake.

The door creaked open a little. Encouraged, Jake planted his foot on the doorframe. He leaned back and heaved with all his might. His muscles were straining from the effort. He felt something inside him flexing as well. It was in the upper part of his chest. It kind of felt like a muscle flexing but not quite. It was something more than that. It felt as if something was shooting out from that new muscle. Most of the sensation was shooting into his head. Another large part was directed to somewhere in his stomach. He felt jolts shooting through his arms and legs as well. He felt stronger than he ever had before. The door grudgingly opened a little at a time. When it was about a foot open, it swung easily on its hinges. Jake had been pulling so hard that when the resistance disappeared, he lost his balance and fell back into Kimberly. He was surprised at how strong she was. She recovered quickly and was able to keep them both on their feet.

"Sorry about that."

"No problem," she said.

Jake's grip had slipped off the door handle. Somehow, he knew that he had to keep the door open. If it closed, it wouldn't

Levels

open to the same place. He didn't understand why he knew that he just did. He lunged forward and caught it. He was afraid that if he were to let it close then the other…what? door…portal… would close as well. Whatever it was, he was determined to hold it open.

"Go ahead," he said to his dad. The rest of the group followed Derek through the doorway. Jake knew Kimberly had to help him keep the door open until the others had passed through. He was the last one to cross over. Once he stepped over the threshold, the sound of the blaring alarm ceased. One second it was there, and the next it was gone. There wasn't even the usual feeling of a vacuum from the lack of sound. The alarm was blaring away, and then there were the usual sounds of a busy store. There was no fading or merging. It was just one sound, and then it was gone.

The heavy smell of smoke was gone too. He hadn't realized how bad it was until it wasn't there anymore. Well, it wasn't in the air anymore, but it was still all over him.

The group had gathered a few feet into the store, in the direction of the elevator. Jake quickly looked around. They were in the men's clothing section. In front of them was the boy's section then the exit onto the shopping promenade. To their left, along the back of the store, was the area for the smaller kids. He knew from the earlier visit that the shoe section was on the far side of the floor.

The cash register they had paid at earlier was unmanned at the moment.

"What should we do now?" asked Nancy.

"We need to try to figure out what is going on here," said Derek.

Nancy looked around. "Where's Khalid?"

"I was the last one through the door," said Jake.

No one could say that they saw him on this side.

"Maybe he's checking this place out," said Jake as he shrugged his shoulders. "I don't know about you guys, but I'm going to find a bathroom and clean up." Jake held up his filthy hands.

Hanging over the cash register was a sign pointing the way to the different sections on the floor and the regular sign for the bathroom. It pointed them to the back of the floor. It turned out to be right next to the changing area for the little kids.

Derek picked out some clothes for Jake to change into, a pair of shorts and a T-shirt would do for now. He paid for them before going into the bathroom. They hadn't noticed anything out

Levels

of the ordinary, so far. In the short-time Derek took looking through the clothes, everything looked as expected. There was no odd exchange when he paid either. The other customers looked normal to him as well.

Jake didn't get any bad feelings about this place. He cleaned himself up as much as he could, under the circumstances. The cut on his head had looked much worse than it was. The water from the sprinklers had made the blood run down his face. He washed his face over the sink before inspecting the wound in the mirror. He leaned forward to get a better look.

It was still bleeding a little. He used a paper towel as an impromptu bandage and applied pressure on it for a few seconds. That did the trick. He'd probably get a nice bruise out of it, but the bleeding had stopped.

He stood in front of the sink looking at his reflection. He had a strong feeling that another person was staring back at him. The person in the mirror looked the same. Dirtier and definitely more tired since the last time he'd seen his reflection, but the same. He wasn't the same, though. He'd changed a lot. He shook his head and turned the water back on. Throwing his inhibitions to the wind, he took his shirt off and began washing in earnest. If somebody came in and thought he was weird or homeless, so what?

Jake looked up at the mirror and saw his dad looking at him.

"I got you some clean clothes."

"Thanks, Dad. These really stink!"

"Can you help Tommy clean himself up?"

"Yeah, we're good."

"Tommy, I'm going. . ."

He stopped when he heard the lock slide on the stall door.

"I heard you. I'm not a baby. I can clean myself up."

"Okay, you boys take care of yourselves. I'll be right back, okay?"

"We got this, right, Tommy?"

Derek didn't take long picking out clothes for himself and Tommy, just a pair of jeans each and a couple of T-shirts would fix them right up. He was happy to see Nancy standing over by the cashier station.

"I see you had the same idea," she said looking at the pile of clothes in his hands. "The girls are changing and should be out in a minute."

He finished the sale and thanked the cashier.

Levels

"I'll hurry the boys along. We'll be right out," he told her.

Jake was handing fresh paper towels to Tommy. "Can you wet some down for me too?" Derek asked Jake.

"Thank you, son," he said when Jake handed him a wad of wet paper. "I'll be just a minute," he said before he went into the stall. He quickly did what he needed to do.

When they were as clean as they were going to be, the freshly scrubbed group formed up far away from the cashier, so their conversation wouldn't be overheard.

Clare noticed how Jake was looking at her. "Do I look too silly?"

"No, it's just that I wouldn't have guessed you were a fan of the Teenage Mutant Ninja Turtles," he replied.

"What, you don't like the Turtles?"

"I do. I, well. . ." He decided just to let it drop. He didn't know what to say that wouldn't sound rude or stupid or both.

"I'm just messing with you, Jake. Nancy came in with some clothes and we just kind of made do with what we had. In case you didn't notice, this is the boy's department, not the girl's." She saw the blush rising in his cheeks. "It's cool. I like the Turtles too."

"What do you think we should do now?" asked Nancy.

Jake was surprised to see that she was talking to him. He glanced over at Kimberly to see what she thought. She shrugged her shoulders.

He stood a little straighter. "We need to see if there's anything weird going on here. Has anyone seen anything? Anything that seems, you know, different?"

He looked at the other kids first. They all shook their heads. "Nancy, did you notice anything about the clothes or the prices?"

"No, in fact, I spent a little bit of time going through the racks looking for anything different. Nothing stood out to me. How about you, Derek?"

"No, me neither," he said shaking his head. "I was looking for differences too. Nothing seems strange to me here."

"Maybe we're back to normal then. Maybe this nightmare is over," suggested Angie.

Her cell phone started to ring, surprising all of them.

"Finally, a signal," she exclaimed. She pulled the phone from the pocket of her baggy boy jeans. The color drained from her face when she saw the number displayed on the screen. It went so pale Jake was afraid she was going to faint.

Levels

Clare stepped closer and looked at the display. She looked up at Jake. "It's Melissa," she said with a quiver in her voice.

"Hello," said Angie, answering the call.

Clare leaned in close, so she could hear too.

"Where are you girl? I've been waiting like five minutes already."

Angie said the first thing that came to her mind. "I'm sorry." It came out as barely louder than a whisper.

"Just hurry up girl! I'm by Ladeaux."

Angie stood there, looking at the phone in disbelief.

"It was Melissa," said Angie, still looking down at the phone in her hand.

Angie made a decision. She turned and began walking toward the exit from the store. The perfume store Ladeaux was two stores down on the left.

She stopped a few feet short of exiting the store. Less than a hundred feet away, leaning against the rail, texting on her phone was Melissa. Her concentration fully on her phone, thumbs on the fly, so she didn't see the group standing just inside the store.

The scene looked so normal, shoppers walking by with bags in their hands while a teenage girl leaned against the rail texting away on her phone. A scene so very normal, except that this teenage girl had just died.

Clare put her hand on Angie's arm. She was trembling.

Angie turned her head to look at Clare. "How?"

All Clare could do was shake her head. She didn't know any more than Angie. Somehow, in this reality, Melissa was still alive. That much was evident. It was the how that she didn't have a clue about.

Shoppers were walking past paying them little, if any, attention.

Clare looked at Jake for a sign. All he gave her was a shrug of his shoulders.

Angie made up her mind and hurried from the store. She quickly closed the distance to her friend. Clare kept up with her, but the rest of the group held back.

When they were still about fifteen feet away from where Melissa was standing Clare grabbed Angie by the hand and stopped her. Angie whirled on her. The pain was easy to read on her face.

"Angie, I understand you have to know. Just be careful okay. She probably doesn't know what happened. Maybe for her, this has been a normal day."

Levels

A tear slid from Angie's eye. "I know," she said, nodding her head. She squeezed Clare's hand then turned back toward Melissa. She wiped the tear away and tried to put a smile on her face.

"Sorry I took so long," said Angie.

Melissa stopped her texting and turned to her friend. "It took you long—" she stopped when she saw the look on her face. "What happened? Did you and your mom have another fight?"

"No, it's nothing," said Angie wiping her nose with the back of her hand.

Seeing that, Melissa reached into her purse and dug around until she found a tissue. "Here you go, girl, that's nasty."

Angie couldn't help herself, she half laughed, half snorted.

"You're such a classy chick," said Melissa. She rolled her eyes over to Clare. "So, you're babysitting again?" she said as she hitched up her left eyebrow.

"Hi, Melissa," said Clare. She'd been through way too much to be bothered by such petty things.

"No, I'm spending time with my sister," said Angie. She took Clare's hand and held it.

Melissa looked from Angie to Clare. "I didn't know you two were so close," she said with a snarky edge to her voice.

"She's my sister," said Angie simply.

"Well, you just missed it. Jason and his friends just walked by. Guess who was with him. You're not gonna believe it: Sara! And not even Sara Thompson. Sara Smith! She's only a sophomore. Can you believe it?" She looked at Angie and stopped.

"What's so funny? You've been crushing on Jason forever. And now he's with her, and all you can do is smile? Are you feeling okay?"

Angie really shocked her friend when she reached out and hugged her. "I thought I lost you, you crazy bitch."

"What are you talking about? We just hung out last night." She looked over at Clare. "Did she bump her head?" She turned back to Angie. "Are you on drugs, girl? If you are, they must be good. Give me some!"

Clare looked behind her and saw that Jake and the rest of the group were hanging back just far enough not to be obvious. She reached out and squeezed Angie's arm and gave a tilt of her head, indicating she was going to go over and talk with the rest of the group.

Angie reached out her hand and held Clare's for a minute before nodding her head a little. Clare walked over to Jake.

Levels

"Everything okay?" he asked.

"Yeah, she's still going on about the same boring stuff. If this place is different, it's not very different. At least she's not. Did you guys find anything out?

"No, it all looks pretty normal. Nothing stands out as being different. At least not yet. Well, except for the obvious that is."

Clare got a confused look on her face. She got the point when she followed Jake's eyes to the very alive Melissa. "Yeah, except for that."

"Listen, Clare, I'm going to go to the coffee place where we left my mom. I've got to know."

Clare nodded her head that she understood.

"What are you going to do?" he asked her.

She looked over at Angie. She was fully involved in her conversation with Melissa. "They'll be like that for a long time. Mind if I tag along?" she asked.

"Sure." Jake looked back at his dad to make sure it was okay. Derek nodded that it was.

"Jake, do you think she would have just stayed there waiting for you guys to come back for so long?"

"Maybe not," he said. "Then again she might still be there. Sometimes she gets caught up talking on the phone with work," he explained with a small shrug of his shoulders and an attempt at a smile.

Derek looked over at Nancy. "So, we made it this far. We're going to go over to that café' that serves coffee. I think it's called Patrini's. We left my wife there before all this began. I don't have any idea if she's still there." He laughed a little. "After all that's happened, I don't even know if we do find her if it will be her," he said as he was looking at Angie talking with her not-dead friend.

Nancy saw where he was looking. Her hand twitched toward his. She wanted to reach out and hold his hand. She wanted to tell him that she understood. She didn't do either of those things. She didn't feel that it was right. She didn't want him to misinterpret her attempt at comfort for something more. Derek was trying to get back to his wife, and all she wanted to do was support him. It was her nature to empathize and solve problems. It was what she was good at. It was a tactic she used in her business dealings. It's what made her such a great success. She took care of her people. Her people took care of her. That synergy was what made her company so successful and by association her as well.

Levels

The group moved out. They spread out in smaller groups. Derek and Jake were walking side by side with Clare right behind them. Nancy was holding Tommy by the hand. Kimberly was on the other side of him holding his other hand.

They were walking past the directory sign, the same one that Jake and Derek had stopped at earlier to get their bearings when Derek had an idea. He'd seen a couple of security guards walking in the opposite direction on the far side of the promenade.

"Jake, hold up here a minute," he said before walking back to Nancy.

He stepped up to her and said in a voice little more than a whisper: "I think we should check with security. I'm sure Tommy's mom has to be going crazy with worry about him."

"Yeah, you're right. She probably reported him missing. I'm surprised we haven't been stopped yet," she said.

Tommy had been following their conversation. His little head swiveling back and forth between them. "We don't need to talk to the police," he said.

Not understanding what he meant by that Derek tried to reassure him. "It's going to be okay. I think they can help us to find your mom. We'll just go to their office and see if they found a lost mommy, okay?" he asked.

"She's not here," said Tommy.

"You didn't come here with your mommy?" asked Nancy.

"Yeah, but she's not here."

"You think she left you?" asked Derek.

"No, she's not in this 'here.' She's in the other 'here. The one with the bad people," he explained.

Nancy knelt down, so she was on eye level with the little boy. "What makes you think that?"

Tommy shrugged his small shoulders. "I don't know. I just do. Sometimes, I just know things. My grandma says that I got the gift." He shrugged his shoulders again. He shrugged them up so high they almost touched his ears. "We shouldn't talk with the police. If we do, there will be trouble."

Nancy looked up at Derek before standing. She reached out her hand and ruffled Tommy's hair. "Okay then," she said. "We won't go visit the police. The last thing we need is any more trouble," she said nodding her head to Tommy. She was happy that he nodded his head too, a big smile spreading across his face.

"Okay, so we keep going to the café," suggested Derek.

Levels

Jake scanned the crowd, looking for the most familiar face to him. He thought he saw her so many times along the way. He thought he recognized her hair until the woman turned around. He thought he saw her again, but his eyes were playing tricks on him. The closer he got to the café, the worse it became. He wanted it to be her so bad. He knew the odds of her still being there were small. He even knew that the odds of them being in the right "here" were small. He couldn't help hoping, though.

She wasn't there. Jake was disappointed but not surprised. He looked back at his dad.

Derek saw the look on Jake's face. He knew he was deeply disappointed. "Hey, kiddo, what do you say if we just give her a call?"

He was happy to see Jake's face light up.

Derek pulled out his phone and checked to make sure he had service. Fortunately, three bars were on display. He gave a reassuring smile to Jake and pressed the button to call his wife.

The phone was sounding the busy signal. It wasn't surprising. She was usually busy.

"Sorry, but it's busy."

"Did you leave a message?"

He hadn't thought of that. But what could he say? *Sorry, we missed you. We were in alternate realities for a while. What've you been up to?*

He was startled when the phone rang. He hadn't even thought about her returning his call. He had just thought of it as being unsuccessful. He brought the phone up to his ear and answered it along the way. Before he even got the phone to his ear, he could hear her voice.

"I've only got a minute, Derek. I'm in between calls. Is everything okay? Is Jake okay?"

He said the first thing that came to mind. "Jake's okay. We were just looking for you at Patrini's, and when you weren't here, we thought we would call you."

"Why would I be at Patrini's, Derek? This is your weekend with Jake. I'm at the office working. Are you sure everything's okay? Let me talk with Jake."

Derek waved his hand for Jake to come to the phone.

"Hi, Mom."

"How are you, honey? Is everything okay? Dad said you were looking for me at Patrini's."

"It's nothing, Mom. Where are you?"

Levels

"I'm at work, Jake. You know I've got that big project I've been working on. I figured since it was your weekend with Dad, I'd put in the overtime and try to get ahead of as much of this as I can. I want us to have a good time next weekend, and I don't want work getting in the way."

When Jake didn't say anything, she continued.

"I know what you're thinking. It won't happen again. I won't cancel this time. I'm looking forward to you and Ken getting to know each other."

Who the heck is Ken?

"You'll get to like him if you just give him a chance, honey. Oh, listen, I've got to go. I've got another call coming in that I have to take. Call me later. I love you."

Okay, that was weird. This is definitely an alternative reality. A bad alternative.

Nobody said anything. It was obvious the call hadn't gone as hoped. One look at Jake or Derek, and it was plain to see how awkward it had been.

"Okay, so what now?" asked Nancy.

Jake wasn't surprised when everyone looked to him for the answer. He thought about it for a minute. *Maybe it's this place that's making it happen? We've already been to every floor* except the first floor. What if we look around down there? If everything looks the same, maybe we should try to go outside and see if that brings things back to normal."

Before he'd even finished, Kimberly was shaking her head. "I tried that before, in the other place, or whatever. Remember I told you that I went out to scavenge around. It was all the same. Plus, remember I crossed over from my house, not here."

"Maybe this is different," offered Clare, shrugging her shoulders. "I think it's worth a try."

Kimberly just looked at her. She didn't have anything more to say. Clare could be right. She didn't feel that she was, but then again, none of this made any sense.

"Okay, so we go down and see what we find. Then we check out the exit. If it looks safe, we can explore a little. Does anyone else have any ideas?"

Nobody did.

"Okay," said Jake. "So, what's the closest way down from here?"

"The elevator," said Kimberly pointing back the way they'd come.

Levels

"Probably not a great way to go," said Derek. "We'd have to pass Melissa and Angie to get there. That might get awkward. I think it would be best if we avoid that."

"Okay, so where's the next closest elevator," asked Nancy.

"The stairs are a little farther down," said Clare.

"That works," said Jake.

He looked at each member of the group and seeing no objections, led the way to the stairs.

The promenade was bustling with shoppers. It wasn't so busy that it was difficult to navigate, but there was a steady flow of people going about their business. Jake's attention was focused on cutting through the openings in the crowd, so he could get to the stairs.

Derek, as usual, was watching the people around him. He focused on what they were wearing, how they were acting and interacting with each other. He was even looking at their shopping bags, looking for any unfamiliar stores. He was doing what he always did. He was paying attention to what was going on around him and trying to understand the story being told. So far, nothing seemed to be out of place. At least nothing for sure. There may have been some stores logos on the bags he didn't recognize, but that was to be expected. He had never been a big shopper, and he didn't invest a lot of his time at the mall.

An older man sitting on a bench caught his eye. He was relaxing and watching the people passing by. The old man looked right at Derek and smiled. Derek couldn't help himself and smiled back. He closed the distance between them and the man stood up. His motion caught Nancy's attention.

"Khalid?" she said.

He nodded his head. "One and the same," he said with the big smile still on his face.

"I thought we lost you," said Derek.

"I was checking out some interesting inconsistencies when I noticed you all weren't there any longer. It is quite interesting how we are here, though," he said.

"We looked around for you in the store. Where'd you go?" Derek asked.

Khalid looked puzzled. "I didn't go anywhere. I looked around for you, and when I didn't find you I decided to see if you had ventured this far," he said shrugging his shoulders.

His story didn't make sense to Derek, but then again not much was making sense. He let it go and looked over Khalid's

Levels

shoulder. He saw that Jake, Kimberly, Clare, and Tommy were almost to the stairs.

"Khalid, we're going to the first floor and check things out down there. We can trade stories along the way."

"That sounds interesting. I've encountered some very peculiar things since we last spoke."

Derek couldn't help but laugh. "Yeah, I believe it."

"Come on. I don't want to lose Jake and the kids," he said.

Jake and Tommy were leading the girls, and they had already gone down a couple of steps. Kimberly and Clare were following about five feet behind and were about to take the first step.

The first flight of fifteen tan colored marble steps ended at a wide landing. On each side of the stairs, a stainless-steel handrail was mounted above a glass barrier. The glass helped give the impression of openness to the structure. It allowed the people to see what was around them and decide sooner where they wanted to go. The second flight ended on the right side of the first-floor promenade, next to a smoothie stand on the left and a women's clothing store on the right.

Jake and Tommy were about to step onto the top of the second flight of stairs, and the girls stepped onto the landing when they disappeared.

Derek had made up the distance and was at the top of the stairs. One second, they were there, the next they weren't.

"Jake!" he called out, startling the shoppers around him.

He rushed down the stairs to the landing, frantically looking around for any sign of Jake. There was none. He knew what had happened. He knew Jake wasn't there anymore. He also knew that he had no way to get to him. He was powerless.

Derek felt his knees go weak. He sat down on the step and took a deep shuddering breath.

"He'll be back, my friend," said Khalid.

Derek looked up at him with red-rimmed eyes. "How can you know that?"

"He will find a way. He did before. And this time he's not alone."

Derek nodded his head. It was true. He wasn't alone. He was with the other kids.

"How did you know that, Khalid?" asked Nancy.

"Know what?"

Levels

"That he came back? When he did, you weren't around. How did you know?"

Khalid gave her his big smile. "He was just here, so he had to have come back."

His answer made sense but for some reason, Nancy felt that he knew more than what he was saying. She decided to let it go, *for now.*

"Well, it seems like we have some time to kill. Does anyone else feel like a smoothie? We can sit down and discuss all of the interesting things we've been through," said Khalid.

"Maybe we'll get a better idea of what in the hell is going on," said Derek, looking at Khalid pointedly.

Khalid nodded his head and smiled that enigmatic smile of his.

Chapter 10

Jake felt the now familiar sensations coming over him. He looked back and saw the surprised look on the girls' faces. He tried to hold the feelings back as things around him lost their focus. He looked up to his dad as his image faded away. The stairs they were standing on dimmed in color. Things in his peripheral vision became blurry, and little things flitted around the edges. He tried harder to suppress the feelings. He looked over at Kimberly. "Try to push it back," he said.

"How?"

"Try to stop the feelings."

"Okay," she said. She closed her eyes and concentrated on doing what he had said.

Jake did the same. He closed his eyes and concentrated on stopping the feelings.

He was startled out of his concentration. Something bumped him from the right side, hard. A woman, overloaded with shopping bags and trying to manage two toddlers, continued on her way. She didn't even bother turning back when she threw a

Levels

parting shot over her shoulder. "Why don't you kids get out of the way," she said as she hurried on.

"I want a smoothie, Mommy," hollered one of the kids. "Me too, me too." The other one joined in.

"I'll get you a smoothie if you promise to be good," she said.

Jake looked away from the departing family and back up the stairs, hoping to see his dad. His heart fell. He wasn't there. They'd crossed over.

Jake ran back up taking the stairs two at a time. Nausea hit him hard. His guts clenched, and his mouth filled with a metallic taste. Spit filled his mouth, and his throat tightened. His breathing was reduced to shallow gasps as he tried not to hurl. His foot didn't clear the step, it caught on the top edge. His hands reflexively reached out, arresting his fall. He lay there, sprawled on the steps, trying to catch his breath. Lights danced in front of his eyes. He shook his head, trying to clear his vision. All it got him was a stronger wave of nausea. His guts clenched so tight he thought he was going to pass out or crap his pants, or both. *Yeah, that would really impress Clare.*

After what could have been a few seconds or a few minutes, he realized he was on his hands and knees, and there was a comforting hand on his shoulder. He could do without the shaking that hand was giving him. The nausea was still there, but it was better.

His vision cleared enough for him to see that he was looking at a filthy step. His vision was blurry because his eyes had filled with tears. He knew it wasn't from his smarting knee. He looked to the right and saw trash on the side of the stairwell. He wanted so bad for it all to be over. All he wanted was to go back to how it was before.

"Jake! Jake!"

More shaking from that hand. How could he have thought it felt comforting? That shaking was threatening to make him lose his cookies if there was anything in there to lose.

"Alright, alright, I'm okay now."

"We've got to get out of here, Jake," said Kimberly. The panic in her voice was barely controlled.

"She's right. We've got to go," Clare said with an uncharacteristic shrill tone to her voice. He'd heard Clare when she was scared. This was more like barely restrained panic.

It brought him back as surely as a bucket of cold water would have.

Levels

When he focused, he could hear the uproar that was coming from below them. He looked down the stairs and saw them. A large group of Enforcers surrounded what looked to be a makeshift camp site. A camp had been set up inside the store. Tents of various colors and styles were placed haphazardly across the open promenade.

Jake turned and sat down on the filthy step. He didn't trust his legs yet. He looked at Kimberly. "We need to get back. If we both focus really hard on my dad, we can get back to him. I know we can," he said.

She didn't look as convinced, but she nodded her head anyway. She'd do just about anything to get away from here. She'd seen what the Enforcers did to people and wanted no part of it.

They gathered at the top of the stairs, away from the rail so that those below couldn't see them. Jake and Kimberly each held hands with Tommy and Clare, making a circle. They all closed their eyes, all but Tommy who was too curious not to see what was happening.

Jake didn't feel anything. No nausea. No dizziness. No sense of things blurring out. He concentrated harder, trying to focus on the place that those feelings came from. He felt that he was getting in touch with that source, but there wasn't anything there now. He focused harder, scrunching his face up with his effort. Sweat began to bead on his brow and his top lip. He didn't have any idea how long he stayed like that. His concentration was finally broken by Kimberly's voice.

"It's not working. I don't know why. I don't even really know how, but it's not."

Jake let go of their hands and walked down a couple of stairs. Without saying a word, he turned and ran back up. He knew it probably wouldn't work, but he had to try. His wounded knee protested with every step. He'd hoped that he would climb back to where his dad was. It didn't happen. He hadn't even felt a twinge of the power or sensation or whatever it was. He looked around for his dad anyway, trying to find some sign of him.

"I don't think we're going to find him here," said Clare. She had followed him without him realizing it. He'd been so focused on getting back to his dad that he hadn't paid attention to what went on around him.

Jake turned to her. She could see that he already knew it. "I think we need to do something here," she said.

Jake nodded his head. That seemed to be one of the things that they'd figured out. There wasn't any going back. They had to

Levels

keep going forward. Wherever forward may be and to whatever lay ahead. Even though he knew it wouldn't do any good, he gave another slow look around. The only thing he saw was a litter-strewn expanse that moments before had been clean, well lit, and vibrant with life of all walks going about their business. Now it was dirty and tired. He took a deep breath and resigned himself to seeing this thing through so that, somehow, he could find his way back.

He turned and wasn't altogether surprised to see that Clare was right there, waiting for him. Knowing she was there for him helped him to feel better. In that moment, looking at her profile, he fell in love with her. Of course, he didn't fall very deep, but he fell nonetheless.

They moved to the side of the walkway. They needed to understand what was going on.

He heard voices coming from behind them. He waved his hand for the others to run.

He kept an eye out. He wanted to give the others a chance to escape. If he needed to, he'd try to lead them away from his friends.

A group of Enforcers came out of the store and started walking down the promenade. They looked relaxed, talking freely with each other.

Jake kept his back as close to the wall and crab-walked as fast as he could. He moved back into a recess for one of the stores. It would block him from their direct view. He was hoping they would turn and walk over to the other side or go down the stairs. He pressed back against the metal gate that was blocking the entrance into the store behind him.

He hadn't seen where the rest of the group had gone. He hoped they didn't come back looking for him.

Don't look over here. Don't look over here, he kept thinking. He was ready to run. His heart was beating a mile a minute.

Something tugged the jeans on the back of his leg. He kicked his leg away out of reflex. He was a split second from darting away from whatever had grabbed him.

"Jake," whispered Tommy. "We're in here. Hurry!"

Jake looked down and saw Tommy's face looking up at him from behind the gate. His little arm was waving for him to come in from the space between the bottom of the gate and the

Levels

floor. Someone had forced the barrier open just enough to squeeze through.

Jake lay down and rolled under the gate. Tommy led him back into the darker shadows.

Clare and Kimberly were there, hiding behind the checkout counter.

Jake's eyes adjusted to the darkness. Gradually, he could make things out from the shadows. They were in what had been a women's clothing store. The display racks were mostly empty. Clothes lay on the floor, haphazardly discarded. He looked up and saw that the junk jewelry was still fully stocked. *I guess when the world falls apart, the interest in earrings goes with it.*

They hid in the darkness for what seemed like forever. Jake kept checking his watch. Ten minutes passed without any sign of the Enforcers. "Did anyone check and see if there is a stockroom in the back? Some way we can get out of here?"

"No," said Kimberly. She stood up. "I'll check it out," she whispered.

"I'll go with you," said Clare.

Jake knew better than to insist he go. There would be that whole, "just because he was the guy, he had to do it thing." He knew Clare could handle herself. If she needed him all she had to

251

do was call out. Plus, somebody had to keep a lookout. Clare caught him looking at her.

"Be careful," was all he said.

She nodded her head, and they were off.

The attention span of little boys is not very long. Having nothing better to do, Tommy leaned against Jake and fell asleep.

Jake listened for any sound. He tried to breathe as quietly as possible, so he wouldn't miss something. It had been a while since he'd heard anything from the girls. At first, he'd heard them whispering to each other. One of them must have used their phone as a flashlight because it lit up the area and light spilled back into the store. The circle of light receded into the back as the girls went deeper to investigate. Their whispers faded with the departing light.

Jake hadn't heard anything for almost ten minutes. He didn't want to wake Tommy up. He knew he had to be exhausted, but he really wanted to get to the front of the store. He needed to see if the Enforcers were still out there. Had they left or were they just out of sight?

Where could the girls be? It can't be that big back there.

The gate at the front of the store rattled loudly causing Jake to jump. He scooted closer to the checkout counter pulling

Levels

Tommy with him. The boy had bolted awake at the noise. Jake held his finger to his lips for him to keep quiet.

"Go on, get your skinny ass in there."

"Why don't you go first?"

"I outrank you, now go."

"Bullshit! We're both corporals, and you know it."

"Yeah, but I've been an Enforcer longer than you."

"You finished training one class ahead of me."

"There you go. Now get your skinny ass in there and check it out. Sarge said to sweep this area."

"Fine, but your fat ass goes first next time."

Jake pushed Tommy away from him and pointed to the back of the store. "Go Tommy. Go find the girls. I'm right behind you," he whispered as quietly as he could.

Jake watched Tommy crawl back into the storage area. Once he was clear, Jake followed. He heard the Enforcer walking around the front of the store. The guy had a flashlight. The beam was sweeping randomly back and forth. Jake looked back to the front of the store. There were only two of them. The guy inside was looking at something over to the left.

Jake began to crawl again. He must have been too focused on the Enforcer instead of watching where he was putting his hand. It landed on something metal. Maybe it had been part of one of the display racks. Whatever it was it rolled. Of course, it wasn't perfectly round. That wouldn't have made much sound at all. It was square and the way his hand caught it made it roll to the next side. It made a muted sound on the carpet.

Jake froze. The beam of light stabbed the air above him. He saw the dust drifting in the air revealed by the beam of light.

"What is it?"

"I think I heard something?"

"I didn't hear anything?"

Jake heard the guy walking closer, the beam from the flashlight moving back and forth, probing the darkness.

"Come on already, there's nothing back there."

The beam of light turned away. "I'm telling you, I heard something. We just caught that old guy. There might be more of them."

Jake took advantage of the distraction and crawled to the back room. Before he made it, he was caught in the beam of the light.

"Shit!" he cursed under his breath and stood up. The guy was coming fast.

Levels

Jake had an idea. It wasn't a great one, but he only had seconds to come up with it. He kicked his feet around till he felt something. He bent down and picked it up.

The guy was almost there. He was out of time. He gauged his move by the brightness of the flashlight beam and the sound of his boots.

As soon as the guy crossed the doorway, Jake wrapped his face up with the shirt he had picked up. Jake jerked down hard and to the side. The element of surprise was on his side, and he threw the Enforcer to the ground. The flashlight fell from his hand, sliding deeper into the room, the beam dancing crazily as it spun around.

Jake made a dash for it and was just able to grab it up as he raced for the door he saw at the back of the room. He didn't see Tommy anywhere. *I hope you already made it out.*

He hit the door fast. He was just through it when holes punched into the metal beside his head.

Jake didn't notice them. His attention was focused on getting away. He was in a big receiving area. He looked to the right and saw shelves and boxes. He looked left and saw Tommy running down the aisle. He sprinted after him.

Tommy turned right. Jake had almost caught up to him when Tommy turned right again.

Jake shot his hand out to push off a shelf and make the turn down the aisle.

The sound of more gunshots ripped the still air. *This guy is not giving up.*

Jake wasn't a gun guy. He didn't know how many shots a gun could fire. Unfortunately, for him, the gun had a large capacity magazine.

He caught up with Tommy and scooped him up in his arms.

"Hey, buddy, you're really fast."

He didn't see any sign of the girls. "Did you see where the girls went?"

"We need to go that way," said Tommy, pointing to the left.

Jake didn't question it. He turned left at the next break in the shelves then poured on as much speed as he could.

The sound of the gunshots had to have alerted any Enforcers in the area. *They're probably closing in right now.* He knew that the guy chasing him was only a few steps behind. *Think! Think!*

Levels

"Go there," said Tommy pointing down a side aisle.

Jake pivoted and turned to where Tommy was pointing.

"Over there," Tommy said pointing to a big cardboard box.

Jake stopped just short of the box, not sure what Tommy had in mind.

Tommy squirmed out of his arms and climbed on the shelf, hiding behind the box. Jake followed him.

Jake tried to get his breathing under control. He strained to hear where the Enforcer was.

Tommy moved over to the next row and onto the other side of the box, startling Jake. He followed him. When he came around the corner of the box, Tommy turned to look at him.

"Quiet," mouthed Tommy.

Jake nodded his head.

Tommy pointed at the box. "He's here," he mouthed.

Jake's eyes widened reflexively. He felt the threat in the air. He wanted to turn around, but he was afraid of making any sound that would betray their presence. He twisted his body and craned his neck to see past the box. He saw the back of the same Enforcer he'd taken down at the store. He was getting to the end of the row, looking from side to side. He was leading with his pistol. It was chilling to know that this guy wanted to kill him.

He made it to the end of the row and checked the cross aisle.

Tommy tugged on Jake's shirt. He saw Jake look at him, so he turned and went around the edge of the box. Jake quickly followed him.

Movement to Jake's left drew his eye. A group of Enforcers was moving down the aisle toward them. That must have been who the guy had signaled to. He was waiting at the end of the row. Jake heard muffled voices as they met up.

He closed his eyes, so he could focus on the sounds around him. Would they continue down the main aisle or would they come this way? There were too many of them. If they caught him and Tommy, there would be nothing he could do. He tried to come up with an escape plan. Nothing. He looked at Tommy. The boy didn't look scared. In fact, he gave Jake a little smile then slid out from their hiding spot.

"What are you doing?" Jake mouthed to him.

"Come on," said Tommy. He didn't wait for Jake. He crept across the aisle and through the shelves to the next aisle.

Jake followed as quietly as possible.

Levels

They crossed over two more rows before Jake led the way to the end of the aisle. He paused there with his back against the shelves. Somehow knowing it was time, he walked across the main aisle without looking to see if it was clear. Jake followed but wasn't as bold as Tommy; he took a look before crossing. The group of Enforcers, Jake estimated at least six of them, had moved further away.

Tommy surprised him when halfway down the row he asked Jake to lift him up onto the shelf. Jake hesitated and looked back in the direction they had just come from.

"Come on. We have to climb up there now."

It had worked so far, Jake reasoned. He lifted Tommy onto the shelf then climbed up behind him.

"One more, Jake."

When Jake made it to the top, Tommy was already lying on his stomach.

"Quick, they're here."

Jake flattened himself out on the shelf. His movement disturbed the layer of dust, tickling his nose. He grabbed his nose and squeezed the bridge to stop the sneeze. They'd be caught for sure unless he held it in. He squeezed his eyes closed, tight. A tear leaked out of his eye and dripped onto the wood of the shelf.

After what seemed like forever, the sensation passed.

Below them, an Enforcer on each side swept down the aisle. An additional three units of five each had been dispatched to investigate the shooting. They were methodically sweeping each aisle looking for Jake. They didn't know about Tommy or the girls.

After what felt like a very long time Tommy sat up. "We need to go."

"Are they gone?"

Tommy shrugged his shoulders. "We need to go that way," he said pointing back to the way they had come from.

Since the Enforcers had seemed to go the other way, Jake thought it was a good idea to go as far from them as possible.

They carefully climbed down off the shelf. Tommy was content to let Jake lead the way.

Taking a page from Tommy's book, they threaded their way through the shelves. It took longer, but Jake wasn't going to take any chances.

They stopped at the end of the row. The door to the store they had entered from was across the aisle and to the left. Jake was about to cross the aisle when Tommy walked around him. He passed the door and continued down the aisle.

Levels

Jake leaned down close to Tommy's ear and whispered. "Where are we going?"

"This way."

"Okay, but why?"

"Don't know. We just do."

Jake was frustrated, but he trusted Tommy. So far, he'd made choices—right choices. Jake didn't know how Tommy could know these things, but he could. There was no doubt in his mind.

"What's wrong?"

Tommy had slowed down. It looked like he was listening for something.

Jake strained to hear any sign of danger. It was probably his imagination, but he thought he heard footsteps behind them. He looked back expecting to see a bunch of men dressed in black sneaking up on them.

He didn't see anyone.

He shook his head to ease the tension and turned back to Tommy.

They walked past a couple more rows, very slowly.

"I don't hear anything. Where do you think we should go?"

261

"Shhhh," said Tommy waving his hand up and down for Jake to keep it down.

Tommy stopped walking and leaned forward and a little to the right.

Jake waited for him to say something. And then waited some more. Running out of patience and seeing no sign of danger he was about to say something when Tommy darted to the left. Surprised by the sudden change Jake stayed close on his heels.

They ran deeper into the receiving area, past row after row of discarded and broken merchandise. Cardboard boxes and other trash were strewn haphazardly on the floor keeping their pace in check.

Tommy turned left.

Jake saw that the row opened up to a large open area. Across the space was what looked like a cargo elevator. He wasn't paying enough attention and stepped on the end of a pallet jack causing the wheels to slide. He pinwheeled his arms, fighting for balance. Luckily, his momentum carried him over the pallet jack, and he landed on his feet.

Tommy was halfway across the receiving area to the elevator.

Levels

Jake hurried to catch up to him. There was no doubt about it, the Enforcers were back. He could hear them talking to each other. It didn't sound like they'd heard the metallic clunk the tine of the pallet jack made when he accidentally stepped on it.

The platform for the cargo elevator wasn't on this floor. A safety bar was the only thing across the entrance. Tommy easily ducked under it and slid around the corner. He wasn't wasting any time. He climbed down the ladder as quick as he could go.

Jake looked down the dark hole. The platform was at the bottom, at least twenty feet down.

As soon as Tommy was far enough down the metal ladder, Jake followed him, taking one rung at a time. He was climbing quickly for a boy of six.

Tommy surprised him when he got to the bottom. Instead of going into the receiving area on the bottom floor, he went down another ladder, outside.

As soon as Jake pushed through the plastic curtain, the heat hit him like a wall. He squinted his eyes from the bright sunlight. He blinked his eyes to adjust from the darkness of the elevator shaft.

Jake just saw Tommy go around the front of a semi. The truck was backed up to the loading dock, so Jake had no choice but to follow him around the front. For a little guy, Tommy could really move. He was running as hard as he could, staying in front of the trucks.

Jake caught up to him. Tommy was losing some steam. They were about a hundred feet from the end of the loading zone. The last two bays were empty.

Jake was surprised again when Tommy veered to the right, angling for the bay door of the west tower. "Why there?"

"It. . . feels. . .right."

"Okay. We're almost there," he said encouragingly.

Tommy ran out of gas about twenty feet from the bay door. Jake scooped him up and swung him onto his back. When they got to the bay, he sat Tommy on the bumpers.

"Hold on. Let me make sure nobody's waiting for us, okay?"

Tommy nodded his head.

Jake scaled the three-step ladder then moved to the side of the door. He didn't want to expose their position, and he wasn't about to just walk right in. For all, he knew the Enforcers could be inside on a lunch break. *Lunch sounds good. Focus!*

Levels

He was being cautious. He knew the Enforcers had been heading this direction. Hopefully, they'd been satisfied after their sweep and had headed back to wherever they had come from.

He didn't see any movement. They couldn't risk staying here any longer. They were too exposed. He looked to Tommy to make sure he didn't have any last-minute premonitions or whatever it was that he felt.

Tommy understood the look and nodded his head that it was okay to go in.

The receiving bay was much smaller. There weren't nearly as many shelves. Most of the space was marked off with lines on the floor. Judging by the big empty boxes inside the painted lines, they were for staging the merchandise when it was taken off the trucks.

At the far side of the room, there were two big doors, one on each side of a cargo elevator like the one they'd climbed down before.

One look at Tommy confirmed that they wouldn't be taking the elevator up.

"Wanna ride on my back again?"

The boy nodded.

Jake looked back at the receiving door. He didn't want anyone sneaking up behind them if he could help it. He didn't see anything to worry about.

Jake paused at the door and let Tommy get down from his back. He cupped his hand behind his ear and mouthed listen, to him. They both put their ears up to the door, straining to hear any sounds. After a couple of minutes, Jake was satisfied that there wasn't anyone on the other side. He cracked the door enough to look inside.

It was dark. He couldn't make anything out. He had enough presence of mind to know that the light he was letting in from the door behind them was betraying their presence to anyone on the inside of the store.

"Come on," he said to Tommy, hurrying through the door and then closing it quietly behind them.

It was dark. Really dark. The little light that came in from under the door was enough to move to the side without them tripping over anything. Jake led them down the front of a display counter, letting his hand slide along the edge—*OW!* He pulled his hand back from the sharp pain and looked at the cut.

Oh yeah! Dark! Can't see anything.

Levels

A piece of glass from the broken display case had sliced his finger open. He did the only thing he could under the circumstances. He used his thumb to put pressure on the cut, and they continued on to the end of the counter. With the display case on one side and the wall behind their backs, they crouched down and waited for their eyes to adjust to the dark.

Jake's senses were on high alert. The throbbing in his finger made him aware of the sound of his heartbeat in his ears. He strained to hear any sound that would signal they weren't alone.

Time has a way of stretching out. Sitting in the dark, expecting danger to fall upon them at any second, it seemed to take forever for their eyes to adjust. Gradually, they made the transition. Shadows started to gain definition. Vague shapes came into focus out of the gloom.

Clothes hung from circular display racks on the other side of the aisle. To the right, he could make out what looked like compound bows on display. He couldn't see any deeper into that area. The display shelves blocked out what little light there was.

After what could have been in as little as ten minutes and as many as thirty or so, not that it mattered much, Jake decided to risk moving again. Sitting there without anything to do other than let his eyes adjust to the dark, he tried to make a plan. He wanted to take Tommy by the hand and try to cross back over to where his dad was, but he didn't want to abandon Clare. He'd gone over all sides of the argument in his head. He knew there was a good chance that she'd told Kimberly that the most likely thing he would have done was to return to his dad.

It was true. That was what he really wanted to do. He just couldn't do it. He couldn't just leave without looking for the girls. He decided to scout around. Maybe he'd find a reason why all this was happening.

They crossed the aisle, staying low, and made it to the first clothes carousel without any problems. They took it slow, listening and scouting out their next step before taking it. He was deliberately staying in the middle of the section, away from the aisles.

"Hey, over here."

Jake's heart stopped. He frantically looked for the person who called out. It sounded like a girl, but he wasn't sure. It also sounded like it came from in front of where they were. He couldn't make out anything in the darkness. *It didn't sound like Clare or Kimberly, but who else could it be?*

"Who are you?" he whispered.

Levels

"You need to follow me. It's not safe here."

Jake looked at Tommy hoping he would tell him what to do. Tommy just shrugged his shoulders.

Jake had no idea if he could trust her. If it even was a her. Then again, the Enforcers didn't whisper. They didn't hide. They came right at you, from what he'd seen of them. So, she wasn't an Enforcer. In Kimberly's journal, she'd written that there'd been people hiding from the Enforcers. She'd avoided them. He thought that was a good idea. Then again, maybe this girl could help them. She probably knew her way around.

He decided to take a chance, a guarded chance.

"Come on, Tommy," he said. He carefully looked around. He didn't see any movement. Plus, Tommy wasn't saying not to follow her. That was a pretty good sign. Then again, he wasn't saying that they should follow her either.

They crossed the aisle and walked, crouched over, to where he thought she was hiding.

"Over here, come on," he heard to his right. She sounded like she was about twenty feet away.

He took it slow. The deeper they went into the store, the darker it got. He felt as if the darkness had a physical weight to it, pressing on him from all sides. It felt like something was going to

269

grab him at any time. His eyes could only adjust to the dark so much. He was navigating between dark and even darker. He used his hands out in front to prevent them from bumping into too many things. It wasn't easy. The place had been trashed. Shelves and empty display racks were everywhere. Tommy held onto Jake's back pocket. Each time his little hand bumped into him, Jake jumped a little. He couldn't help it.

A couple of times, he thought he saw her. A shadow separated itself from the others and crossed the row in front of them. He couldn't be sure. It happened so fast and could have just as easily been his imagination playing tricks on him.

"Over here, come on."

This time there was no doubt he saw her. She was down low to the floor. He saw her waving her arm for him to hurry toward her.

She was holding a door open for them. He couldn't see what was on the other side. It was too dark. He decided to follow through. He really hoped that Tommy's sensors would feel if it was a trap.

She must have closed the door because what little light there had been was cut off.

"Close your eyes," she said.

Levels

There was no way he was going to do that. He felt too exposed already. He regretted that decision a split second later. Light flooded the room. It was too much for his eyes to take. His vision was washed out. He shut his eyes hard. Bright colors danced across his vision.

"I warned you," she said.

He put his hands over his eyes and tried peeking through tightly slitted eyelids. No use! It was still too much.

"Just give it a minute. It'll be okay," she said.

Jake nodded his head.

"Why are you helping us?" he asked her.

"You're the first people I've seen in a while. Plus, you looked like you could use it."

"We can take care of ourselves," he said. He was blinking his eyes. He could see her, but with the colors and bright shapes floating in his vision plus the tears in his eyes she wasn't more than a shape. The more he blinked, the more defined she became. She looked like she was a couple of years older than him. She seemed to be about as tall as him and had short dark hair.

"I'm sure you guys can. It's just that I haven't seen you around here, and you looked like you didn't know your way around."

"What makes you so sure?"

"Well, for starters, you'd know to stay away from the loading dock. They patrol there all the time. Then you wouldn't have stopped where you did when you came into the store. They always sweep down the main aisle. And, like I said, I haven't seen you guys before."

Jake was finally able to see without blinking like a fool. The light came from a flashlight she was holding. They were in a maintenance room. Fuse panels lined the wall to the left of the door. They looked like the one at home but a lot bigger. Shelves on the right had light bulbs and other junk.

"Come on," she said, leading the way.

The room was about twenty feet long to the back wall. Jake was surprised to see that it was long. It looked like it went the whole way down this side of the building. Along the back wall was a long workbench. Some tools were still on the pegboard. The bench also doubled as office space from the look of it. Computer stations were at various stations along its length.

They walked along the back aisle and had gone past ten or twelve rows of shelves when they came upon a break area. A couple of couches, tables, and chairs dotted the area. On the far side was a kitchen area with a fridge and microwave.

Levels

Judging by the blankets and general look of the place, this was where the girl lived.

"Yeah, I know it ain't much, but welcome to my humble abode. Have a seat," she said waving her arm to take in the splendor of the accommodations.

Tommy didn't waste any time and hopped onto the couch.

"Okay, since this is my place and you two handsome boys are my guests, I'll go first."

Jake was immediately worried. First at what?

"How rude of me. I'm sorry. My name's LouAnne, but everybody calls me Lou."

"I'm Tommy."

"Hi, Tommy. How old are you? No, don't tell me. Let me guess. Nine? No, you're too cute to be nine. Ten, right?"

"No, I'm six and three-quarters. I'll be seven in October," he said proudly.

She smiled at him. "Nice to meet you, Tommy."

"Jake," he told her.

"Hi, Jake," she said looking at him. She took a deep breath. "Okay, so I'm actually from here, born and raised. My mom's a professor at VCU. Well, she was. She taught Anglo American studies."

Lou got lost in her memories. She sat like that for a couple of minutes before she remembered what she'd been doing.

"That was before." She shook her head.

"Things stayed pretty normal for a while. I still had to go to school. Mom went to work. It didn't last long. We started running out of gas. There were long lines at the gas stations. Cars waited in line for hours. There was a committee in place. Some of the members were what was left of the city government before the walls. Others, like my mom, were volunteers trying to make a difference. They tried to work with the government. They were told that it was nothing but logistic issues and they'd be fixed. 'Just be patient,' they'd said. That was when the Enforcers came. Well, you know. They were always here, but then they arrived in force. Were you guys here for that?"

"No, we came after," he told her.

She nodded her head. "I'd say you were lucky, but from what I've heard, the same thing happened in all of the exclusion cities. We still had electricity. We could watch TV. Even the Internet was still working until that day. My mom and I talked about it. Everybody was talking about it. People had been protesting about the conditions and the fact we were illegally imprisoned. It was the uprising in St. Louis that did it. That lit the

Levels

fire. Some people thought the right thing to do was to fight back. My mom sided with the peaceful way."

Jake waited for her to continue. Tommy had drifted off to sleep. Jake focused on the boy's steady breathing. He let his eyes wander around the room. She kept it clean. There wasn't anything out on the countertops. The metal lockers had clothes in them. Somebody passing through wouldn't see that anyone was living here at first glance. Pretty smart.

"It didn't do any good. Three days later, the buses arrived with the Enforcers. The angry crowds met them, demanding gas, food, water. They didn't care. I wasn't there to see it. I was one of the only kids still going to school. By then, most of the teachers weren't going either. My mom, the professor, wouldn't hear of me skipping school. I'm glad I wasn't there. They used their clubs and just started beating people. The first wave beat them down. The second wave picked them up and put them on the buses. A friend of mine showed me pictures he took. It was terrible. They beat them bad. When people realized they were being put on the bus, they tried to fight it. The area beside the bus door, on each side, was red with blood. They tried to hang onto the side. At first, the Enforcers just shoved them in, overpowering them. After the first couple of buses, they decided that it was slowing them down too much, so they posted an Enforcer on each side. Whenever a person was conscious enough to resist, the Enforcer would club their arm down.

"Once the bus was full, it pulled away. I don't know where they brought them. I do know that nobody ever came back. There was talk they were brought to a military base, maybe Fort Lee or Langley. There was even talk that they might have been brought to Norfolk and put on a ship back to Europe. Nobody really believed that one, though. It was just hopeful thinking. Others said they were brought overseas to fight in the war. Some people thought they might be sent to work in the coal mines as slaves, maybe to the south to work on the farms. The worst idea was that they were taken someplace and killed. I don't know where they all went, but those buses kept taking people away.

"Three days after the crackdown began, my mom and the other leaders were able to get Governor Baker to come to a meeting. They held the meeting at his mansion. Mom wouldn't let me go with her. She felt it was a good sign that the governor had agreed to attend, but she wasn't convinced. She didn't say it, but I think she knew it was a trap. Things were pretty bad. The Enforcers patrolled the streets in force. Groups of people protested their harsh crackdown, which only gave them a reason

Levels

to round up more people. And the buses kept running. They didn't even bother washing the blood off the sides of the doors.

"Mom left me at the VCU campus. She told me I'd be safer there. She left me with a couple of faculty friends of hers. Some of the staff and students had been stockpiling supplies and re-enforcing the dorms since the Enforcers started their crackdown.

"I never saw my mom again. I don't know what happened at that meeting. That night, the Enforcers raided the dorms. There was so much noise. Kids were being pulled from their rooms screaming. The sounds of fighting out in the hall. I don't know how you know the difference between the sound of a fist hitting flesh and the sound of a club, but you do. There was plenty of both. It lasted for hours. At one point, they broke down the door of the room I was in. I was hiding under the bed, as far back as possible. There were plastic storage boxes with stuff in them. I hid behind them and covered up with some blankets. I don't know how they didn't see me. The guy even used his club to poke at the blankets I was hiding under.

"Hours later, it was over. I didn't hear anything. I stayed under the bed for a long time. By the time I worked up the courage to climb out, it was day again.

"I crept closer to the door. They'd really done a number on it. The part with the door handle had been completely ripped out of the door, and the top hinge had the screws torn from the door case. I stayed inside the room, listening for any sign of people moving around, talking, anything. Nothing. It even felt empty.

"I must have waited like that for at least ten minutes before I dared to take a look. The place had been ransacked. Broken furniture, clothes, even a broken guitar littered the hall. I carefully checked the other rooms to make sure I was all alone. I went back to the room I'd spent the night in and looked out the window. Twelve stories down I could see Monroe Park. It looked like it did during the running of the Monument Avenue 10K. Tents were set up in the park, and people were everywhere. Buses were lined up along Belvidere to collect their human cargo. The interstate was only a few blocks north. The park made for a convenient processing hub. So many people!

"I stayed in that room for two weeks. Well, not the whole time, of course. I scavenged some water and food when the coast was clear. They were thorough. They did random sweeps through the building. They almost caught me one time. There was this one Enforcer that was roaming around on his own. Maybe he was

Levels

looking for things to steal. I don't know. I came down the stairs and turned into the hall on the seventh floor, and there he was. I'd grown careless. I was very lucky that he was walking away from me. All I saw was his back, and that was more than enough. I eased back into the stairwell and climbed those stairs as fast and quiet as I could.

"And you know the rest. More sweeps. Less food, less water. Fewer people. There were fewer Enforcers too. I guess they needed to do more ethnic cleansing in other places." She was sitting forward on the chair with her forearms on her thighs, shaking her head from side to side. If she was trying to clear the images from her head, it didn't look like it was working.

"I came upon this place about three weeks ago. The door was open, so I came in to investigate, you know, scrounge up some supplies. I found a key that worked to lock the door."

Tommy woke up from his nap and stretched his arms and legs.

"Feel better, handsome?" asked Lou.

He sat up and nodded his head.

"Do you guys have any water?"

"No, we were looking for some when you found us."

"I didn't think so, but a girl's gotta try, right? So, what's you guys' story? Are you two brothers?"

"No, we just look out for each other, don't we, Tommy."

Tommy spun around on the couch looking back at the door they'd come in.

"We need to go, fast," he said turning and looking at Jake.

"It's okay, buddy. I locked the door."

Tommy shook his head. "We need to go," he told her.

Jake stood up from the couch. "Is there another way out of here?"

"There's nothing to be afraid of. I locked the door," she said.

"Lou, I've learned that when Tommy says we need to do something, we really need to do it. Now, is there another way out of here or not?"

"Follow me," she said turning right and walking further into the maintenance room.

They all heard the door handle rattling. Someone was trying to get in.

"Don't worry. I've heard them check it before. They'll move on," she said confidently.

She was wrong.

Levels

Loud thuds were followed by even louder booming sounds. They wanted in and weren't going to stop until they did.

Lou picked up the pace. "Hurry," she said.

She took the metal steps of the staircase two at a time making no sound. Knowing that Tommy couldn't keep up, Jake picked him up and swung him around to ride on his back. "Ready buddy?" he asked.

He felt Tommy nodding his head.

"I need you to not squeeze my neck so tight," Jake said to him. He felt the pressure ease up. Jake couldn't take the stairs two at a time, but he hurried as fast as he could. They were on the last flight before the next floor when the door gave way. Jake slowed down and took the last seven steps as quietly as he could. He watched through the open-backed staircase as the Enforcers stormed in. Their flashlight beams cut through the darkness and marked their progress. Jake counted six of them. Once through the door, they broke off into three teams of two and efficiently began sweeping the area.

Jake reached the landing for the first floor and went through the door. Lou was to the right of the doorway and at least thirty feet away. He quickened his pace to catch her. He managed to avoid most of the obstacles in his way. He was almost to her when the light went out.

He kept going in the same direction. He was sure he had to have reached her by now. He didn't want to say anything. He didn't think the Enforcers were here yet. He thought for sure that he'd be able to see their flashlights.

A strong hand grabbed his arm. His heart nearly leaped out of his chest and his breath seized in his throat.

"Follow me," she whispered. She moved her hand down his arm till they were holding hands. It was crazy. He could breathe again, but his heart was still racing. She was cute, but this was *so not* the time. He took a deep breath hoping to calm down.

She obviously knew where she was going, even in the dark. She led them to the stairwell. Not the maintenance one they'd just used, the fire escape one like in the other building. She looked through the glass in the door. Satisfied that the coast was clear, she eased the door open and waited.

Jake hadn't expected that. He bumped into her.

Tommy bumped his head on the doorframe. "Ow! That really hurt."

Lights lit up the stairwell walls from below. The sound of boots pounding up the steps filled the air.

Levels

Jake didn't know whether to go back into the store and hide in the dark or to go up the stairs. Lou made the decision for him.

She pulled him along behind her as she darted up the stairs.

She has to have a plan. She knows what she's doing.

He was going as fast as he could with Tommy on his back. The boy didn't weigh a lot but still…

She threw the door open to the third floor and raced in. Jake stayed close on her heels, more from the fact she was still holding his hand than his ability to keep up with her. She went to the middle of the store. Like she told him before, the Enforcers stayed to the main aisle.

She led them to a checkout counter. Tommy climbed inside, and they both squeezed their bodies as close to it as they could. They'd just gotten settled in place when the stairwell door banged open. Beams of light cut through the air. They were moving erratically, bouncing up and down and swinging quickly around. The sound of pounding boots filled the air.

Just like Lou told them, the Enforcers kept to the main aisle. They let their flashlights probe the middle part of the store while they quickly completed their circuit.

Tommy pushed his way out from under the counter. He actually pushed Jake over onto his side. He grabbed Jake by the hand, leading him back the way they'd come from. Jake held Lou's hand and followed Tommy.

The lights were moving back toward them, down the right side of the store. The same side where they had been hiding.

Tommy stopped right before a beam of light crossed in front of them. If he had continued, they would have been caught in the beam. It turned away from them, probing other shadows.

Jake felt the breath she'd been holding when Lou let it go.

Tommy led the way to the left side of the store and off toward the side. The store was a big sports store that specialized in golf equipment. He led them to an area that had golf clubs on display. They hid behind one of the displays. The club heads pointed up and were arranged by type. The drivers were on the left of the display with the hybrids next to those and the irons following them down.

Jake was worried because the shafts they were hiding behind allowed him to see out at the rest of the store. If he could see out, then someone could see in. They could see him. He trusted Tommy, but this had him really worried. This and the

Levels

incident in the stairwell. He'd saved them from being caught in the light, but still, he was scared.

Tommy must have felt him trembling or heard his fast breathing. Something gave Jake away. Maybe the smell of his fear was pouring out from his pores. Maybe that would be what got them caught. Maybe the Enforcers would smell his fear. Or, maybe Tommy just wanted to tell Jake what they needed to do.

"We have to stay here. Don't move."

Jake leaned close to Tommy and whispered, "Okay."

He leaned the other way to Lou and whispered in her ear, "Tommy says we have to stay here. Don't move." Her hair tickled his nose.

She turned her head. Their cheeks were touching. He felt her hot breath when she whispered back, "Are you sure?"

"Yeah," he said, nodding his head.

Time in the dark is not the same as time in the light. The dark plays games on you. Jake's eyes were looking for threats, trying to see if a shadow was just a shadow or if it was something else.

He tracked the progress of the Enforcers through the store. Their lights sent up a glow around them. He watched the ceiling to track roughly where they were. He watched that glow as it slowly and inexorably came closer to them.

Lou squeezed his hand back. He hadn't been aware of how tightly he was squeezing his hands. He must have been crushing Tommy's little hand in his. He made his hand relax its grip and took a deep, albeit quiet, breath.

He watched their approach. Two Enforcers were sweeping their side of the aisle while two others were focused more on the center. They were taking their time. Occasionally, they would go off the aisle and investigate something. The tension was terrible. He was sure they were going to be caught.

The pair finished their inspection of the row beside them. Jake watched the beams of light dance on the floor back to the main aisle then they swung their way. They swept the area keeping their beams chest high. Shadows from the club shafts danced crazily depending on the angle of the light hitting them. The light hit Jake full in the face, hurting his eyes. It passed over him as quickly as it had found him. He cast his eyes to the ground to avoid it happening again.

His vision must have been more distorted than he thought. It looked like he could see the floor through Lou's hand. He blinked his eyes. No, it wasn't just her hand. He could see

Levels

through his too. He looked the other way and saw the same thing with his left hand holding onto Tommy's hand.

He turned his head back to look at Lou and was astounded to see through her. She caught him staring. He was so amazed his mouth was open.

"What?" she mouthed silently.

All Jake could manage was a shake of his head.

The Enforcers continued their sweep, somehow passing them over. Jake tracked their progress by the glow on the ceiling. The group formed up at the back of the store and then split again to take each stairwell. As the sound of their boots faded, the darkness closed in. Out of options, for the time being, they decided to wait where they were.

It was Lou who decided that they'd waited long enough. She led them back to the stairwell. Jake was amazed at how good she moved through the dark. She either had eyes like a cat or knew this place like the back of her hand. Maybe it was both.

She reached out her hand, feeling for the door she knew had to be in front of her. What she touched wasn't metal. It was hard plastic. A hand shot out of the dark and grabbed her arm. She reflexively jerked it back. The grip was strong and whoever was holding on wasn't letting go.

Jake bumped into her when she'd stopped. He was still holding Tommy's hand so when the feelings came over him suddenly, he was in physical contact with Lou and Tommy.

"Stop! Stop! Stop!" The feeling passed quickly. They were in a well-lit store. The door to the stairwell was right in front of them. So was the Enforcer, still holding onto Lou's arm. He had a look of disbelief on his face.

To their left was the shoe section and to the right racks of lady's golf clothes.

"What do you kids think you're doing?" asked a middle-aged woman. "You know you can't bring your Negro in the store. He has to wait downstairs in the colored area."

Jake looked around quickly, trying to assess the situation. He said the first thing that came to him. "Yes, ma'am. Daddy said to have him carry the new set of clubs down to the car."

"Hmpf," the woman said and walked off in a tiff.

The Enforcer had recovered enough of his wits to note what the woman had said. "What's a Negro?" He looked around the store. It was too much for him to take in. Not only had they gone from a pitch dark and deserted store in a way he couldn't comprehend, but the store was filled with only white people. There weren't any black people around.

Levels

"I don't know what the hell's going on, but I'm bringing you guys in. Come on," he said roughly.

"Get your hands off of the kids!" a commanding voice boomed from behind them.

The Enforcer looked up and saw two men dressed just like him, black beret and all. He didn't understand how they could be Enforcers and be white, but the uniform was right.

"I'm glad you're here. I'm bringing these three in. Then you can fill me in on what's going on."

"How about you let the girl's arm go and step away from the kids. Now!"

The other Enforcer spoke for the first time. "I don't know how you got your hands on the uniform, but I promise you're gonna regret it. You better not have hurt one of my brothers or sisters or your negro ass ain't gonna live to see the end of this day."

They rushed him. The man let go of Lou and fought the two men. They were a blur of black uniforms with splashes of white skin peppered with dark.

Jake had seen enough. Taking Tommy by the hand, he ran away from the fight, with Lou close behind. He went straight to the elevator and pushed the down button. It was time to go. This was not their reality. Here, it seemed like slavery never ended.

Lou was trying to look at everything around them. She had no idea how this could be happening, but it was. They were the only ones waiting for the elevator to arrive.

"What's happening? And why don't you look very surprised?"

He quickly looked around to see if anyone was paying them any attention. "Crap!" The woman was at a counter talking with one of the store employees. "That's them," she said shrilly, pointing an accusing finger at the end of her bony arm. "They are the ones that brought that Negro here."

Jake saw that the Enforcers had their hands full with the one that had crossed over with them. They'd subdued him and were walking him across the store, away from them. The employee the woman was talking with was saying something into the phone.

"Come on, come on." Jake urged the elevator to arrive.

His hopes were answered by the reassuring chime and the light indicator above the door changing to three. They were able to board the car without any further difficulties.

Levels

Jake pushed the button for the first floor so hard it hurt his finger a little. The car didn't move when the doors closed. There was no falling sensation. Nothing.

"What's going on?" asked Lou, more than a little freaked out by the sound of her voice.

"It's a lot to explain and no time to do it, so I'm just going to say it, okay? We just crossed over to a different reality. It looks like in this one slavery is still very much alive and whites are the majority instead of blacks like where you are from."

Lou didn't say anything for a few seconds as she processed what he had just said. She shook her head. "Wait, you just said from where I am from. You aren't from there? You're from somewhere else?"

"Not somewhere really. It's all the same where and it seems to be the same when. It's just things are different. Some places there's not much difference, but others, like here, it's really different."

The doors began to open then just stopped. Complete darkness enveloped them again. Nobody moved. The only sound was their breathing.

She whispered, "What now?"

"I think you're up again. You know this place even in the dark. Can you get us back to the stairs?"

"Yeah, come on." She reached out her arm and hit his chest.

"Sorry." She moved her hand along his arm then taking his hand in hers. "Ready?" she asked.

"Okay, Tommy?" he asked.

"Okay, Jake."

Levels

Chapter 11

They made it out to the second floor of the promenade without any problems. Jake had been thinking of a way to talk to Lou about what he was sure he'd seen in the golf store. He wasn't sure how he could casually ask someone he barely knew if they were part chameleon.

They were walking along the promenade, staying close to the wall in case there was anyone on the bottom floor looking up, when he just asked her directly, "So, how long have you been able to do that?"

"Do what?"

"You know. Back at the golf store. How long have you been able to do that?"

"Do what?"

"That hiding trick?"

"I didn't. Remember? Tommy led us there. He's the one that hid us," she said smiling at Tommy.

He nodded his head. "Tommy led us there, but you hid us. I saw what happened. It was awesome!"

"Seriously, what are you talking about?" She'd stopped walking and was now standing in front of him.

He looked right back at her. "You made us disappear, well not disappear exactly," he said thinking through how to say it best. "More like fade away so they couldn't see us."

She didn't say anything. She just looked at him.

Is it possible she doesn't know she does it?

"It's nothing like jumping realities. That was incredible!"

They walked a little way in silence, but it wasn't awkward at all. They had more than enough to think about.

"Jake, wait up," he heard a voice whispering behind them.

He whirled around to see Clare and then Kimberly roll out from under a store's security gate. He ran back to her and gave her a hug. Kimberly joined in too. Clare let go of Jake and picked Tommy up in a big hug.

"Who's she?" asked Kimberly.

"Kimberly, Clare, this is Lou. She's been helping Tommy and me."

"Okay," said Kimberly.

"Hey," Clare said, sizing her up.

Levels

"So, what happened to you guys?" asked Jake. "We waited for you in the store till a couple of Enforcers came in. Did you hear the gunshots?"

"What? Are you hurt? Did they shoot you? Tommy are you okay?"

"We're both okay."

She looked down and saw the blood on Jake's hand. She grabbed it and held it up to see the damage.

"It's just a cut. Really, we're both fine. What happened to you and Kimberly?"

"We went out into the receiving area. We were just checking things out, you know? We heard voices. A group of Enforcers were hanging out by the cargo elevator. They were on break or something. A couple of them were smoking. Anyway, we were backing away when I tripped and fell. We ran, but they caught us. They said they were taking us to the processing station, whatever that is."

Lou spoke up. "I've seen those places before. They take people they catch, and then those people get on a bus and disappear. Well, they used to use buses. They probably don't need to anymore. There's almost nobody left."

"Well, I didn't think it sounded like where we wanted to go." She looked at Lou, trying to gauge how much she should say. "Kimberly got us out of that, though. We had a hard time finding our way back here."

"We crossed over with Lou. She knows," Jake told her.

"Okay," said Clare again.

"I couldn't make it work again. I kept thinking about you and Tommy. There wasn't any, you know, feelings at first. But then I started feeling it. I think they might move, Jake. Maybe they are farther away sometimes, or something?"

Jake thought about what Kimberly had said. It sounded like she was onto something, but he didn't know enough about it to know if it was right or not. "It sounds right, but I just don't know either," he said. "The important thing is that we are back together. Now maybe we can get back to where we started." Jake realized what he said a second too late. He turned to look at Lou. She wasn't from the same place as the rest of them.

"Hey, I don't want to stay here. They want me gone? Fine! Let's get gone," she said. "I'm sure it has to be better where you guys came from, or you wouldn't want to go back. I'm in."

Levels

Chapter 12

They continued down the promenade, keeping quiet and close to the storefronts. Jake took the lead. He went ahead of the group to make sure the coast was clear. Lou was in the back of the line. She kept an eye to their rear to make sure nobody snuck up and surprised them.

Jake edged to the side. He wanted to see if there was any activity below them. He looked up and down the lower level of the promenade. Seeing no Enforcers, he went up to the railing and leaned over to see if there was anyone below them on this side. All clear.

He looked ahead. There was a crossover to the other side about fifty feet away. A coffee place was in the middle with some chairs and tables around it. A staircase in the center went down to the lower level. He didn't see anything to worry about from here. He looked back. Everyone was looking at him, waiting for him to lead them. Lou was looking behind them and walking backward. She looked over her shoulder and gave him a little smile and nod of her head. Kimberly watched him, waiting for him to move or tell them to hide. Either way, she was ready. She was holding Tommy's hand. The little boy smiled at Jake and gave him a small wave of his other hand. Then there was Clare. She was right behind him. Well, not exactly right behind. She was about twenty feet away, but she was next in line and ready to back him up if he needed it.

Jake moved away from the rail and to the middle of the walkway. He kept his eyes ahead, on the crossover and on the far side of the promenade. It wasn't easy looking everywhere at once, but trouble could literally come from anywhere.

He came even with the crossover. Something was wrong. A pair of legs were sticking out from the other side of the counter. Someone was sitting in a chair and had their legs stretched out. They were wearing khaki pants and a pair of brown loafers. *Okay, so he's not an Enforcer, but oh, I hope he's not dead. Would they just leave a body there to rot? I don't want to see a dead body.*

He angled to the far side of the crossover to provide distance between him and the person in khakis. That way he'd be able to see him sooner too. He stepped quietly not wanting to give away his presence just yet.

The legs pulled back.

Jake froze.

"Hello, my friend." A man stepped into view.

"Khalid, you really scared me."

Levels

"Sorry about that, Jake." He looked over Jake's shoulder. "I see everyone's here. He paused when he saw Lou. The questioning look faded away, and a smile returned. He extended his hand toward the group. "Shall we?"

"Is my dad with you?"

"I'm sorry, but no. This is not his journey."

That's a funny thing to say.

Khalid closed the remaining distance to the group. He reached out his hand and mussed Tommy's hair. "How are you, Tommy?"

Tommy smiled up at him. "Did you find my mommy?"

"I sure did. I told her we'd be right back. I just need you to help us out here first, okay?"

Tommy nodded his head that it was.

Khalid looked at Kimberly next. "I'm very happy to see you, Kimberly. I wasn't certain you were going to make it out of that grocery store."

"You were there?"

"I was the one that led them away from you. You are a very important young lady. We can't afford to lose you." He looked at each member of the group before continuing. "Any of you. You are all very special." He looked directly at Clare. "You

299

too, young lady." He tilted his head as if pondering something. "Yes, very special indeed," he said smiling his brilliant smile.

He looked at LouAnne last. "I don't know you, miss."

"She's LouAnne, but she goes by Lou."

Khalid's neutral expression slowly returned to a smile. He got a distant look on his face as if he was listening to something. "Everyone needs to stay calm." The man shook his wizened head. "This is the way it needs to be," he said quietly.

Jake looked confused. "What?"

Behind Khalid, a group of five Enforcers walked around the corner.

He looked over to the right and saw another group of five closing in. They must have just seen them too because they broke into an easy run to close the distance.

Jake whirled around and was about to run away when a pair of strong hands grabbed both of his shoulders.

"Stay calm, Jake," Khalid said from right next to his ear. "You need to stay strong and do not panic. The others are looking to you for guidance. Stay strong! This is what must be."

"You sold us out?"

"No. That will never happen. I am always here for you." Khalid looked at the rest of the kids. "All of you."

Levels

"Be strong. You will know when the time is right to do what you know is the right thing. Listen to each other. You are stronger when you work together. This is very important. Not just for the here. This is an overlap event. What happens here will affect myriad realities."

He was interrupted by the arrival of the Enforcers. They had closed in from all sides. Another contingent of five had closed off their escape on the stairs.

The group on the right arrived first. They were wearing full riot gear. Protective plating covered their chests, legs, and arms. The visors on their helmets were down, covering their faces. It gave their voices a distorted, muffled sound. Muffled or not their message was clear.

"DOWN! DOWN! On your knees."

The first Enforcer to arrive must have thought Khalid was moving too slow. He thrust out his left arm and hit Khalid in the head with the butt of his rifle. It was a glancing blow, but it knocked him on his back. Two Enforcers that had converged from the right were on him. They flipped him over and trussed his arms behind his back, securing them with zip ties. It was amazing how quick they did it. It was obvious they were well practiced in the maneuver. With his hands secured, they pulled him up and shoved him forward. Khalid slouched down on his knees. His head bowed forward, chin resting on his chest. Blood flowed from the wound above his right eye.

They quickly secured the rest of the group. The zipping sound of the zip ties signaled their captivity before the plastic restraints bit into their flesh, securing their hands tightly. They at least let them leave their hands in the front.

Jake watched the face of the Enforcer as he secured his hands. He seemed to be only a few years older than Jake.

The Enforcer noticed Jake looking at him. His upper lip curled at the corner of his mouth, and his eyes squinted tighter. A look of complete revulsion came over him.

Jake saw the blow coming. He tried to tighten his abs, but it didn't do much good. He didn't have much in the way of ab muscles to begin with. The punch knocked the wind out of him, and he doubled over from the pain.

The Enforcer grabbed him by the shoulder and forced him back up.

Jake struggled to breathe. He gasped, taking in small sips of air as bright spots of color danced in his vision. He was sure he was going to pass out.

Levels

"Don't you ever make eye contact with me, Whitey! You!" He looked over Jake's shoulder at the rest of the group. "All of you, are less than animals. You don't deserve to look on the pure."

Two very big Enforcers hauled Khalid up.

"Get on your feet!" Jake couldn't tell who gave the order. He tried to stand, but he was still gasping for air and simply didn't have the strength for it.

The same guy that had punched him was back in his face. "You were ordered to stand! Are you stupid or are you resisting arrest? Captain, I think this one's resisting arrest."

Jake was hit again, hard. This time the blow caught him in the left eye. It immediately started to swell. The cut on that side of his head re-opened and blood flowed into his eye. He was unceremoniously hauled to his feet. His knees buckled. His head was swimming. His legs felt like rubber and his lungs were on fire. The feeling deep in his gut was so bad he didn't know if he was going to puke, pee on himself, or crap his pants. He would have been afraid of doing all three if his brain was capable of forming a coherent thought. The Enforcers kept their strong grip on him and dragged him along with the rest of the group.

They went down the stairs to the first floor. Somewhere along the way, Jake was able to proceed from being drug along, to shuffling along, to stutter stepping. The Enforcers led them to a makeshift processing station. It was set up in what had been the food court.

A group of forty or so people was loosely surrounded by Enforcers, who were armed with assault rifles and dressed in full riot gear. They had the escape lines closed off.

The perimeter guards parted to allow them to pass. Khalid wrapped Jake's arm around his neck and supported his still wobbly legs. Khalid led the group to a couple of booths that were vacant.

A man in his mid-thirties brought them some bottled water and sandwiches. "Do as you're told. Don't resist them," he said looking over to the armed Enforcers. "We'll be done processing you soon. The bus is already here. In just a couple of hours you'll be in the safe zone," he told them. He had a nice face. He didn't look cruel, he actually looked like a doctor. He looked like he wanted them to be reassured by his words. He sounded like he believed what he had said. Jake kept thinking about what Clare had read to him from Kimberly's diary. The Enforcers had assaulted that woman in the street for no better reason than that

304

Levels

they could. Then Lou's story about what she'd seen. He had a strong feeling that there wasn't going to be any safe zone.

A touch on his left arm surprised him. Tommy's small hand was gripping his forearm.

The little boy was looking directly at him. He wasn't scared. At least he didn't look afraid. "Not yet Jake." He turned and looked out at all of the Enforcers that had them closed in.

Jake took a deep breath, as deep of a breath as his sore lungs could manage.

The Enforcer that had hit Jake walked over with an older one beside him. He tossed Kimberly's backpack on the table. Her hands moved so fast they were a blur. She easily caught it, arresting its momentum before it could strike her or skid off the other side and fall to the floor.

The smirk vanished from the brute's face.

"There's nothing in there that's contraband," said the older of the two. He tilted his head back to the perimeter before turning on his heel. The other one reluctantly followed.

"What are we going to do now?" asked Clare. She was looking at Khalid. The right side of his face was covered in blood.

"We need to do what the doctor said. We need to do exactly as they say. These guys are not playing around." He looked pointedly at Jake. "Don't even make eye contact with them if you can help it. There is so much hatred. Anything can set them off." He turned his attention to Tommy. "We'll know what to do when the time is right."

While Khalid had been talking, Kimberly had been rummaging through her backpack. She held a pack of baby wipes up to Khalid.

"Lean forward a little. Let me clean some of that off you."

Lou inspected Khalid's wound, applying pressure to try to slow the bleeding. Kimberly and Clare cleaned up as much of the blood as they could. Jake and Tommy, having nothing better to do, began eating a sandwich.

"You should eat too, girls. I understand you might not have much of an appetite after everything that's happened, but the truth is, we don't know how long we'll be here, and we don't know when we'll have another chance to eat," Khalid said.

Kimberly just kept looking out at the circle of Enforcers that had them trapped. Jake couldn't tell whether she was lost in fear or if she was just watching to see what would happen next.

Before he knew it, the sandwich he'd been eating was gone. There was only one for each of them, so he resisted taking another one.

Levels

"Go ahead, you can have mine," said Khalid as Clare finished wiping the last of the blood from his face. "I'm not as young as I once was, but I still remember how big my appetite was at your age."

"Thank you, but I'm okay."

"Go ahead, Jake. Seriously." Khalid nodded his head.

"Stay still please," said Clare. "I'm almost done."

"Yes, ma'am." Khalid flashed his bright smile.

A few minutes passed while Clare finished up. Jake had polished off the second sandwich before she was done. Tommy had finished his too by then. Kimberly was still watching what was going on around them.

"Jake, come over here and sit next to me," said Clare. "Let me clean that blood off you too."

Jake hadn't realized he was bleeding. He raised his hand up to the cut on his forehead. It was tender to the touch, but it had stopped bleeding. He focused on what was happening around them while Clare helped clean him up.

Several people wearing white lab coats were moving through the crowd. They were bringing people, in groups of two or three, never from the same groups, into the back of what used to be the prep area.

"We need to get out of here, Jake," Kimberly said turning to face him.

"We tried. It didn't work, remember?"

She rolled her eyes as only a teenage girl can. "Of course, I remember. It didn't work then. That doesn't mean it won't work now. We have to try. We have to get out of here."

Jake couldn't argue with her. It was all he could think about too. He didn't feel that thing, that power, inside of him. Maybe it was there. It was all so new.

"Okay, let's try holding hands again," he said.

"No, Jake. We have to wait," said Tommy.

"Why?" Jake asked him.

The little boy shrugged his shoulders. He didn't know the answer. He just knew it wasn't time yet.

Jake looked to Khalid for direction.

"If Tommy says to wait then that's what we need to do," said Khalid. He ruffled Tommy's hair affectionately.

Tommy broke out in a big smile. It was so cute because he was missing a couple of teeth.

Khalid looked at Clare and became very serious. "Clare, you need to trust your feelings. You are very special. You have no idea just how special you are. Very soon you are going to need to

Levels

let go of your feelings. Don't hold them back. Don't be afraid of them. Don't doubt. Don't think. FEEL."

They heard a commotion from the other side of the group of captives. "I'm going with her. I'm her father."

"No. You are not. Sit back down," said one of the men in the lab coats. He was very slim and had a long, sharp nose. When the father didn't immediately comply with his order, he nodded his head toward the ring of Enforcers.

A big man separated himself from the others and walked menacingly toward the disturbance.

"You're not taking her away from me. Just let me go with her. She's just a little girl."

"I recommend you sit down. Your daughter will be back out in just a couple of minutes."

"No, I won't sit down. I won't just sit down and take it. We've got rights, damn it!"

The doctor grabbed the girl by the arm and turned to walk away with her.

"Get your dirty hands off her!"

"My dirty hands!" the man blustered. "How dare you talk to me like that?" A smile turned up the corner of the doctor's mouth.

The Enforcer had closed the distance and had the butt of his rifle in position to hit the man in the back of the head.

A bottle of water arced through the air, hitting the Enforcer in the head. It harmlessly bounced off the riot helmet startling him. He flipped the rifle around so fast the black weapon was a blur. He snugged it firmly into his shoulder. The muzzle centered on the thrower's face so fast the man's hand was still extended, the index finger pointing at the enraged Enforcer. Flame shot out of the end of the barrel. Two slugs slammed into the man's head before he realized what was happening.

Clare couldn't see the shooter's face. His back was to them. She could see the faces of the others that encircled them. What she saw froze her to the core. The anger. The hatred. The disgust was so plainly on display. They didn't even see them as people.

Time slowed. Her focus was drawn from one Enforcer to the next. Despite the distance, she saw their faces clearly. She could see their eyes through their face shields. She saw so much more as well. Somehow, she could see, feel, and know what they were feeling.

Levels

She focused on each one for an instant, for an eternity, before moving on to the next. Her focus was inexorably drawn to one man. There was something about him.

Something stirred inside her. It was a vaguely familiar sensation, but it had never been this strong before.

"Don't resist it, Clare. Let it go." Khalid's voice filled her mind. "You know what you must do."

She was confused. She didn't know what to do. She didn't even know what was happening. Her focus started to pull back from the Enforcers face.

A disgusted look came over the man. His brown eyes blazed their hatred out at her.

"Why do you hate me so much?" She raged at him in her mind. Her focus zoomed in tighter on the man. The power surged within her. Her body was pulsing with its force. "Why do you hate me?" She saw his cheek twitch but didn't think anything of it. Why do you see me as less than you?" she wondered. "We are the same!"

The man's eyes flared wide with hate. It was like he heard her thoughts.

His hatred was a thick evil mass pushing toward her. She felt it as if it was a physical force. She pushed back at it. That feeling surged up within her, this wave stronger than any before.

"We are the same!" she shouted at him. "Why can't you see me?"

Some of the Enforcers were leaning forward. Their forward leg bent, the knee pointing at their intended target. The back leg braced to absorb the force of the recoil. Their trigger fingers were itching to apply the last amount of pressure. They were eager to unleash their judgment on their captives.

The power surged up from within her, growing stronger by the second. She thrust her chest forward and let it go. "See us. Really SEE US!"

Jake couldn't believe how loud she was yelling. He didn't think it was possible for anyone to shout that loud. He looked around to see if everyone was as surprised as him. He could barely see Lou. She had faded away. She was standing there, but he could barely see her. Remembering what had happened back in the golf store, he reached out and took her hand. She was still holding Tommy's hand. The little boy was faded too.

"Tommy, hold Kimberly's hand," he said.

Levels

The expression on the faces of the Enforcers changed. They looked like they'd just woke up from a dream. Some shook their heads from side to side. Others were looking at each other with horror. A few stood there, staring down at their shaking hands. It was like they were just now realizing how terrible a thing they had just about done.

Not all of them looked repentant. The kid that had hit him wasn't showing any remorse. All Jake saw was hatred.

Tommy looked up at him. "Jake, we have to go. We have to go now!"

He didn't question the boy. "Kimberly! Now!" He shouted so she could hear him. A staccato of automatic weapons fire ripped through the air.

People frantically struggled to get clear of the barrage without much success.

Clare was locked in a fierce battle. The fear, anger, and hate coming off the Enforcers was thick and cloying. It tried to engulf everything in its path. Clare changed her focus from the hate to the men. To the young man that had punched Jake.

She focused on one feeling. She projected a feeling of acceptance. Accept each person for their uniqueness. For what makes them special. Accept yourself because you are special too.

She felt the barriers coming down. She felt the tide of hatred stall, then it began to diminish.

Most of the Enforcers had thrown down their weapons and were stepping back from the carnage. The now unarmed Enforcers closest to the shooters turned on them, bellowing for them to stop shooting. When that didn't happen, they attacked them in an attempt to stop the slaughter.

Clare watched the young man as realization dawned on him. He threw his rifle on the ground and turned to walk away.

Jake reached out and grabbed Clare's hand. Khalid grabbed Jake's shoulder. As soon as the circle was closed, Jake shut his eyes and concentrated as hard as he could. He focused on one thing, a clear picture of his dad's face in his mind.

Levels

Chapter 13

The power surged within him. He felt it building, expanding in size until it felt as if he was rising from the floor. He was hit with another pulse of power. His head jerked back, and he yelled out.

Kimberly's power rushed into him, amplifying his power to all new levels. The additional surge was almost more than he could take.

He tried to keep his focus. He tried to concentrate on the image of his father in his mind. It was impossible. There was too much sensory input. The power pulsed through him making his muscles sing. It blinded him to everything, it was so strong. It was all he could do to keep from splitting apart. The power consumed him. All he could see was a bright yellow light. He couldn't hear anything except a roar in his head.

The light didn't so much fade as his eyes adjusted to the intensity. He was able to see like he'd never been able to see before. Images flashed by at the edge of his vision, as they had before. It was like looking into a mirror at a fun house. The kind that made you feel like you were looking into an infinite version of you. Each layer was thinly separated from each other, like the pages of a book.

Each of the images were separate, he somehow knew that each one was a different reality. He was looking at reality after reality existing so close to each other yet distinctly separate and different. If he concentrated, he was able to focus on each one separately. He could not only see it, and what was happening inside it, he could feel it. Each one was humming at its own unique pitch. His mind latched onto that fact, and something clicked into place, he could hear sounds begin to separate from one another, becoming distinct and separate from the overwhelming hum.

He felt a tug, then a tiny voice from far away. The tugging became more insistent and stronger, and the voice more distinct and urgent.

"Jake, we need to stop. I can't hold on much longer," said Kimberly.

He tried to pull back from those thinly veiled worlds. He knew he had to stop but the desire to stay was almost overpowering. He wanted to know more. He needed to know more. The sensations which had been so intense, and overwhelming were now in tune with him. He wanted to keep

Levels

experiencing them, all at once and separately, for just a minute more.

He felt the tug again and looked to Kimberly. He saw an image that he knew was her. She'd fallen to one knee. She was straining to hold on.

Jake realized with a shock that he couldn't feel whether he was still holding onto Khalid and Tommy. He couldn't let go of them. His fear of losing them brought him back into focus. He strained to maintain contact, to focus on his hold on them. He forced his concentration down to his hands. He strained to feel his hands touching them.

He opened his eyes. It was too bright. Pain stabbed into his brain. It felt like he'd been stabbed in the eye. He shut them again, squeezing them tightly closed. He tried to make sense of what he'd been able to see in that brief glimpse. It was no use. There was no making sense of it. It just was. His understanding of everything had changed. He didn't know everything. Quite the opposite. He'd seen so much that he knew he never would know more than a scintilla of the potentialities that abounded. He understood and accepted it without question.

He focused on the touch with the others, the connection to them. He focused on his right hand and the contact of his hand on

Clare's skin. Her arm was warm, her muscles tense. He slid his hand down her arm. Her hand was clenched tightly in a fist. She opened it and took his hand in hers, holding it firmly. She had a nice strong grip. He concentrated on pulling the group to him, not with his muscles but with his power. He focused on holding them tighter.

The additional power that had flowed from Kimberly was suddenly gone. His eyes flew open. She was gone. Tommy and Lou were too. Clare was looking at her empty hand.

He didn't have time to think about it. Khalid had let go too. He was down on one knee with his head bowed down, his left hand pressed to his side.

Jake looked around to see if they were in any imminent danger.

The food court was busy but not packed. People were going about their business. So far, they hadn't drawn any attention. Jake put his arm around Khalid and helped him stand up. He let out a groan. With Clare's help, they were able to help Khalid walk over to a nearby booth. He collapsed onto the bench once he could.

"Clare be a dear and get me some napkins, please." He looked at her with a little smile.

Levels

She nodded her head then turned and looked around for the bathrooms.

"How bad is it?" asked Jake once she'd left.

"I think it's just a flesh wound," said Khalid. "Contrary to popular belief, we have quite a bit of open space inside of us. I'm hopeful that nothing serious was hit. There are not too many things in this area that will cause a quick death," he said flashing that brilliant smile.

Jake wasn't buying it. He'd felt how weak he was, how much they had to hold him up. If it wasn't serious yet, it soon would be. They had to find help, fast.

Clare returned with the napkins. "Scoot over, Khalid," she said sliding in next to him. She took his left arm by the elbow and gently raised it until it was resting on the table. Khalid leaned forward on the table top.

Clare reached over and pushed back his sports coat. The white shirt was dark from halfway down to where it was still tucked firmly into his belt. Clare tugged the shirt free and wiped away as much of the blood as she could. She had seen the blood on Jake's hand, so she had made some of the napkins wet. She'd even brought some ice, just in case.

There was a small hole in the back and a larger, ragged looking hole in front. Clare had taken some first aid classes when she was training to be a babysitter. None of the training covered what to do with a bullet wound. She did the best she could with what she had.

She smiled at Khalid. "Well, I have some good news for you."

He nodded his head and smiled back at her.

"It looks like it went clean through."

"Well, that is good news. At least I won't die from lead poisoning." He gave a weak chuckle at his joke and immediately winced from the jolt of pain.

"Jake, can you get some more paper towels?" asked Clare. "Make a few wet, if you would?"

"Okay," he said, standing up to go.

"Jake?"

"Yeah?" he said turning back to her.

"Don't forget to wash your hands, okay?"

He looked down and saw what she meant. He clenched his hand into a fist and walked off to the bathroom.

Clare went back to work on the wound. She took some napkins from the dispenser on the table and stacked them

Levels

together. She made another stack from ones she tore in half. Satisfied that she was as ready as she was going to be, she told Khalid what her plan was.

She helped him take the belt out of his pants. While he held the napkins in place over the wound in the front, she held the smaller stack in place on his back. It was awkward, but they managed to get the belt in place over the makeshift bandages. She tightened the belt up another notch. Khalid inhaled sharply from the pain. The color drained from his ordinarily dark complexion. He looked ashy. She was sure he was going to pass out.

"Here," she said handing him an ice cube. "Chew on this. You need to hydrate. You may be going into shock a little."

"I'll be fine," he assured her. His voice was barely more than a whisper.

"Of course, you will," she agreed. "You're just going into shock a little bit. It probably has nothing to do with the bullet wound. It's probably just a reaction to being around so many teenagers. I know I find teenagers shocking all the time."

Khalid couldn't help himself from laughing. He immediately regretted it as the pain washed over him.

Jake came back from the bathroom and settled in on the other side of the booth. Khalid cleaned his hands as well as he could with the wet paper towels.

Clare took her turn in the bathroom. She was washing her hands, scrubbing them vigorously to get the blood off them when she looked up at her reflection. She took a deep breath to keep herself calm. Despite her efforts, she started to shake. She couldn't help it, after everything that had happened. She took some deep breaths to get herself under control. *You can worry about all of that when this is over.* She wiped the tears from her eyes. She laughed when she realized all she had done was make her face wet. It felt good to laugh. It had come out sounding like a strangled croak, but that was okay.

She turned the water on full blast and all the way to the coldest setting. She cupped her hands and let them fill with water. She raised her hands and sunk her face into the fresh cool water. It didn't take long for the water to escape from between her fingers. It was all she needed, though. She washed her face vigorously and then dried off. When she got back to the booth, she saw that Jake had managed to get a cup of water for Khalid.

"Have you tried calling your dad yet?" she asked him.

Levels

He was shocked that he hadn't thought of it on his own. He'd been so focused on taking care of Khalid that everything else faded in importance. Now that he was as stable as they could make him, they could focus on the other critical issues. He took his phone from his pocket. He was glad to see that there was still a charge and it hadn't broken after all they had been through. It even had service. He stood up and walked a few feet away from the booth before he pressed the redial for his dad. His hand shook as he brought the phone up to his ear.

After the third ring, he realized he'd been holding his breath. He stubbornly didn't let it out. He was afraid that if he changed anything, his dad wouldn't answer. After the eighth ring, he exhaled and hung it up.

"I'm sure there's a simple reason he didn't pick up," said Clare when he sat back down in the booth.

Jake nodded his head. He didn't trust his voice right then. He sat up straighter and hit the redial for another number.

It was answered on the second ring. "Where are you? I'm tired of waiting here, Jake. If I drink another cup of coffee, I'm going to vibrate right off my chair."

He was so relieved to hear her voice. "I'll be there in a couple of minutes, Mom. Have you seen, Dad?" He could hear the background noise coming over the phone, but there was nothing but silence from his mom for a long time. "Mom are you there?"

"Are you okay, Jake?"

"I'm okay, Mom."

"Okay, hurry up and get back here. We need to get going."

"Mom, we can't leave without Dad. I lost him." He heard his mom start to cry. "What's wrong?"

"Jake, I don't know what's going on with you. You know Dad's not coming back, honey. You probably just saw somebody that looked like him."

Now it was Jake's turn not to say anything. His mom waited for a little before she continued. "Honey, I know it's only been a couple of months since the accident, but you need to accept that he's not coming back. I'll meet you at the fountain, okay?"

"Okay, Mom. I love you."

"I love you too, honey. Let's go home."

"Okay, I'll be right there."

He ended the call and absently wiped a tear from his cheek. He knew that they were in an alternate reality. A pretty crappy one. One that his dad wasn't in. What would happen if he

Levels

just left? Would the version of him that was supposed to be here go back to his mom? Where was that other him? Did they become one when they traveled to other realities? Was it only the soul or spirit or ka or whatever that traveled? This was so frustrating! There were so many things he didn't know.

"What is it?" asked Clare.

"My dad's not here. He died in a car accident a few weeks ago."

She didn't know what to say to that. She looked down at her shoes and waited for him to say something. When that didn't happen, she asked him the most important question. "So, what are you going to do?"

He looked back at Khalid. He was resting his head on his arms. He looked peaceful.

"I can't just leave him. My mom will have to wait a few more minutes." As much as he wanted to see his mom, he was surprised to find that he wasn't in any hurry to face a reality where his dad wasn't in it.

Jake sat down next to Khalid. He was careful not to startle him from his slumber.

"Do you think we should call an ambulance?"

She thought about it.

"I mean, he did lose a lot of blood. He might need to have surgery."

She nodded her head that she agreed with him. She reached out her hand and put it around Khalid's wrist. She closed her eyes, so she could focus on counting the seconds and counting his pulse. She moved her fingers around a few times. He had lost quite a bit of blood. It was to be expected that it would be hard to find a good pulse. She took a deep breath and searched with her fingers for the tell-tale pulsating feeling.

A few minutes passed quietly. Jake looked around at the other people, people who had no idea how close the next world was. It was literally closer than the thickness of a piece of paper, but it was so far out of reach for them. These people were going about their day like it was any other day. For them it was normal, while sitting only a short distance away was a young man that had lost each of his parents at different times and saw people being gunned down by maniacs, maniacs with and without badges. He'd saved the lives of a woman and her child from a fire and he'd fallen in love. Now, he was sitting next to a man that was a complete mystery who looked like he was going to die. All of this while these people went about their typical day. Here he sat,

Levels

within the same veil, and yet he was still in an alternate reality. All of their group was forever changed from these other people.

His attention was brought back to their table. Clare sat up and looked around at the people around them. It didn't look like anyone was paying any attention to them. The booth they were sitting in was toward the back of the food court. It wasn't next to the trash, so people didn't approach them to clear their trays. The food court wasn't very busy.

"Change places with me, Jake," she said as she got up and slid around to sit next to Khalid.

She wrapped her arm around his neck. "Come on, Uncle Khalid, wake up. We need to get going," she said close to his ear. She looked like a tender niece with her sleeping uncle. She was hoping her voice would wake him up. She feared it wouldn't. Her left hand was searching for the pulse in his carotid artery.

She palpated her fingers. She could feel his windpipe. The vein should be right here she thought to herself in frustration. She pressed her fingers down harder, hope fading fast that she'd find it.

She leaned him forward and lay his head down on his folded arms. She still held out hope that his pulse was too faint for her to feel because of his blood loss. She slid her finger up along his arm so that it was just under his nose. By now she wasn't thinking about how this would look to anyone watching.

She watched the people eating their food, talking with each other, laughing with each other. She didn't say anything. She sat that way for what felt to Jake like a long time. It could have been a couple of minutes. It could have been more than five. Eventually, she sat back and looked at Jake.

She didn't need to say anything. She saw the look on his face and knew he understood.

"What do we do now?"

"Khalid told me to trust my feelings," she said. "I never did before. I never trusted myself. I always thought someone else knew better, you know? My mom had all the answers until she didn't. Teachers had all the answers." She shook her head and continued, "I'm just a kid. I'm supposed to do what I'm told to do. My sister thinks she has all the answers. Well, she thought she had all the answers until today. I doubt she's so sure of herself now. I do know that I can trust how I feel. I trust that Khalid knew what he was talking about. I felt something come over me back there. I'd felt it before. Not like that, though. Sometimes, I understood just how somebody else felt. I thought everyone did the same. You know, being empathetic? Just reading the situation

Levels

and the other person's body language. Now I know it was something more."

She'd been looking around at the people around them as she'd talked. She turned her focus full on to Jake. "I don't feel you should stay here. I don't know why but it doesn't feel right. No, that's not true. I don't feel that this is your place. You aren't supposed to stay here. I have the same feeling when I think about me staying here."

Neither one of them said anything for a minute or so.

"I've been thinking about where we should try to go," said Clare. "The only idea I feel attracted to is following Kimberly. Strangely enough, I feel that we'll see Khalid again."

She looked at Khalid's face. He looked so peaceful with his head resting on his arms.

She looked back at Jake. "I feel that we'll see your dad again too." She smiled at the hopeful look that came over Jake.

"I think we'll see Angie again too. I just hope she's not still hanging out with that self-absorbed friend of hers."

"Okay, so we go," Jake said with a small nod of his head. He didn't have the feelings Clare did, but he felt that it was the right thing to do. He was as determined as ever to find his parents, his real parents, not some alternate reality imitation parents.

He extended his arms across the table, palms up.

Clare took his hands in hers and gave them a firm squeeze. "Let's go see what the next reality's like."

"Mommy! Mommy! They disappeared!" said the little girl.

"Sure, they did, honey."

"No, Mommy, they really did. Look!"

The woman looked up from her phone long enough to glance over to where her daughter was pointing. An old man had his head down on the table and was sleeping the afternoon away.

"Hurry up and finish your cheeseburger, Sam. We need to get a move on if you're going to make it to soccer on time."

THE END

Levels

Dear reader,

Thank you for taking the time to read Levels.
I hope you enjoyed it as much as I enjoyed writing it.
I wanted to bring to light that the issues of prejudice and racism are not exclusive to any color or culture. These are issues of power. People try to minimize others, so they feel superior.

Unfortunately, there are examples to be found all throughout history and they are still occurring today. It's hard to believe that we are so technologically advanced, the most educated humanity has ever been, and still some of us choose to judge based upon color, gender, culture, or social standing.

These are issues that are straining our society and holding us all back. All you need to do is turn on the news to find current, deplorable examples. People in positions of leadership say derogatory statements that belittle and undermine sections of society.

I pray that soon we all will judge each other based upon individual merits and actions.

Each of us is amazing for who and what we are.

Embrace the differences that make humanity so wonderful. Only then will each person's potential be able to be fully realized.

All the best,
TL Scott
04 November 2018

T. L. Scott

 T. L. Scott grew up in a small Midwest town. A fan of storytelling from a young age he could always be found with a book in hand. The written word fired his young mind with adventures of lands both real and imagined. He has traveled to places great and small and to this day he can still be found with his nose buried in a good book.

Levels

Also by T L Scott:

Fault Line - Bill has come home to see his little sister get married. He brought along some of his Army buddies to enjoy this slice of small-town America. They were looking forward to getting some rest and relaxation away from war. Unfortunately, war has found them here, on the streets of small-town America.

The tranquil setting is interrupted when a man forces a woman down on her knees in the middle of Main Street. When he brings the muzzle down, just inches from her beautiful face, the soldiers are forced to take action.

This fast-paced novel has the soldiers teaming up with local law enforcement and agents from the FBI to eradicate a gang that has invaded the very fabric of this town. They couldn't have become so embedded without help, help from someone in a position of power, someone is at fault and has definitely crossed the line, the Fault Line.

A Life Worth Living - tells the story of Dave, a hard-working man that has made sacrifices for his family, but his work-a-holic ways have driven a wedge between him and his wife, Debbie. All he wants to do is provide a good life for his family. When a tragic accident strikes, he must face the consequences of his choices.

T. L. Scott

A Scary Story – When Carrie was little, and people would ask her name, she was always in such a hurry the words smooshed together and it came out itscarrie and sounded like it's Scary. Naturally it became her nick-name. She decided to be the bravest girl there was. In the first story, she finds herself on a path on a dark night. She's confronted with scary sounds. She has to find out what they are to know if she's in danger.

The second story, Ride With The Wind, has Scary falling asleep in her bed when she hears a sound at her window. She must be brave to find out what it is. She discovers a flying unicorn outside her window. They become best friends and go on many amazing adventures together.

Levels

Excerpt

Fault Line Chapter 1

Late summer is a wonderful time of year. The sun has eased back from the blistering intensity of July. It now warms the skin instead of frying it like an egg in a skillet. The air has lost some of its sweltering quality. A cool breeze stirs the air and then rolls gently through the park.

This green oasis of nature is a favorite place for kids of all ages. People play catch with Frisbees, while others toss a baseball back and forth. Tired mothers stand at the ready, keeping a watchful eye on their tireless toddlers at play. Young couples lay on blankets, basking in the sun as much as they are basking in their love. People feed the ducks by the pond. Joggers make their way along the path which winds around the promenade and continues on its serpentine route through the park. The rhythmic cadence of their footfalls add to the natural rhythm of the day. At the south-eastern corner, a black lab races along the green expanse of grass and launches into the air to catch a Frisbee with effortless grace.

Bill is taking it all in. It feels good to be back home. The smell of fresh-cut grass combined with the morning breeze helps him to relax like he hasn't been able to do for so long.

"Man, you gotta get the Shelby. If you're going to get a Mustang, you might as well get the best," said Sam. He was from Virginia Beach and had grown up around muscle cars. His dad taught him some of life's most valuable lessons while tinkering under the hood of one project after another. When it came to cars, Sam knew what he was talking about. His favorite project had been rebuilding a 442 with his dad and uncle. It was the first time his dad had involved him in the restoration of the engine and transmission. Before that, he'd mostly done body work and been the one to fetch what the men needed. In fact, looking back, it was that restoration more than anything else which had led him to decide on being a 63B, light vehicle mechanic.

"Listen, man," said Sebastian, "I still haven't made up my mind. Yeah, I love the Shelby, but that Camaro is awesome too." He held up his hands to forestall the complaints he knew were coming. "Before you say that it can't compare with the Mustang, think about after-market work. With some fine tuning and a little

Levels

tweak to the computer chip, she'd be sweet! Now toss in a new
transmission, and it would scream!" Sebastian was an Army brat
and had spent most of his childhood in Germany. He had always
been good with electronics and had initially come into the Army
to do that. Once he was in the Army, he learned about the things
the guys in EOD did so he cross-trained and became an 89D.

"It still wouldn't be the same," grumbled Sam.

"To tell you the truth, I'm leaning toward the Beamer.
I've been reading about the M3, and it's a complete package. I
like the way it rides so low to the ground. It really hugs the
road." Sebastian scooted to the edge of his chair while he was
talking. "It's got 425 horsepower pushing around 4,000 pounds.
Get this man, it goes zero to sixty in four-point-five seconds!"

"Your right man," said Tommy, "that M3 is sweet." He
was leaning back as usual. His pose and attitude, as usual, was
relaxed. "For me though, I'm going to get a Range Rover."

Tommy was from Atlanta and would be going there to
visit his mother after the wedding. Like the rest of the guys, he
hadn't been home in over eight months. He was an only child
and in-spite-of his tough exterior, he had a soft spot for his

mother. She had made a lot of sacrifices for him. His dad died when he was young, and she'd raised him as a single mother. He owed her a lot and tried to respect her sacrifices by becoming the best man he could be. He had big shoes to fill. His father had been a great man. Tommy constantly strove to become better. One day maybe someone would think that he'd been a great man as well.

"You're all crazy," said Raul. "The classics are the best. I'm gonna get me a '78 Monte Carlo and trick it out. Picture it man, lime green, chrome rims, at least 32's, and full hydraulics, a true hopper." He crossed his arms and sat back with a smug look on his face. When none of the guys showed any reaction, he quickly sat forward on his chair again and put his hands on his knees.

"You've got to be shittin' me guys. You don't know what a hopper is?" He held his hand out, palm down, and bounced it up and down, small at first then bigger and bigger. "Sweet right?" he asked, leaning back again with a big smile.

Raul was a proud New Yorker. As much as he loved his city, he knew he had to leave her to find himself. He'd seen too many friends die over stupid things. He wasn't afraid to die.

Levels

Dying was easy, he wanted to make something of himself. That was hard. He had to work at it all the time.

He knew what he needed to do the first time he heard a presentation by an Army recruiter. He'd never been good at school. He wasn't bad at it; he was a C student. He just wasn't interested in what they were teaching him.

Most of his teachers tried about as hard as the kids. Everybody was coasting through. School was a place he had to go to so he could get out of there. He knew that drop-outs never got away. He had to finish High School so he could get away and make a difference. The Army needed soldiers. It turned out to be a good match.

Once he enlisted, he decided he liked the camaraderie and worked hard to become better. He graduated at or near the top of his classes. He found that he liked to learn. It was different than school back at home. This was stuff he wanted to know. The instructors really cared about teaching you. They got up close and personal. The lessons were going to keep him and his buddies alive. He decided to try some college classes after he settled into his first posting at Fort Bragg. He finished his

Bachelor's degree in three years and was working on his Masters in Adverse Psychology. Along the way, he also completed Army Sniper training. He had a real knack for observing and analyzing. He was also very good at taking action when it was the right time.

Bill sat back and listened. He was usually the quiet one of the group. These were his friends, and he knew he was damn lucky to have them. It was funny that two years ago they hadn't known each other. They came from different walks of life. Each man had decided to join for his own reasons. At the core of it, they were looking for the same thing. Each of them wanted to become better than what they were. They'd become as close as any brothers. Being in battle together does that; especially when they'd saved each other's lives too many times to count.

Bill watched the tranquil scene of normal life play out in the park across the street. A large, black crow was working on a crust of bread. It would attack the prize a few times with its beak, then raise its head, darting it from side to side to make sure his perimeter was clear. The crow was cautious. He made sure his prize was still safely his. Satisfied, it returned its

Levels

attention to the bread, stabbing its beak into the crusty morsel. Suddenly, it dropped the meal and launched into the air.

The unmistakable crack of a gunshot shattered the tranquility.

Instinct and experience guided Bill's eyes over his left shoulder. Reflex and muscle training guided him as he gracefully turned his body, rising fluidly off the chair, his eyes searching for the aggressor. He dropped to a kneeling position to minimize his exposure to the potential aggressor. His right knee hadn't made contact with the red bricks of the patio before his eyes locked on the target. His right hand clasped the grip of his Sig Sauer SP 2022 Nitron. Having identified his target, he began clearing it from the holster. His left arm, now clear of the seatback, came around for a two-handed grip. His sights locked on the confirmed threat.

A man stood over a woman in the middle of the two-lane road. She was down on her knees, gesturing with her hands fiercely. Bill couldn't make out the words they were saying from this distance, but it was obvious he wasn't asking her out on a date. The man was holding the stock of what looked like an AK

47 with his right hand, waving it around menacingly, while shouting at the woman. His long, stringy, brown hair whipped around his head. He punctuated his agitation by thrusting the gun up and down.

The woman raised up off her heels and said something. Whatever she said caught his attention. He closed the distance between them then bent his thin frame down so his face was inches from hers.

She shrank back from his leering face. Whatever it was she said next, he must have found amusing. He tossed his head back and laughed, then started dancing around her. He was doing a kind of high-step, his knees pumping high while he jabbed the rifle sharply up and down. He was really getting it too. He completed his circle of her and stomped his heavy boot down, ending his dance. He threw his head back and howled like a wolf. Bill had to give it to him; the guy had some good lungs.

The man took in a deep breath as he rolled his body back forward. He snugged the butt of the gun into his shoulder and sighted in on the woman. The black barrel ended inches from her upturned face. Her jet-black hair blew back from her face in the

Levels

gentle breeze. It, and the angle she was facing prevented Bill from seeing her face.

Bill admired the way she faced the man that was about to take her life. She looked proud and strong. Even if she was seconds from meeting her maker, she wasn't going to cower. He respected her for that.

Bill increased the pressure of his trigger finger. Seeing the man tense his shoulder and bring his right elbow out to the side triggered Bill to engage fully. A split second before applying the final amount of pressure, the dancer jerked to the right. He fell in what seemed like slow motion, Bill knew better it was what he called battle speed. Bullets sprayed out from the barrel of the AK47 in a deadly arc. It was good that the rifle shot up to six hundred rounds-per-minute. It quickly ran out of ammo before anyone was hurt by this madman. With the guy out of the fight, Bill scanned for more threats. Seeing none, he did a quick check on his friends. Sam and Raul were both covering down on the baddie.

Bill kept his weapon trained on the inert form in the road, from his kneeling position. He cut his eyes over to Tommy and

Sebastian and saw they were taking cover behind the decorative fence that separated the café from the sidewalk. He could see they were at a loss. They were used to being in uniform and reacting as they were trained to do. When their finely-honed reactions came up with a missing weapon, they didn't have an answer for a beat. This wasn't Iraq or Afghanistan; it was Texas, and yet war had found them here.

Bill kept his weapon pointed at the bad guy as he ran over to the woman. She was still on her knees in the middle of the road. The man hadn't moved since he'd hit the pavement. Bill saw why. A pool of blood spread out from his head. The blood looked black on the asphalt road. A smaller puddle was congealing under his torso as well. Bill wasn't taking any chances. He'd seen men get up from wounds that should've killed them outright before.

He slowly circled the body, keeping his eyes on the man's hands. If they so much as twitched, Bill would drop the hammer. His finger skillfully had four of the seven pounds of pressure squeezing the match grade trigger. It would only take a small fraction more to dispatch the man if needed. He kicked the rifle

Levels

away from the corpse and then looked at the woman. She was staring at the body.

Bill couldn't see her face from his angle. Her black hair was loose and partially covered it. He could see that she was shivering in-spite-of the warm air.

A crowd was beginning to form. Sam and Raul were still training their weapons around, searching for any more potential threats. Sebastian and Tommy were keeping the small crowd that had formed back, maintaining a loose perimeter defense. They were doing their best to keep the look-e-loos away from the scene. Of course, in this modern day, most of the people had their phones out, trying to catch it all on video. It would be up on social media before the authorities had a chance to arrive on the scene.

"Are you okay ma'am?"

She raised her obsidian eyes to his and said in a calm voice, "I think so."

"Are you hurt?" Bill asked her.

"No, . . . I don't think so," she replied shaking her head slowly.

"Are there any more of them?" He asked as he cast his eyes around.

"I don't know," answered the woman. "I don't know who he is."

She looked down at her lap, and her body sagged down. The steel that had held her up seemed to leave her. "He was really going to kill me," she murmured.

They both knew she'd spoken the truth. Bill didn't see any need to say anything further on that point.

"What's your name ma'am?" He asked her in a gentle tone as he reached out his hand to help her up.

She took it and let him help her to her feet. Once she was sure she wasn't going to fall back down, she squeezed his hand a little and responded; "My name is Isabella, thank you." She said looking him in the eye.

"You're welcome," he replied simply.

There was something about this woman, something more than her beauty. There was a feeling of strength that radiated from her. He tore his gaze from her beautiful eyes and looked around at the scene developing around them.

Levels

More people had gathered on the sidewalks on both sides of the street. Traffic was at a standstill. Cars were lined up with their doors standing open. Their drivers had abandoned them to get a better look at the aftermath of the violence that had played out in their small town. Small children were standing with their parents. Some parents were trying to cover their children's eyes, but the curious little ones weren't having it. Bill wished he could cover the body up. Not to give the man his dignity but to lessen the macabre interest that had overtaken these people. He knew better though; he knew the police were going to conduct an investigation. Back here, that meant collecting forensic evidence. As if on cue, the shrill notes of a siren cut through the still morning air. All together, less than three minutes had passed since the first shot had been fired, and the discordant wail sounded the arrival of law and order.

Fault Line Chapter 2

In the time it took for that terrible scene to play out, on what ironically was Main Street, the crow had made it to the edge of the small town, and a very bad man knew that things had changed.

Sound travels well over the dry air. To a trained ear there is no mistaking the crack of a rifle. When a person was as experienced with weapons as this particular man was, they can even tell the type of rifle fired.

He knew the sound had likely come from one of his men. The wind whispered the story into his well-trained ear. The answering report of pistols told the next chapter. It was the ensuing silence which told him the conclusion of this drama had played out. His man was probably dead. If not dead, then he would soon be locked up in a jail cell. Regardless, the heat had just been cranked up several degrees.

The warehouse he was standing in was far enough from the road that it avoided attention and was still close enough for quick transportation of the goods he traded in. It had proved to be a good place for a temporary headquarters. It had hills on

Levels

three sides with the front opening out to the road in the distance. The road leading into it wound down into this valley. The warehouse had been built up, so it sat higher than the ground around it to prevent the products stored inside getting damaged during the few times it rained heavily.

He looked out at the gravel road which cut its way out to highway 27. His eye caught the movement of a single bird. It flew, rising on the air that was heating as the sun cut higher into the sky. He stood in the entrance to the warehouse for a few minutes, just letting his eyes and thoughts wander. In time, he saw a cloud of dust rising from the gravel road.

"Have him brought up to the office," he said to his men that were stationed on each side of the door, their weapons at the ready.

He made his way to the east side of the building and looked over his operation as he went. A group of his men was loosely gathered by the trucks. Some of them were working on the engines, but most were just standing around and talking. Another group was gathered around the cages on the other side of the building. He heard some tell-tale sounds coming from the smaller administrative offices. He didn't care if the men had some fun, as long as they didn't damage the product.

Everything seemed to be under control. He climbed the metal stairs to the office, noting the positions of the guards that were up on the rafters. One of the men noticed him and gave a small wave. Miguel forced a smile on his hard face and returned the salute. He had learned over time that some men responded better if there was a sense of camaraderie. All Miguel cared about was that the men did what he told them to and were loyal. Whatever it took to make that happen, he would do.

Once inside the air-conditioned space, he fired up his laptop and started making calls on his phone. He needed answers and knew that the fastest way to get them was to check out social media. He had become friends on several of the local pages. As he had believed, the American love for posting what they saw, heard, thought, or believed online told him what he wanted to know.

This wasn't a big hit to the operation. It could be handled, with some small interventions at the right levels. An unstable man, high on meth, goes berserk on Main Street. That would be

Levels

a good cover. It was sensational and yet believable. It was also not far from the truth. There would be a price to pay for this. He had to send a message to the rest of his men that this was not going to be tolerated. They had to stay focused on their jobs and, above all else, stay invisible.

His guest was coming to get an update on the operation. The man had been useful while setting up this operation but he had to be put in his place. He thought that his public standing afforded him a right to control how things were handled. He had to be made to understand that he wasn't in charge. He was only a tool to be used. He was still a useful tool, so he had to take care of him and handle him appropriately. A time was coming when his position and sources would no longer be necessary. He would then be discarded. Today was not that day, but it wasn't far away.

"How in the hell did this happen," the man demanded to know. "You said there wouldn't be any problems. You said there wouldn't be anything to worry about," he said, pacing back and forth. He was really worked up. His face was turning red.

Miguel enjoyed watching the man work himself up. When he talked the skin under his chin flopped around. It made Miguel think about the waddle on a turkey. He fought to control his smile.

"Well, guess what? I'm fucking worried." The man stopped and braced his hands on the table opposite Miguel. "I thought you had control over that group of fuck-ups!" he demanded. The man's voice had a plaintive note to it that wasn't present when he was talking to the press.

Miguel knew this man liked to be in control. He wasn't in control of this and was just beginning to realize how little control he had.

"Careful amigo, you wouldn't want someone to hear you? They might question your loyalties. You wouldn't want that would you?" he asked as he leveled his gaze on the agitated man.

The man glared at Miguel. He didn't like to be challenged. That hard look melted away under the cold stare that was locked on him. He could feel the cold blue eyes as they bored into his

Levels

soul. They held no compassion, no warmth. They were dead eyes and until that gaze passed the man couldn't breathe.

"Come, sit down, have a drink. All this pacing and shouting will not change what has happened. It changes nothing." Miguel waved his hand dismissively. He picked up the bottle from the silver serving tray. It was such a contrast, the fine silver sitting on the beat-up scarred wood of the table. The man poured the liquor into the fine cut crystal tumbler, carefully measuring out precisely three fingers worth. Once the liquor was poured, he raised his eyes to the man who was still standing.

"I said sit down."

He didn't raise his voice. He didn't need to. His voice, like his eyes, held no compassion.

"You know," Miguel said once his guest was seated, "I have come to truly appreciate fine Scotch. Many of my countrymen only drink tequila."

He slid the tumbler across the table. "Now, don't get me wrong my friend, I like my tequila too, but a fine scotch, now, that is something else altogether. You see, tequila is like a scorpion. It comes right out and stares you in the eye. It says fuck you *esse* and then it stings your ass. It might kill you. It will make you sick. But you definitely will remember its bite. Now, take this fine Scotch, it has a bite as well," he said pointing at the tumbler. Condensation was forming on the side of the glass.

"The difference is that it starts out with a smooth burn that slowly engulfs all of you. It does not sting you," he said, shaking his head.

He quickly leaned forward, placing his hands on the side of the glass, the ropy muscles in his forearms flexing as he pressed his hands down on the table. "It consumes you. It consumes you, and you don't even realize it until it is too late."

"You see my friend that is what we have done here. We moved slowly. We took our time, set things up one step at a time. We are here. This is our town," he said, sweeping his arm in the general direction of the town. "This problem on Main Street is only a small bump in the road," he said as he dismissively waved his hand. "Yes, we will be careful, but we do not need to stop our operation."

"Drink up my friend and let the beast warm your heart," Miguel told him as he leaned back in his chair.

Levels

The Senator drank down the Scotch, but the chill from his friend's eyes tamped out the fire of the beast. In fact, he'd never felt so cold in his life. He knew that the man had spoken the truth. The beast had consumed him, and there was no going back again.

Made in the USA
Middletown, DE
27 February 2019